"How do you keep everything together?"

"I love the kids, the pets, all of it, so it's become second nature to me. I can only guess what you must think of the chaos that has become my life."

Chaos. That was one description of Lucie's life, but happiness radiated from her. The cat curled its lithe body around Lucie's feet in appreciation.

While Caleb had been away, Lucie had had her sweetheart image shattered and become the town's enemy who housed unwanted animals while starting a business to support this household.

He couldn't help but wonder if Lucie had gained more.

"It suits you." The two times he'd visited this house in the far distant past, the house was exactly that—a cold residence with impeccable interior design highlighting good bones.

Lucie had created a home.

What would it be like to find his way home every night to this?

But while he'd love nothing more, her home couldn't be his...

Dear Reader,

Thank you for taking a return trip to Hollydale. Some books are a pure joy to write, and Lucie's story was one of them. I found myself rooting for Lucie, who forges a new path to turn her life around. When times are tough, she scrabbles a family together consisting of her twins, her friends and a menagerie of pets.

She's reunited with her childhood friend Caleb, a park ranger turned reluctant hero, who returns with a mission but is often diverted by Lucie and her messy life. Hidden treasures of love and redemption may be the most meaningful and most elusive for him.

My favorite scenes revolve around Fred and Ethel, a pair of miniature pigs. Ethel immediately cozies up to Caleb, recognizing his true worth, something Lucie needs to be reminded of. I couldn't resist paying tribute to my alma mater, the University of Georgia, by including a bulldog named Ladybug.

Thanks for picking up *A Ranger for the Twins*. I hope Lucie and Caleb touch your heart like they touched mine. You can reach out to me on social media or at tanyaagler.com. I love hearing from readers!

Tanya

HEARTWARMING

A Ranger for the Twins

Tanya Agler

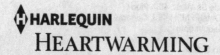

HARLEQUIN

HEARTWARMING

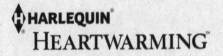

HARLEQUIN®
HEARTWARMING™

ISBN-13: 978-1-335-88992-8

A Ranger for the Twins

Copyright © 2020 by Tanya Agler

Harlequin Enterprises ULC
22 Adelaide St. West, 40th Floor
Toronto, Ontario M5H 4E3, Canada
www.Harlequin.com

Printed in U.S.A.

Tanya Agler remembers the first set of Harlequin books her grandmother gifted her, and she's been in love with romance novels ever since. An award-winning author, Tanya makes her home in Georgia with her wonderful husband, their four children and a lovable basset, who really rules the roost. When she's not writing, Tanya loves classic movies and a good cup of tea. Visit her at tanyaagler.com or email her at tanyaagler@gmail.com.

Books by Tanya Agler

Harlequin Heartwarming

The Sheriff's Second Chance

To the treasures of my heart: my four children (including my set of fraternal twins), who bring me joy and show me the beauty of the world every day. Thank you for the adventures, the chaos, Mother's Day chocolate and, most of all, the love.

To Jeanine, who went with me to my one and only yoga class, and to the Writing Sisters for the icing and keeping me on track. Thanks to all of you for reminding me it's all about the emotion.

To the parents of twins. Some say the first six weeks are the toughest. I'm not so sure about that, but I'm thankful for the stories and encouragement you've shared with me and to those who've listened to my stories about Cupcake and Chunk, who gained me admittance to this group.

And to park rangers everywhere for your service and dedication.

CHAPTER ONE

A DROP OF beige paint landed on Lucie Decker's arm. *Perfect.* Now more paint dotted her and her overalls than remained in the can. She replaced the roller in the tray and wiped away the offending glob. Streaming afternoon light from the bay window overlooking the Great Smoky Mountains revealed no trace of the gosh-awful burnt-orange color that had graced the lodge's reception area earlier this week. One task down, forty-four left before the grand opening of the Hollydale Training and Wellness Center in a mere thirty days.

A glimpse of something brown on the window ledge caught Lucie's eye. How did a mouse manage to climb up there? Thank goodness her twins, Mattie and Ethan, were busy in their first-grade classrooms at Hollydale Elementary or they'd be begging her to save the little rodent and add it to the menagerie of strays that lived at their house, five miles away. While Lucie had no problem collecting animals that didn't have a home, including her cat, two dogs, three rabbits and a pair of miniature pigs, she drew the line at mice, especially those that belonged outside in the forest rather than inside her freshly painted reception area.

Since the newly hired maintenance worker wouldn't start for another two weeks, several days prior to the arrival of the rest of the staff, the task of trapping the mouse and releasing it into the wild fell on her shoulders. Problem was, too much had rested there following her ex-husband Justin's conviction and subsequent imprisonment for embezzlement.

No, she wouldn't go there. Her life no longer revolved around her ex. Look how much she'd accomplished in the past couple of months. In just that short amount of time, contractors had helped her transform the former Appleby Wedding Lodge into a corporate training and trust-building center with the latest amenities.

The government had thrown her a lifeline by returning property that had belonged to her parents, declaring it independent of Justin's seized assets. This conference center had to succeed, or she'd have to sell it and start over somewhere else, leaving the only home she and her twins had ever known. This lodge, nearby cabin and surrounding property, along with her family home, were the last links to her parents, who'd died while she and Justin were still only dating.

With a little bit of oil soap and a lot of elbow grease, the woodwork gleamed once more. Her first clients would arrive in four weeks to hopefully strengthen their communication and team-building skills by participating in activities that would foster trust and honesty—she had no time to sit around.

Yesterday, the contractor had finished the high ropes course, accepted the final payment and departed. This morning the last interior worker finished the updates to the kitchen. No more hammering, no more sawing, and no more shattering noise. All that was left was painting and completing the spa area.

She'd have it all finished before her staff reported for duty and a week of practice runs.

But if she didn't do something about that mouse, her clients might cut their visits short and not provide glowing references, which were key to building this sort of enterprise. Her new business would fail before it began.

Lucie ran into the kitchen and found a plate and big bowl. Nearby, on the island, rested the jar of peanut butter she hadn't put away after she'd slapped a sandwich together a half hour ago. One spoonful of the thick creamy substance ought to do the trick. Nodding, Lucie donned her cute black oven mittens decorated with bright yellow lemons and prepped herself for battle.

Satisfied the peanut butter would keep the mouse occupied until she could free him a good distance away from the two main buildings of the training and wellness center, she returned to the reception area and spotted him still resting in the same location on the window ledge.

Sneaking over, she held out the plate with one mitted hand and readied the bowl with the other.

Uh-oh. This was a bat!

Her hold on the plate and bowl loosened and they clattered on the cherry hardwood floor. The bat began circling the reception area, searching for some route of escape.

Lucie sprinted for the foyer and threw open the front door. The cool March breeze chilled her bare arms.

Flushed, she rushed back to the reception area and waved her arms around. One of the oven mitts flew off her hand and she stumbled against the wall. A smear of beige paint left a circular mark on her overalls.

"This way, not that way! Your home is outside. Go find your bat family." Lucie shuddered, hoping its relatives weren't located anywhere inside the lodge.

The bat flew out the front door. Lucie followed and barreled straight into a solid mass. Bouncing backward, she blinked and focused on the man standing there. Short, rumpled dark hair framed a wide and open face partially obscured by a couple days' worth of stubble. Hazel eyes with a twinge of familiarity twinkled at her.

"*Bat family*? You think that bat has a mother and father and siblings waiting outside for it?" A thread of humor laced his words. The man shoved his hands into his jeans' pockets.

Although his question hit her as a little too intimate for a delivery person, she'd tip him well anyway if he'd brought her audiovisual equipment. The speakers and projectors should have been here yesterday. Hard to advertise as a business training and wellness center without the basic amenities.

Then again, he was wearing a plaid flannel shirt, not the brown uniform of her usual courier. Recognition flickered then took flight. Lucie squealed and clapped her hands, the single mitt muffling the noise. "Caleb Spindler! I wasn't expecting Hollydale's hero in person."

He blinked before his mouth fell agape. "Lucie Appleby?"

She reached up and yanked off the bandanna she'd tied over her head to keep the paint from her blond hair. Shaking out her curls, shorter than the long length she'd favored in high school, she stuffed the pink cloth into the side pocket of her overalls. "Believer in bat families for twenty-nine years. I'm Lucie Decker now."

No sooner did she step forward than she paused. What was the right way to greet an old friend? Before Justin's betrayal, she would have hugged Caleb without a second thought. Now? Hugging any male other than her son, Ethan, wasn't on her agenda. She folded her arms, self-conscious of the person standing before her.

"Hello, Lucie Decker. Long time, no see." His voice was deeper than she remembered.

Where was the scrawny teenager who'd kept her on her toes, playing practical jokes even in his darkest moments? In his place stood a man who wore a mantel of confidence. Those shoulders and that straight posture projected solidity and strength, attributes that had gone viral after his rescue of three brothers.

"Everyone's seen you lately. Not many people would put their lives on the line for someone else."

He shrugged, obviously still not comfortable talking about himself. Some things never changed. "He was a little boy stuck in a crevice. Just because he and his brothers snuck into Yellowstone while the park crews were clearing snow off the paths for reopening doesn't mean he deserved a bad fate."

Even when Caleb had been the kid from the wrong side of the tracks, and she'd been the town sweetheart, he'd had a heart of gold, always looking out for wildlife and people alike.

"Just to let you know. You might be the Hero of Yellowstone to most of the country, but in these parts, you're Hollydale's hero."

He shrugged. "I wasn't sure it would even be news around here."

"Considering you rescued the three sons of a baseball legend from Charlotte, a short two hours from here on I-40, it shouldn't come as that big a surprise."

While Jared Engel, who currently served as manager to the team he'd led to the championship title, scouted a top prospect, his sons had scouted trouble. Now Caleb was a hero. And she was…what?

The town pariah, to say the least.

Collecting herself, she raised her chin. She might have lost her money and many of her friends, but her pride was intact. Justin couldn't steal that from her. Besides, as long as Mattie and Ethan were safe and well, she'd manage anything thrown at her.

"Good to see that chin tilt stayed the same. It was definitely worth coming here first, before settling in with Jonathan and his girls." Caleb nodded and glanced toward the foyer, his neck craning as if to see the interior. She'd kept the rustic feel and centered the shabby chic furniture so it faced the massive stone fireplace. "It's been a long time since I worked here."

"We've both come quite a ways since then. What are you doing here in Hollydale? Park service training or assignment? Vacation? Family time?"

"I haven't seen my cousin Jonathan Maxwell and his daughters in too long. He moved back to town not so long ago after his wife died. He's a police officer now. Besides, there's something about the Great Smoky Mountains that called me back. But enough about me. Your email was rather vague. I want to hear more about you."

While she'd emailed him with the express purpose of asking him for a favor—an endorsement of her new center—her mother would roll over in her grave if Lucie welcomed Caleb, home for a visit from Montana, with anything less than full red-carpet treatment. Best to work up to that favor. Besides, Lucie wanted to show off her changes to someone. She bounced on her toes.

"Care for the grand tour?" While the word *grand* might overstate her case, appearances were all she had going for her. She'd keep up the facade of having everything together, especially in front of Caleb. There were few people she wanted to impress anymore, but for some reason, she wanted Caleb to see her in a good light. He'd always been different from the crowd.

"Fresh paint. That's always a good sign of money well spent." He reached over, his finger brushing the top of her forehead before he held it up under his nose with a certain amount of caution. "At least, I hope this is paint and not bat droppings."

"You're the park ranger, so you ought to know the difference." Lucie backed up until her bottom hit the door. "Would you like to start with the main lodge or the cabin? Although, I ought to warn you, I haven't really fixed up the cabin yet. The cabin and the three guest rooms upstairs are part of phase two, which I hope to roll out next year. Having places for guests to sleep will help increase bookings, rather than having them stay at the bed-and-breakfast."

Caleb leaned against the wooden railing and stared at her as if she'd grown an extra head since they'd last talked. "Most people who haven't seen each other in a long time start by catching up."

She fidgeted with the bandanna in her pocket. "My life's an open book for all to judge."

More than ever, she wanted her old friend to see what she had accomplished in the past couple of months. While she'd had to contract out a good deal of the work, she'd saved money and done the jobs herself whenever possible.

"You should know I'm not one to judge. I came here today to find out more about this center."

And not expressly to see her. She should have expected this after not being in touch with him for so long. Too long.

She motioned for him to come inside. "Let me show you the upstairs. Then you can tell me if you like what you see." Buoyed by Caleb stopping by during his vacation, she thought he must be considering her request to endorse her new venture.

Wait a second. Had she outlined that in the email? No, she'd kept it vague on purpose, only half expecting a response.

He followed her up the grand staircase where brides and grooms had posed for photographs, light cascading in from the windows. Summer with local recreational activities like fishing and kayaking had been popular but nowhere near as popular as autumn when the colorful leaves made for a spectacular background.

With some pride and a bit of exhaustion, she chattered nonstop as she showed off the new spa amenities and the accompanying dressing areas before they returned to the main level where most of the group meeting events would be scheduled. The library was rather scarce at this point, but the arts and crafts room was fully stocked and operational. As soon as that AV equipment came, the business area would also be ready for clients.

When they reached the dining room adjacent to the kitchen and the bar, she finally stopped with the main selling points.

"I expected an email rather than you in person, but beggars can't be choosers." The paint fumes lightened her head. That must be why she was revealing too much at once. Keeping this on a business level benefited both of them. Best way to do that was to show off her exterior improvements, as well. Lucie used caution on the porch steps leading down to the gravel sidewalk. "Follow me. I think you'll like the low ropes area."

She didn't look back but strode toward the course on the fringe of the woods, taking care to steer clear of the spiderwebs on the holly bushes. Unable to resist standing on the log held up by long metal chain links, the ends of which were attached to two pines eight feet apart, Lucie climbed on and winced at the oven mitt still resting on her left hand. She clambered across the log, then removed the mitt and stuffed it in her pocket, alongside the bandanna. She jumped off and caught sight of Caleb leaning against the pine farthest from her, surveying the edge of the forest.

"I have to share something with you right off the bat, for full disclosure."

"Do you go around collecting bats now?" Caleb kept his voice low, although his eyes twinkled, his good nature still intact. He leaped onto the log with the ease and grace of a puma and then shimmied across. The chains rattled when he dismounted and stood near her. "The Lucie I knew would have run for cover."

That Lucie of yesteryear, the debutante whose outfits matched her purses, didn't exist anymore. Her father had always chucked her chin and told her she was tougher than she thought. He'd been right. In the past two years, she'd learned how to make Hamburger Helper stretch for three nights and how to accept kindness with a smile.

"That Lucie had to grow up." She kicked some pine straw with the toe of her faded sneakers before she motioned at him. He followed her toward three wooden cubes equidistant to each other, although each was smaller than the previous one. If the coworkers didn't work together to cross the aptly named "alligator pit," they'd all fall into the blue-gravel "swamp."

"That's a shame. That Lucie supported me during one of the roughest times in my life." Caleb jumped onto the middle cube and stared at her. "By the way, you didn't have to email me with a long explanation of our friendship and a request to email back. You're pretty unforgettable, you know, and I'd never send you to voice mail."

"I didn't have your number." She spotted the six-foot plank the teams would use to progress to the next cube. The problem arose when they figured out the plank didn't cross the entire length but instead fell six inches short. A winning strategy required teamwork and communication. And if she wanted Caleb on her team, recommending her center, she'd better stop beating around the hollyhocks and start communicating. "And I wasn't sure you wouldn't send me to voice mail when my name popped up. You disappeared out of my life rather quickly after Justin and I announced our engagement."

"About that. I introduced the two of you. I'm sorry. If I'd had any idea of his true character, I'd have done things differently for both our sakes." He shifted his weight. "Well, I'm here now."

He was apologizing to her?

"Thank you, but you did nothing wrong."

Lucie jumped into the alligator pit and crossed to the plank, checking for any damage to the long wooden board. Finding none, she shrugged. "Enough about me. Here I am monopolizing the conversation, same as always."

"I like it. Besides, listening to the sounds around me is a cornerstone of my work."

"Speaking of work, I'm surprised you could get time off right now. How long is Yellowstone loaning you to us?"

"I'm back for good."

Her hand slipped and the plank thudded into the dirt, the hard collision puffing up a cloud of dust before the echoes died in the surrounding woods. Fine particles lodged in Lucie's throat and she coughed. For once, the Hollydale grapevine must not have had wind of a true scoop: Caleb's homecoming. If she'd known he was returning for keeps, she'd never have emailed him. A long-distance entreaty was different from an in-person request somehow. She didn't want to be lumped in with everyone else asking him for a favor.

However, his recommendation might lead to bookings in May. The more bookings, the sooner she'd pay back her aunt Rosemary and Mitzi.

She pointed to the wood benches that edged the perimeter of the low ropes course. "Want to sit down and talk? I've been on my feet painting all day." Getting the meeting room in shape had consumed most of her morning.

"I've been doing nothing but sitting for thirty hours over three days." Caleb stretched and smiled. "When Jonathan moved back to Hollydale, I requested a transfer. It finally came through. As soon as I finished packing, I drove straight to North Carolina, only stopping at night."

And he'd come here to the Hollydale Training and Wellness Center first? He was a true friend. He could have gone anywhere in town, his favorite trail overlooking Timber River, his cousin's house, or Sal's Pizzeria for the best slice this side of New York. Her eyes misted and she stopped herself from giving him a hug.

"You don't know how much that expression of friendship means to me." She thumped her fist over her heart. "There are people in this world who are your true friends, and you're one of mine, Caleb Spindler. You might be the best friend I've ever had."

He reached up and stroked his stubble. "Lucie…" He paused and licked his lips.

"Some friend I am when you went out of your way to make me feel special again. I haven't offered you anything to drink, although your choices are water or the juice boxes I keep on hand for the twins. My food and beverage deliveries aren't for a couple more weeks."

She turned in the direction of the main building, but he tapped her arm and cupped his right ear with his hand. "What was that?"

Silence pervaded the air until the sound of three faint pecks traveled their way, followed by a hoarse shrill call. "I hope that woodpecker isn't tapping on my chimney again."

"It's coming from the woods." He lowered his hand and stretched his back. "Have you spotted the Timber River woodpecker?"

"Except for penguins and chickens, most birds look alike to me. All I know is this one bird likes my chimney." Although she loved animals, she was thinking of making an exception for the aggravating woodpecker.

"If you can, take a picture the next time you see it. That bird is endangered."

With her luck, it figured the one bird she criticized was endangered and protected. They'd taken a few steps before she stopped and tilted her head sideways. "Is it just me or are you limping?"

"The long car ride must have aggravated the titanium rods in my back. I'm fine."

His quick response sounded a little defensive but understandable given his first visit was to her.

"If I know you, being out in nature is the best remedy for what ails you."

The cool wind whistled across the tops of the pines. In an instant, the temperature seemed to drop; a sure sign spring didn't have a tight-fisted hold on this part of the state yet. Pine straw and gravel crackled under her footsteps. Nearby squirrels chased each other and scurried up a tree. Peaceful moments like these gave her hope this whole venture was worthwhile.

Without another word, Caleb stopped on the path and raised a finger to his pursed lips. Then he pointed to the clearing in front of a line of camellia bushes that separated the ropes courses. Two deer, one bigger and presumably mother to the smaller fawn, graced the far-off distance. The mother deer sniffed the bush and the fawn copied her before they scampered off into the woods.

"How beautiful," whispered Lucie.

The wildlife around here was one of the main reasons she hadn't accepted offers for the land. One speculator had wanted to raze the lodge and construct a series of condos. Another had wanted to build a bigger hotel alongside the lodge since there was direct access to the Timber River and nearby amenities. But the Great Smoky Mountains held an important place in Lucie's heart. Protecting this sanctuary for Mattie and Ethan, as well as for Hollydale's residents, was the least she could do. Keeping this site off-limits to real-estate developers was the best way she could ensure this area would remain a sanctuary.

Besides, under the terms of the limited liability corporation she'd signed for the venture, the lodge and cabin were collateral for the loans Aunt Rosemary and Mitzi had given her to fund the necessary changes and pay the contractors. The first three clients' down payments covered the staff salaries.

Unlike Justin, though, Lucie intended on paying her investors back.

They reached the side entrance and she pulled the lanyard with the security keycard from the bib of her overalls. Swiping the card through the new security system installed last month, she opened the door and waved Caleb inside.

Since the kitchen hadn't been renovated in the ten years since the car accident claimed her parents' lives, Lucie had sunk a pretty penny into updated appliances and code compliance. The whole center had been fitted with modern décor over the past few months. She'd also tested the Wi-Fi and added an extra signal booster since they were five miles outside of Hollydale and a fifty-minute drive north of Asheville.

The next two weeks were for the finishing touches her mother had especially taken pride in handling. Ironing the tablecloths for the main dining area and putting up the remaining window treatments topped her list.

Lucie filled a glass with water from the new refrigerator filtration system and handed it to Caleb.

"Thanks." He accepted it with a smile. "Do you know you're the first person all month not to treat me any differently since those three kids had the misfortune of taking the wrong trail?"

"But they did." Lucie filled another glass

and took a sip. "We can't ignore what life hands us. We have to deal with what we're given and adjust. Events change us. Sometimes for the better, sometimes for the worse."

He shook his head. "I don't buy that. We react to events, but we're still the same people underneath."

Lucie Appleby would have smiled and nodded, and the thought of simply being Lucie around him, with no preconceived judgments, was worth more than a spa treatment a couple of weeks from now. "I hope our friendship can survive."

"What do you mean by that?"

He had been gone a while. "Some people in town might not want you associating with the likes of me." Caleb sipped his water and then placed his glass on the counter. "Like I said, I'm the same person underneath. After all these years, we can be honest with each other, right?"

She twisted the edge of the bandanna sticking out of her pocket. "Hate to break it to you, but you're here under false pretenses tied with thread, twine and Kevlar rope. I thought we'd exchange a flurry of emails before I had to get to the point." She stuffed the bandanna as far down as it would go. "As you can see, this is no longer the premier wedding destination this side of the Biltmore."

"You weren't going for the outdoor wedding destination experience?" He clicked his tongue. "Why didn't you continue your parents' business? Why build ropes courses and add a spa?"

The number of reasons would outnumber the remaining Timber River woodpeckers.

"Even though my main focus centers on companies coming in for trust-building exercises, this new setup will encourage other groups to book time here. Church groups, family reunions and others can reserve spots, as well. This location is unique with the Timber River a short walk away and a mere ten-minute drive to downtown Hollydale."

Was she selling herself or him on the center? She wasn't sure as time brought a new guarded edge to his gaze.

"Quite a few changes since I worked here. Those changes don't come cheap," he noted.

"Tell me about it. Thanks to some others, this is a dream come true. In addition to the two ropes courses, there are other outdoor activities like a nature walk and—"

Caleb yawned. "Slow down, Lucie. The drive is starting to get to me."

If she'd been on the road for three straight days, what would she do first? Sleep? Eat? Greet her pets and get a shower of doggie kisses? Caleb had chosen to see *her* first. That type of loyalty and friendship was beyond rare. "Get some sleep. I'll get to the point of my email—"

Her phone pinged and she held up her index finger. "Is it already two o'clock?" Digging deep in her other side pocket, she palmed the phone and laughed at her reminder to stop painting and greet Mattie and Ethan at the bus stop. "School's almost out for the day, and the bus will arrive soon. You need some rest, but why don't you join us for dinner later? We can talk about the center then."

She led him through the kitchen, passing the conference rooms and ballroom before arriving at the reception area.

"Do you still make the best macaroni and cheese in the world?" Caleb opened the front door for her and she smiled as they made their way onto the front lawn.

"You remember my cooking?"

"I could never forget anything that good."

"It's because I use cheddar, Gruyère *and* mozzarella—" She stopped when the familiar pecking sound she'd come to dread reached her. "There's that woodpecker again."

She pointed up to the chimney, where a dotted brown-and-black bird made a racket.

"That is the Timber River woodpecker." Something akin to awe laced his words.

As much as she'd like to delve into her sales pitch, asking for his endorsement would have to wait. With her two children, the only family she had left in the world, depending on her, she had to focus on them. "If you arrive late for dinner, your chances of getting a full plate will be *endangered*. See you at six. I live in my parents' old home now."

He nodded, and she strode away without looking back. She never looked back anymore. Only forward.

CALEB SPINDLER SHUT his cousin Jonathan's front door, double-checking the lock before heading out toward downtown Hollydale. He didn't need his windbreaker, the cool weather luxuriously warm compared to the frigid temperatures he'd left behind in Montana.

Though he'd loved Yellowstone with its sweeping vistas, there was no place he'd rather be in spring than right here in North Carolina. The sweet scent of rhododendrons filled the air, the vibrant colors of pink and purple in the passing yard catching his eye. While hollyhocks were his favorite, they wouldn't bloom until late summer. This year he'd see them again at last.

On the sidewalk, Caleb stopped and tied his boot. When he straightened, he spotted a neighbor, who waved and called out, "Welcome home, Caleb. Way to go saving those boys. You made Hollydale proud."

The neighbor's name eluded him, so Caleb waved back with a smile, a simple "thanks" his only response.

He kept on strolling along Oak Street. If memory served him right, Lucie's house was within walking distance of his cousin's place. The thought of hopping in his car, even for a short drive, had turned his stomach.

Almost as much as the decision before him. Oh, for a hiking stick and his camping gear, as a night under the stars usually helped him focus and come up with solutions.

It had sounded so easy on the drive. Dig around into Lucie's life to see whether his parents should invest in an attorney to broker involvement between the authorities and whoever was in charge of a restitution account, however small, to see if they could

recover the fifty thousand dollars Justin had
swindled from them.

Spying was the more accurate word, but
that was harsher to his ears.

Then came the words he'd never expected
to hear after all these years.

Lucie considered him her best friend.

Friends didn't spy on each other.

Friends didn't lie to each other.

Yet his father, Drew, expected information for his impending decision, which would
necessitate his parents traveling here from
Atlanta. While his mother, Tina, reveled in
being alive and second chances at life, Drew
wasn't as forgiving toward anyone whose last
name was Decker.

Had Caleb known on that fateful Friday
morning that they'd turn over a substantial
portion of their savings to Justin and his
phony investment corporation in the hope
of solid returns, what would he have done
differently? Argue with them? Beg them not
to trust the man they'd fed so often when
he'd come home with Caleb during college
breaks?

Not one of them had had any idea the authorities would swoop in and arrest Justin
before Caleb's parents completed the paper-

work, which would have provided enough proof they, too, had fallen victim to his schemes.

After Drew had been transferred to Atlanta, Caleb had begged his parents to go to the authorities, but they had insisted no one would hire Tina as a bookkeeper if the word got out that they'd trusted a swindler.

Then came the phone call that still sent a shiver up Caleb's spine. Tina had delivered the devastating revelation of her breast cancer diagnosis. For their peace of mind, they'd focused their energy on that battle, especially after Justin was convicted.

Now, the truth hit him hard. Any wisps of hope their savings might still be recoverable were just that. Wisps in the wind that wouldn't pay the mortgage or the remaining doctor bills. They also would never get back the money for that trip to Australia his mother had saved a hundred dollars for every single month.

His boots slapped against the pavement with each step as he remembered childhood winters when his mother had needed a new coat and she'd shrugged on her old one, saying it would be warm in Sydney when she and Dad set foot in the Southern Hemisphere. If he didn't change his attitude and think with a little more optimism, they wouldn't recover anything. A little legwork on Caleb's part couldn't hurt, and it might result in enough of a windfall for his parents to regain their nest egg with some left over for that dream vacation. If he played his cards right, Lucie might not even know. Lawyers were expensive. He'd just observe a little longer and then report back to his parents.

Stretching out his spine, he ignored the tingle below his scar. Driving thirty hours over three days hadn't done his backbone any good, but walking and stretching might alleviate some of his discomfort.

He cut down Timber Road, the spire of Hollydale's oldest church rising high. Made with timber that put Hollydale on the map, the church with its stained-glass windows attracted visitors interested in local history.

Heading west on Maple Drive, he took his time, soaking in the old and the new. Corner Grocery had been there forever; it had always been his first stop—for a bottle of orange Fanta and a Moon Pie—after he cashed his paycheck from his landscaping job at the Applebys' wedding resort. He'd held the job during his junior year until he'd had to quit when the doctors decided surgery was his only option.

Caleb turned onto First Street and caught sight of Hollydale's famous gazebo, where generations of high school seniors had posed for class photos, although he hadn't had such a chance. A staph infection following his scoliosis surgery had sidelined him for the first six weeks of his senior year, and a recurring infection had sent him back to the hospital at the end of the year. On Caleb's graduation day, while his classmates partied, he'd gazed out the hospital window, thankful just to be alive.

"Caleb?"

A familiar voice from behind stopped him in his tracks. He turned and found Jonathan heading his way, his navy police uniform a contrast to Caleb's informal flannel shirt and jeans. In the short time since they'd last seen each other, fine lines had been etched into his cousin's forehead, no doubt on account of the grief following his wife's death.

Caleb waited until Jonathan caught up with him and, after a quick embrace, Caleb clapped his cousin's back. "Great to see you, Officer Maxwell. Thanks for letting me stay with you until I find my own place. Let me guess—the room with duct tape down the middle isn't my bunk area?"

"Izzy can't stand Vanessa's stuffed animals on her side of the room, and Vanessa complains about Izzy's soccer cleats on hers, so that was my solution." Jonathan rolled his eyes but not before Caleb caught the love shining through. "An airbed in the office was the best I could do on short notice."

"Best price around, too." Caleb smiled at how well Jonathan adapted to adjustments. Caleb had never been happy about change— it always seemed to herald something bad.

Then again, Caleb had traveled two thousand miles to start over. If that wasn't a pretty steep change, nothing was. And Lucie had made a good point earlier. Nothing stayed the same forever. Even Hollydale had changed. From here, he could see a new outfitters' business he'd have to explore soon. And Lucie herself was changing her parents' wedding destination into an event and wellness center.

"Earth to Caleb, come in." Jonathan waved his hand in front of Caleb's face. "Are you headed out somewhere, or are you going back to my place? I'll make sure the girls keep it down to a dull roar if you need sleep."

"Thanks, but I have dinner plans out."

Caleb turned and started walking in the direction of Main Street, and Jonathan fell into step beside him. "I'll catch up with you and the girls tomorrow night. I'll admit, I didn't think you'd move to Hollydale after Anne died."

"I had to do something about Izzy. She's a chip off the old block. Eleven going on twenty-one. Thank goodness Vanessa is two years younger than Izzy."

His cousin's raw emotion caught Caleb off guard. It made him feel that much better about his decision to move back and support Jonathan. Family supported family. Always. Sometimes it stretched incredulity that Jonathan, who'd never been the embodiment of law and order, now wore a police uniform.

"And what's this about dinner out?" Jonathan asked. "You've been back long enough to make plans already? Won't Leah What's-her-name be upset?"

A bitter taste coated his mouth at the thought of Leah, who'd lied to him and used him. Her betrayal had made the decision to move to his hometown that much easier once his transfer had come through. Jonathan and his daughters had only sweetened the decision. "Leah stayed in Montana, and I came to

Hollydale wiser for the wear." Caleb glanced at his watch. "I've got to run."

"You're not getting away that easy. First chance we get, I'll take you to the new bar on the outskirts of town—they make great nachos. How about Saturday?" Jonathan folded his arms. "Wait. That won't work. Izzy has a soccer game. We'll figure out a time later. Once you hear about her latest stunt, you'll be buying the first round."

Caleb couldn't even remember how their game had begun, but both men would dump their sob stories. The one whose load was lighter had to buy the other a beer. By the time they left, his wallet was always lighter than Jonathan's. This time would be different. The Leah story alone was worth a few bottles. "Nachos sound good."

Jonathan's radio crackled, and he turned to Caleb. "Gotta go. The girls and I won't wait up."

Caleb turned left on Main and kept walking.

"Caleb Spindler? Is that you?"

He didn't recognize the voice and glanced over his shoulder.

A man held up his thumb. "Way to go. You

made Hollydale proud!" The man grinned before he entered the post office.

Then another person yelled out their congratulations and waved, and Caleb shuffled his feet before waving back. Lucie's house wasn't as close to downtown as he remembered. Of course, everything had seemed shorter and sweeter when he was younger.

In less than a quarter of a mile, the business district gave way to century-old residences, many of which were two-story Victorians with gingerbread trim. He'd always loved this section with its bright colors and brighter gardens. Timber had offered a good livelihood for many in Hollydale. So had the apple orchards, especially for the Appleby family.

His parents had lived a couple of miles away in a house that resembled most of the others in their modest subdivision.

A yellow Victorian caught his eye and he slowed his pace. Then he squinted at what used to be the most impressive house in town. Paint peeled off the second-story shutters, one of which was slightly askew, while the white picket fence bordering the front yard needed pressure washing. He read the sign on the fence: Don't Let the Pigs Out. He rubbed his eyes and reread the words. He hadn't made any mistakes.

Low-pitched grunts piqued his curiosity, so he stepped onto the soft green grass and peeked over the fence. Rubbing his eyes, he stopped and focused on one miniature pig rooting in the ground while the other scratched its back on a wooden post in the garden. A border collie completed the picture, running in circles around the other two animals.

Lucie Appleby, debutante and homecoming queen, now owned pigs? The surprises kept coming.

Caleb tore himself away from the sight and strode along the sidewalk leading to Lucie's front porch. Good-natured barking signaled his approach. He wasn't quite sure what he was walking into. The wellness center sparkled, but the condition of Lucie's house verged on disrepair.

Caleb knocked and the door opened to reveal a young boy. "We're not allowed to talk to strangers. Goodbye!"

The front door slammed in Caleb's face.

"Ethan," a girl's voice, laced with disapproval, came through loud and clear. "You shouldn't say that. You should have said we don't want any and talked about Ladybug. Salespeople don't like big dogs."

"But Ladybug loves everyone."

The front door flew open and Lucie stood there, her mouth agape, holding on to the bright pink collar of a giant brown-and-white bulldog with slobber hanging down the sides of its mouth. "Caleb. Come on in before the house gets cold."

Who could resist an invitation like that?

Caleb entered, and Lucie released the bull-dog, who grunted and settled on its haunches right at his feet.

"This is Caleb, the old friend I was telling you about. We went to high school and college together."

The little girl in a sparkly tie-dyed T-shirt and bright purple leggings came up to him and held out her hand, her blond hair curling in every direction. "I'm Matilda Grace Decker, and I'm seven. I'm older than Ethan by twenty-two minutes, and pink and purple are my favorite colors."

Out of nowhere, a small gray bunny hopped into the middle of the conversation, and Matilda paused to pick the animal up.

"Now, Harvey, you're not supposed to be out of your cage. Excuse me!" She curtsied and held the bunny to her chest, murmuring endearments while she climbed the stairs.

Lucie smiled and turned to the boy—with his dark brown hair and wide cheeks, he looked exactly like a younger version of Justin. "This is my son, Ethan."

"I gotta help Mattie. She's bad at closing doors, and Harvey'll get out." Ethan escaped and followed Mattie.

This was his opportunity to start digging. Best to ask questions when the twins weren't within earshot. He hadn't counted on how he'd feel probing with them around. They were innocent in all of this.

Still, his father wanted to know if it would be worth it to hire an attorney. With his parents in Georgia, that left him to look for answers.

"Lucie..."

"The timer's about to buzz, and I need your advice. Ladybug, get off Caleb's foot." Lucie waved for him to follow her, and he navigated the obstacle course around the book bags and shoes left at the front door. "Ladybug's a darling. Mattie named her after she was abandoned. Ladybug, that is. Mattie never wanders far from my side. She keeps

Ethan in line. Ethan named our other dog Pita. She's outside with the pigs right now."

The bulldog plodded after him as if he was her new best friend, while Caleb gathered his wits about him. First the wellness center had thrown him off track, and now Lucie's home flustered him—warmth reigned here, with a dollop of controlled chaos. Unlike the brand-new stuff at the center, the furniture here looked lived in and older but still comfortable, in keeping with her style.

Caleb settled on one of the stools at the laminate counter, the delicious aroma reminding his stomach it hadn't had anything homemade in quite some time. He glanced down to find Ladybug, her tongue lolling, watching his every move. Great, a canine chaperone who probably wouldn't take kindly when he asked subtle questions that might come across as accusing her owner of stealing to pay for her kibble.

Lucie handed him a cucumber and a peeler. "No one eats for free here. You'll be working for your dinner."

He was used to hard work. That might have been the hardest part of his hospital stay. Not the surgery, not the infections, but having to be still. Without his two part-time jobs, he'd been at his wit's end until Lucie had arrived with books, crossword puzzles and herself to keep him company. Lucie and his sketching had saved him.

He peeled the cucumber and decided to start small. "How long before the center is open for business?"

"One month. While we're fully booked for the first three weeks, I was thinking someone with a little clout might be a draw until there's some word of mouth. Catch—" She threw two tomatoes at him and he caught them.

One thing was for sure—she was as unpredictable as ever. He'd missed that about her.

"Slice those for the salad but leave them on the side. Mattie loves fresh tomatoes, but Ethan only likes them once they're processed in the form of ketchup." The oven buzzed. Lucie opened the door and waves of cheesy perfection wafted his way.

His stomach grumbled and he considered letting Lucie off the hook, especially with her children in the house. But as much as he'd like a fresh start, his parents deserved answers. "You have a pretty impressive setup, Luce."

She walked over to the refrigerator and

emerged with two bottles of salad dressing. "Italian or ranch?"

"How much did it cost?" Wariness entered his voice, the same tone he heard whenever someone asked him whether the animals running through Yellowstone were really wild.

"A couple dollars each. When you have twins, sometimes you have to splurge." Lucie laughed and set the bottles on the kitchen island.

"The ropes courses and the new business."

She met his gaze and the laughter faded from those morning glory eyes of hers. "More than a couple dollars." She reached for a towel and wiped off her hands. "Why?"

"Where did the money come from?"

Her smile faded. "If I didn't know you were a park ranger, I'd guess you were with another branch of the government right now…"

"Mommy, is dinner ready? I'm starving." Ethan ran into the room and reached for a crouton, popping it into his mouth.

"You and Mattie can play on the Nintendo system for ten minutes." Some of the softness came back when she addressed Ethan.

Caleb already missed that softness directed at him.

"Yesss." Ethan fisted his hand and brought

it toward his chest in a victory motion. "Hey, Mattie," Ethan yelled, "we can play games until dinner."

"I get to decide which game first." Mattie's voice called out from the other room, and Ladybug sauntered out of the kitchen.

Lucie closed the door and crossed her arms, her cold gaze chilling the air. "Spit it out, Caleb. Why did you really come here tonight?"

Guess he would have made a lousy spy.

Even after years apart, she knew him better than anyone else. Including Jonathan.

Still, family was family.

"There's been a lot of work done at the wellness center. You claimed in the news stories that Justin wiped you out, but if he left you with nothing, how did you afford those improvements?"

Lucie gazed upward before running her hands through her hair and looking his way. "For two years, I've been accused of every crime imaginable. There's nothing like finding out your husband, who's now my ex, is a first-rate scumbag." Lowering her voice, she glanced toward the living room and clenched her teeth. "So many people didn't believe me. So many times, I thought I wouldn't get to see my children grow up because I'd be behind bars. So many times, I thought of you and missed my friend, the person who always treated me with respect."

"Lucie."

"Did you come here for dinner?" There was that chin tilt again. "Or to interrogate me?"

One thing was for sure. She wasn't lying. The one time she tried to lie to him in the hospital was a memory in and of itself. He'd given her caramel clusters as a thank-you gift, and she hemmed and hawed before admitting caramel made her break out in hives. "I made a mistake."

"A mistake is picking up a bag of decaf instead of the real stuff. Those questions were deliberate."

Friends didn't dig into places they weren't welcome, and friends didn't make friends feel that bad.

"Maybe we should start over." He stepped toward her, hand extended. "Hi, Lucie Appleby. It's been a long time. Too long."

"Not tonight. I don't want you to slip and ask any questions in front of the twins." She opened the kitchen door and Ladybug was sitting there, a forlorn look in her brown eyes as if she, too, regretted making Caleb her new best friend. "Just go."

While he'd been in the hospital, only one person other than his parents had come to visit every day, the same person whose gaze reflected so much hurt right now.

Tomorrow might be soon enough to start over. At the front door, Caleb looked back at the warmth and love in the chaotic house. It was everything he'd dreamed of having while he was in the hospital, and nothing he'd ever been able to work hard enough to deserve.

CHAPTER TWO

LUCIE TUCKED HER laptop under her arm and opened the door of A New You, her favorite of the two beauty salons in Hollydale. The tinny bell chimed her presence bright and early on this Wednesday morning. Aerosol spray and perm solution overcame the fresh mountain air as she crossed the threshold, searching for the owner, Mitzi Mayfield. What she would have done these past two years without Mitzi, she didn't know.

At first, Mitzi had been the only person willing to give her a job after Justin's arrest, even standing by her when some of the salon's most loyal customers left for Mitzi's competitor. That kind of loyalty set Mitzi apart. Gratitude didn't even begin to cover her debt to her mother's best friend. If Mitzi hadn't stepped up to the plate, Lucie would have had to move, leaving the house that had been in her family for four generations, away from the only home the twins had ever known.

The only positive to come out of the past two years was finding out who her true friends were. Max O'Hara fixed her car and let her work on Sundays to pay off the cost of repairs before Georgie returned to Hollydale and found love with the newly elected sheriff, Mike Harrison. Another one of her mother's friends, Odalie Musgrove, had hired her part time during a particularly rough patch when the bills had almost overwhelmed her. Lucie had considered Caleb one of those true friends, even though they'd lost contact with each other. Last night had proved her wrong.

"Lucie! Save me. They waylaid me. Mitzi wants to do something to my hair that involves some sort of lights that aren't headlights." Her friend Georgie's wail carried over the dual sounds of blow dryers and canned hip-hop music.

Lucie hurried to the back of the salon, where Georgie sat with a cape around her shoulders. Lucie settled her laptop on Mitzi's workstation and joined her friend Natalie, who was standing next to Georgie's chair, her bright pink cowboy boots tapping against the beige linoleum floor.

Natalie turned to Georgie. "We talked about this and you agreed to try something new. Besides, you're a newlywed. You need surprise and spontaneity in your life. Mike will thank you for it."

"You're my sister-in-law and therefore biased. I'm so not going there." Georgie reached out to Lucie and pleaded with her green eyes. "The cars waiting to be fixed in my shop don't complain about my hair, and neither does Mike."

Mitzi breezed over with a rolling station containing her supplies, including foils, a timer and clips. She patted the ends of her gray bobbed hair before placing her long fingers on the back of Georgie's chair. "Georgie, Georgie, Georgie. Trust me. Relax and leave your beautiful hair in my capable hands, and you won't regret it. Ask Lucie here about trust."

What? Of all the people in the salon, Lucie was the worst person to say anything about that subject. Why other folks had the ability to read people and she didn't, she couldn't fathom, but she was infamous for trusting first and asking questions second. Last night had only confirmed that trait. Instead of catching up over dinner with an old friend, Caleb had kept asking about money, giving every impression he'd only accepted her invitation to grill her rather than enjoy her company.

"I don't think I'm the most qualified person to talk about trust."

Mitzi nudged Lucie's ribs and sent her a glaring look.

Lucie shrugged. "Except I can truthfully say Mitzi knows what she's doing. She has great instincts."

"Honey, you do, too." Mitzi palmed the ends of Georgie's hair and rubbed several strands together. "That spa idea of yours for the center is right on the money. I'm yours two afternoons a week, and my niece will work for you the other three days a week. We're going to exfoliate the dead skin off your clients and leave them refreshed. You'll pay my investment back in no time."

At that moment, the blow dryer at the other station ceased and everyone else in the salon turned to Lucie.

A weak smile and wave were all she could muster. "It's never been a secret Mitzi is one of my partners. We have a contract and everything. I'm not taking advantage of her."

When Lucie had approached Mitzi with the idea for the wellness center, Lucie insisted everything be signed and notarized. Aunt

Rosemary, her other partner, who lived in California, had paid for the attorney who'd formed the limited liability corporation and kept the deeds to the lodge and cabin as collateral.

"And anyone who says different will have no choice but to visit Chantal's Hair Emporium. Do I make myself clear?" Mitzi picked up a black comb and her thinning shears and waved them around.

The other stylist and her customer nodded. It was no idle threat to send someone over to Chantal's given how everyone, from toddlers to senior citizens, left Chantal's with the same mullet hairstyle.

Mitzi shrugged, her gray bob not moving an inch, while she combed out Georgie's wet hair. "Georgie, you're more tense than my ex-husband. Trust me." Mitzi started clipping Georgie's hair into sections. "Lucie, sweetie, you'll pay me back. I have confidence in you."

Natalie glanced at her watch and gasped. "It's nine already? I didn't realize it was so late. My first personal day away from my kindergarten class since I've been back in Hollydale, and here I am gabbing the day away." She closed the gap between her and Lucie.

"You look like you've lost your best friend. Would a granola bar help?"

Natalie rummaged through her purse, and Lucie held up her hand. Natalie's purse was legendary in these parts as a bottomless receptacle.

"I ate breakfast. I'm good."

"In case you're hungry later, I have a surprise for you." Natalie picked up a pink box with Night Owl Bakery in italicized script on the side. "My college roommate, Shelby, is moving next door to me today—you're going to love her and her little boy, Danny. Anyway, I ran to the bakery when it opened for a Welcome to Hollydale present. I picked up a box of red velvet cupcakes for Georgie. Yes, you must share with Mike and Rachel. After all, he's my brother, and she's my adorable niece. I also grabbed a box of oatmeal cherry chocolate-chip cookies…"

Her favorite. "For me?"

"Well, they're not for Fred and Ethel. By the way, what were you thinking when you accepted responsibility for those miniature pigs? You have enough going on in your life." Natalie waved her hand while tucking the other box under her arm. "Don't have time to stay and chat. Fingers and toes crossed,

Georgie's hair will look as marvelous as I believe it will. 'Bye!"

Natalie was already halfway out the door when Mitzi turned toward Lucie. "You know I love your visits, but is there something you need?"

"I dropped by to deliver these financial spreadsheets and to see if you have any questions."

"That's my sweet Lucie, always one step ahead of me. My faith in you is as big as my hips, and that's saying something." Mitzi wiggled said hips, and some of Lucie's ache eased. "Is this a good weekend for those inventory lists?"

"Already done. I paid the bills and updated those lists yesterday." The only good thing about last night was that she'd turned her dismay over Caleb's accusation into several hours of productive paperwork, knocking out much of her to-do list in the wee hours of the morning.

"Is that what's causing those dark circles, sweetie? A new cucumber facial came in. Why don't you take a load off, plant yourself in a chair and let me wait on you for a few minutes before you head over to the wellness center?" Mitzi snapped on her latex gloves and tapped Georgie's shoulder. "Do you want me to perform a strand test to see if you like the color enough for me to continue?"

Georgie glanced over her shoulder and sighed. "Never mind. Just do it all at once. Rachel will love that I did something new, and Max said to take my time this morning. We're booked all afternoon." She met Lucie's gaze and reached out and touched her hand. "Mitzi's right, Lucie. You look like a Mack truck ran you over. Everything okay with the twins?"

"They're fine. Ethan was disappointed our guest didn't stay for dinner last night, though."

Ethan's pouty lip had been on display throughout the meal and lingered until bedtime, while Mattie had forgotten Caleb's visit within minutes of his leaving.

Was she rubbing off the wrong way on her daughter? Her trying to put aside people who thought badly of her was one thing, but for her young daughter to mimic her behavior didn't seem right. Lucie stifled her shiver.

"Guest? What guest?" Mitzi halted her nimble fingers before she finished wrapping the last section of Georgie's hair. "Someone who'll appreciate you for you, I hope?"

Georgie echoed the sentiment, and Lucie lost her chance to escape while the getting was good.

Lucie grabbed one of the clips and snapped it. "Caleb Spindler is back in town."

"Caleb? The Hero of Hollydale?" Mitzi started applying the cream mixture to Georgie's hair. "We should approach him about endorsing the center while the curling iron is still hot."

Mitzi laughed at her own joke while Lucie cracked a smile.

"That might be difficult considering I kicked him out of my house last night."

"Oh, sweetie. I'm sure you had a good reason." Sympathy laced Mitzi's voice while she dabbed on more of the cream mixture without even pausing at the mention of Lucie's guest. "We'll get someone else. The endorsements will come through once we open and you and your staff build bridges. We'll do fine without him."

Come to think of it, though, he was moving back to town, so she'd soon be running into him at the grocery store, the gas station and everywhere else. Maybe she'd better get past her defensiveness and tell him the whole story so she could hold her head high around him.

For some reason, she'd unloaded on Caleb last night. It wasn't his fault many Hollydale residents had accused her of biding her time and then usurping the money for herself. What was it about this new version of Caleb that made her react so strongly?

"I'll call you tonight and we can go over everything." Lucie grabbed her laptop along with the cookies. "Wish me luck. I'm going to get the app for the wellness center up and running this morning. See you both later."

For now, though, she'd enjoy the treat of a box of her favorite cookies. Sometimes good surprises did turn up out of the blue.

CALEB HADN'T TAKEN three days off in a row since college. Keeping busy was the best antidote to the fear he'd experienced in his hospital bed. At Yellowstone, Caleb had always donated his vacation time to a fellow employee dealing with a difficult personal or family situation. Other rangers might have grumbled about it, but Caleb gave without regret. Vacations weren't his cup of espresso. Steady work drove out the memory of his hospital stay and kept him strong.

While his back held out, he intended to thrive on fresh air and mountain hikes. Every time he donned his ranger uniform, he did his best to make sure Jonathan's daughters, Izzy and Vanessa, could appreciate the same beautiful world, now and in the future.

When Owen Thompson, the new deputy director for the park, had called and asked him to report late this afternoon instead of this morning, Caleb had agreed. It gave him time to either head north ten miles to hike near Lake Pine Falls, the one with the aptly-named waterfall at the end of the trail, or to check out the improvements to downtown Hollydale that he'd glimpsed last night.

In the end, getting familiar with his home-town again won out. Sitting outside Sal's Pizzeria with a meat lover's slice in hand, he breathed in the mountain air and knew he'd made the right choice. From here, the store-fronts gleamed in the sunlight, the renovations and updates fresher and cleaner than he'd remembered.

Everywhere he turned, change greeted him. Now he counted a whopping four traffic lights instead of a mere three.

His waitress checked on him as he popped the last bite into his mouth. Laughing at the timing, he shook his head and asked for the bill.

It was her turn to laugh. "Already paid. You

missed the fight between two of our regulars about who'd get to treat you to lunch."

He'd only been doing his job. When would the attentiveness fade? Probably when another story caught everyone's attention. He hoped that came soon. He offered his thanks anyway and finished his sweet tea. When she left, he tucked a ten under his plate and started walking.

Since he'd been gone, Hollydale had boosted its efforts to become a tourist destination. Even on a Wednesday afternoon, he saw the fruits of those labors, more foot traffic than he'd expected, not that he could blame anyone who had the time to enjoy this balmy afternoon.

With a little over an hour until his interview with a real-estate agent, since Owen had made it clear the station couldn't offer him housing, he stopped at a new marker in front of the old courthouse. The structure had been built when Hollydale incorporated in the early twentieth century. He'd always assumed the town was named for a woman. Instead, it had been the abundance of hollyhocks in the area that had inspired the name.

If he remembered correctly, there was a bookstore nearby. He might as well pick up some local history books and prepare himself more for the bevy of visitors' questions he'd encounter on the job.

After a trip inside The Book Nook—where Connie Witherspoon threw in one of the local history books on the discount table for free, while he paid for three others—he still had a good half hour before he was due at Cobb Realty.

His wallet lightened a little more after a quick stop at the Corner Grocery where the new owners, Mr. and Mrs. Nguyen, introduced themselves when he purchased a box of Moon Pies to share with Izzy and Vanessa later.

A flyer in the front window of Timber River Outfitters, next door to Cobb Realty, caught Caleb's eye. He stopped and read the details of the second annual Timber River Sunset Soiree. Recognizing the name of the keynote speaker, the noted environmentalist Howard Otto, he nodded his appreciation for a small town snagging such a prestigious name. A little over a week away, the community function, with dinner, a silent auction and dancing, sounded right up Caleb's alley. Once he learned his schedule from Owen, Caleb intended to track down a ticket.

Would Lucie be attending on behalf of the new wellness center? Even though last night had been a disaster of the first magnitude, he'd like a chance to remedy the situation. During yesterday's tour of the center, she'd been articulate, her face glowing as she'd pointed out different features. He wouldn't mind seeing that side of her again.

And not only to find out enough information so his father would know whether to hire an attorney. Lucie's intelligence sparked something inside Caleb, something he would have loved to investigate if it weren't for his parents.

Shaking off his reverie, the window display of the outfitters made him eager to make his wallet even lighter. While he would have loved nothing more than to go inside and peruse the latest offerings, he'd best not take the chance he'd lose track of time and miss his appointment with the Realtor.

Taking a step toward the Cobb Realty office, Caleb winced at the twinge in his lower spine. He went in and, while they couldn't see him until his appointment time, he could leave his packages there. Waving, he returned outside. One time around the block ought to work out the remaining kinks from the drive, not to mention sleeping on the fifth different mattress in as many nights.

The discomfort was worth it, though, since he'd had a chance to connect with Vanessa over breakfast. He'd cherish every moment with Jonathan's family until he unpacked a new bed and mattress in his own place after the storage container company delivered his belongings. Once he moved, he'd invite them over often.

Living in faraway Montana had made family bonds all the more precious. While the green mountains of the Smokies had called out for his return, being this close to Jonathan and his daughters ran a close second. The jury was still out on Lucie.

The famous Hollydale gazebo came into sight, and he heard a muffled bark. Before he could head back to the Realtor's office, Lucie came into view with Ladybug waddling toward him, Mattie on one side of Lucie with a dandelion in her hand, and Ethan on the other.

Ethan's pout turned into a full-fledged smile, and he ran forward. Caleb looked around, trying to find out who'd caused such a reaction, but no one else was there.

"Mr. Caleb! Do you remember me? I'm Ethan." The boy skidded and stopped short of colliding with Caleb by about two inches. "My mom still has a lot of macaroni and cheese left over from last night. She made extra on account of you, but you left in such a hurry. I know hers isn't as good as the type you get in the box, the kind with the bright orange powder that tastes great when you lick it off your fingers, but it's pretty good if you give it a chance."

"Ethan!" Lucie caught up, two bright pink circles blossoming on her cheeks. "I'm sure Mr. Spindler has better things to do with his time."

This interchange was the most fun he'd had in a long time. When you made national news for something positive, people treated you differently. All Caleb wanted was to retreat into the shadows and get back to doing his job. "Not for fifteen minutes."

"Since you couldn't have dinner with us, why don't you share our cookies? Ladybug can only walk for ten minutes at a time on account of she's a bulldog, and she needs a break now, so Mommy made it a cookie break." Ethan kept talking as he led Caleb over to the gazebo, making sure Caleb sat next to him.

Caleb looked to Lucie for confirmation

this was acceptable to her. She gripped Ladybug's leash so firmly her knuckles turned white. Mattie stayed close to her side, almost as though she were protecting her mom instead of the other way around.

Then Lucie sighed and lowered herself onto the opposite bench, Mattie clambering next to her. "The Night Owl Bakery opened after you moved away, and Paige, the owner, bakes a delicious cookie. I'd be a bad role model for my children if I didn't share."

Her underlying meaning was clear. Lucie wasn't welcoming him back into her fold. She was only being polite on account of Mattie and Ethan, her family. This might be his only chance to earn redemption in her eyes, so he'd best make the most of his opportunity.

He shrugged. "And I'd be a worse friend if I didn't make amends for last night."

Lucie reached into her tote bag and pulled out a portable dog water bottle with an attached bowl. With a flick of her wrist, she filled the bowl and held it down to Ladybug's level. The bulldog slobbered at the water, her appreciative grunts breaking the silence. The sound had Caleb recalling last night. He was caught between guilt over Lucie and a sense of disloyalty to his parents, and he couldn't seem to shake either.

Moving back to Hollydale was supposed to fill that family-sized hole in him, the one he'd dug when he moved to Yellowstone, where he hadn't known a soul. While the job was professionally fulfilling, there'd been something lacking. Something green like the pines dotting the Great Smokies. Something deep like the depths of Timber River. Something he yearned to reconnect with.

Or some*one*.

"These oatmeal cherry chocolate-chip cookies were a gift." Lucie's calm voice broke through his thoughts. "And it's wrong to keep a gift to yourself."

"Especially considering my lunch was a couple of hours ago. I walked around downtown, and I'm already starving." Especially for one of those smiles he'd seen yesterday during the tour, the type that showed off the one crooked tooth that did nothing to distract from her pretty face.

He found her far more attractive than he should.

"Far be it for me to deny a starving man a cookie even if his questions were a little too direct…" With a glance at her twins, she stopped.

"Forgiveness is a gift, too. Especially when a person is genuinely sorry for what he's done." Whether he was asking for silent forgiveness from his parents for associating with Lucie or from Lucie for confronting her last night before his suitcases were even unpacked, he wasn't quite sure.

"And there are times when one did nothing to ask forgiveness for." Her low voice urged caution, as if he was treading onto a path she didn't want to travel.

"But you tell me all the time I have to say I'm sorry to Mattie, even when I didn't do anything." Ethan patted his stomach. "And, Mattie, can I ple-ease have my cookie now?"

Mattie hugged Lucie before jumping off the bench and holding out the box to her mother. Lucie held up her finger and pulled something out of her tote bag. "I didn't forget your favorite sweet potato treat, Ladybug." After the bulldog snatched the treat, Lucie pulled two cookies from the box. "Thanks, Mattie. I'll hold on to yours for you."

Mattie crossed the length of the gazebo and delivered a cookie to Ethan before stopping short of Caleb. Her eyes were still wary of him, not that he blamed her. He'd arrived for dinner and left suddenly. Although Ethan had accepted Caleb without a blink of the eye, Mattie seemed an old soul in a pair of rainbow leggings, much more cautious.

Ethan was more like the Lucie of the past, and Mattie resembled her mother now. Caleb yearned to see a glimpse of the Lucie from so long ago, and yet, this Lucie was more beautiful than ever, as though the years had thrown her a curveball but hadn't defeated her. Having Lucie's friendship would count for something. As would Mattie's.

"Thank you. This'll tide me over through my appointment with the real-estate agent." Caleb glanced at his watch. He'd have to leave in a few minutes, another case of talk and run. Somehow, though, he wanted any time he could get with this family. He bit into the cookie, the flavors melting in his mouth. "Not many things are as good as promised, but this is one of them."

"A little tart, a little sweet, but always satisfying." Lucie held up the uneaten half of her cookie before taking another bite, a blissful look coming over her face. Caleb popped the other half of his cookie in his mouth and took his time chewing. This was why he'd made his way back home.

Ethan jumped up, ran over to Mattie and tagged her on the shoulder. "You're it."

Mattie sprinted after her brother, who was already on the steps out to the green space in front of the gazebo, the distraction doing Caleb a world of good.

Lucie peeked into the pink box. "There's one cookie left. Want to split it?"

Ladybug snuffled and made her way over to Caleb as though asking him to split half of his half with her. She nudged her head under his hand, begging for crumbs of affection if there were to be no crumbs of cookie forthcoming. He scratched her head and her tongue lolled. "Will she forgive me if I keep it to myself?"

Lucie plucked the cookie out of the box and broke it in two. "Ladybug looks rough and tough, but she's a kind soul. Mattie's bunny, Harvey, jumps all over her and she doesn't bat an eye." She walked over and held out half of the cookie. "Speak now or forever hold your peace."

For honesty's sake, he should spill the whole story about his parents' savings now. The revelation of another one of Justin's lies should come from him rather than anyone else. With the twins occupied on the lawn around the gazebo, playing tag as if they didn't have a care in the world, there'd never be a better time.

But seeing those blue eyes hurt again held less appeal than another thirty-hour drive.

"Thanks." He reached for the cookie, but she pulled it back.

"What if this cookie comes with strings attached?" She knit her eyebrows together before laughing and shaking her head and extending his half. "The cookie is free, but I do need to get something off my chest about the wellness center. I need a favor. That was the point of my email. Nowadays, I try not to hold anything back anymore."

His breath caught as he accepted the proffered half. Whatever she had to say couldn't top his revelation. His phone chimed, the reminder his appointment was a mere five minutes from now. "Can this wait? I'm meeting with Robin Jennings, the newest agent for Cobb Realty, in a few. My cousin's been great about letting me stay with him, but sharing a bathroom with Jonathan and his two daughters on school mornings is already getting old. After I tour possible rentals, I have a meeting with my boss."

"Do you have a few minutes tomorrow morning?" Lucie rummaged through her purse before pulling out her phone. "I have an interview with a potential employee at eight at The Busy Bean. I'll buy you a cup of your favorite espresso to celebrate your move."

"The Busy Bean? Is that new, too?"

Lucie nodded. "The downtown revitalization project has been a godsend for the town. More and more tourists are coming for the Independence Day parade, and then it's bumper-to-bumper until fall. Hollydale is becoming quite the attraction."

That made his job with the Park Service all that more important. Caleb didn't know what time Owen would want him to report tomorrow, and he didn't want to turn around and cancel plans with Lucie. Then again, Jonathan's coffee left something to be desired, and Caleb didn't have the heart to tell him. "I'll try. I can't promise anything, though. Thanks for the cookie."

Walking down the gazebo steps, he glanced over his shoulder and waved. Reconciling his future with his past had seemed so easy in Montana, but here?

Had he betrayed his parents by sharing a cookie with Lucie and her kids? Sure felt that way. Since he was staying in Hollydale for good, he'd have to figure out how to keep Lucie at a distance. So far, he hadn't been succeeding.

Somehow, he'd have to give Lucie a wider berth in the future.

Sometime after tomorrow.

THE MILE MARKERS to Lake Pine Falls gleamed in the setting rays of the late-afternoon sun, the Park Service logo at the bottom right. He swung into the employees' parking lot, a childhood dream come true. While most rangers dreamed of Yellowstone or Yosemite, the Timber River Park represented the pinnacle of success for Caleb. Taking care of the animals and environment in his backyard was all he'd ever wanted.

Getting out of his SUV, he winced at the back twinge that was becoming too much a part of his everyday life. He'd aggravated it when he pulled the youngest boy out of the crevice, and he should have known better than to drive ten hours a day, but the thought of reuniting with Jonathan and finding out information to give his parents had spurred him to keep his hands on the wheel. The sooner he signed a lease and slept on a good mattress, the sooner his body would recover.

Caleb strode to the rear of his SUV and opened his first-aid kit. He chased two ibuprofen with a sip of water while composing himself for his meeting with Owen Thompson, who'd insisted he arrive in plain clothes rather than the standard park ranger uniform of starched green pants and beige shirt.

Caleb zipped up his favorite forest-green jacket, the insignia badge front and center the same found in the gift shops, and forged on into headquarters positioned alongside the visitor center. Waiting in the lobby was Owen, his thinning gray hair the only difference from his picture. Caleb would have known him in his sleep.

"You must be Caleb." The deputy director approached him, his hand extended. "My office is at the end of this hall."

After the niceties were complete, Caleb relaxed, confident he'd chosen the right path. "What time would you like me to report tomorrow?"

Owen placed his elbows on the metal desk. "I heard you never waste time." He laughed and pulled out a file folder. "Yes, I'm old-school paper and files, and yes, I talked to your former supervisor. He said you slow down for meals, and that's all you slow down for. We talked about you at some length."

Even now, the world beyond Owen's office beckoned through the window, the dark brown dirt of the trails, the verdant green of the pines and the slight breeze swaying their tips. Spring was a time of rebirth and discovery. About now, wildflowers would start to unfurl their petals, bears would straddle out of their hibernation dens, and tourists would dust off their backpacks for excursions on Timber River and the Appalachian Trail. Caleb wanted to be a part of all of that.

"Then you should know I'm itching for a tour of the facilities. Spring is the best time to come on board and get to know the staff."

"Whoa! First things first. Lodging accommodations. Like I said on the phone, we don't have a cabin on-site for you, so you'll have to commute. My daughter Ashleigh and I occupy one of the two cabins near our main facility. The senior ranger, Mindy Ellison, lives with her family in the cabin that's farther away from Hollydale. You're taking quite a pay cut without a housing stipend."

"It's almost like you're trying to get rid of me before I even start."

"Not at all. Just wondering if this will seem tame in comparison to what you're used to."

What he was used to was hard work. He'd prefer to do that where he felt comfortable. Caleb leaned forward, his arms on his knees. "I've been in touch with Cobb Realty. My agent knows I need something close by."

"Great. Then there's the little matter of your routine physical." Owen opened the file and handed Caleb a stack of forms.

Caleb wrinkled his brows while he inspected the paperwork. "I just went through all of this last October in Montana. Everything should be in order." That small twinge near his tailbone kicked up, and he shifted in his seat. "Blood work, EKG, the whole kit and caboodle. I should be good to start tomorrow."

"You know it's routine at any transfer." Owen leaned back and linked his arms behind him to form a pillow. "And you've had a busy month, what with the rescue and the trip here. Take the rest of the week off. Get reacquainted with Hollydale."

Caleb rubbed his right ear before laughing. "If you're worried I'm going to preen and carry myself off as a hero, don't. I'm a team player. What we do at this station, we do together."

"That's not the problem." Owen sighed and moved to an upright position. "You know the turnover rate in our line of work. I've seen park rangers console the loved ones of hikers who had fatal heart attacks on the trail. I've seen tourists who are convinced our safety signs and procedures don't apply to them and get hurt—or worse—when they disregard our regulations.

"Since you're coming from Yellowstone, I don't need to tell you about the campers who believe grizzlies are real-life teddy bears. I've seen burnout firsthand. Going in for your physical, taking the rest of the week off and getting settled will help your fellow rangers and yourself. We're a family here, and we look out for each other."

As much as Caleb wanted to argue, he understood those stories—he'd seen all of that firsthand, too. But this mandatory vacation irked the part of him that wanted to be out on the trails helping others and ensuring someone looked out for the animals.

Even if Owen was just looking out for him.

Caleb rose from the chair and extended his

hand to the deputy director. "I'll be here Monday morning bright and early, as energetic as the Timber River woodpecker at Lucie Decker's training and wellness center."

Owen motioned for him to sit back down and Caleb did so. "You saw a Timber River woodpecker? Are you sure?"

"Positive." Caleb pointed to a framed sketching of birds of the region next to a bookshelf. "If you look closely at that print, you'll see the initials CAS in the corner. I drew that and presented it to the director before I left for college. Local ornithology is something I care about." Sketching and Lucie were the two things that had kept him sane after his surgery.

Owen glanced over his shoulder and smiled. "For the record, I had to twist the director's arm to leave that behind. So, you know your birds. When did you see it?"

"Yesterday afternoon."

Owen tapped his fingers together. "I haven't seen a Timber River woodpecker in the year I've been here. They're critically endangered. As a matter of fact, we're the main sponsor for the Sunset Soiree, which will help fund efforts to save them and start a nature conservancy in Hollydale. If you see one again, take a picture and send it to me, along with the exact location. Once there's confirmed proof, we'll map their habitat and go from there."

"Lucie says the woodpecker has fallen in love with her chimney." His stomach churned at how he might be throwing Lucie under the bus—if there was a Timber River woodpecker nest on her property, there'd be park rangers combing the area, enough so as to make her corporate retreats a sight more difficult.

"Then I definitely want a picture. If her land holds the migration and nesting site of an endangered species, the Park Service will monitor the situation and go from there." Owen stopped short of declaring any further intentions, but he didn't have to.

Caleb knew too well what Owen's next steps would be if the woodpecker had chosen Lucie's property as its own personal nesting site.

Eminent domain could tear Lucie's center away from her before it had a chance to succeed.

Owen stood, as did Caleb. Pausing at the door, the deputy director motioned for Caleb to walk ahead of him. "Between the physical and your first assignment of sending me a photo of the woodpecker, it seems like you aren't getting away from work, after all." They reached the employees' entrance and Owen patted Caleb on the back, hard enough for that sore spot to ache once more. Caleb did all he could to keep from jumping. "Your supervisor was sorry to lose you. Hard workers are a rare find. See you Monday morning."

Caleb waved goodbye and walked out to the parking lot. He pressed the key fob and unlocked the driver's door, then stopped. The concern of confiding the plight of the Timber River woodpecker to Lucie brought a moment of panic.

Being with her again was a gift horse that could rear up and kick him in the mouth if he wasn't careful.

CHAPTER THREE

THE AROMA OF coffee and cinnamon added to The Busy Bean's allure and bolstered an already good Thursday morning. The twins hadn't argued once, and Lucie was on time to interview Sierra Hernandez. If this went well, she'd have her employment roster rounded out today before she started cleaning the fire pit area, followed by an afternoon of supervising the AV equipment installation.

Was Caleb's return heralding a change of fortune for her? While the jury was still out on Caleb, his arrival might be a reminder that rainbows could peek through storm clouds. In his case, he'd seemed to sail along on calm seas after that turbulent senior year almost sank him.

Unsinkable. That was Caleb. She could learn something from him.

Scanning the shop, Lucie spotted Sierra, the recent college graduate who wanted to stay in Hollydale but hadn't found anything that would dent her student loans. While Lucie wouldn't be able to offer the same compensation package as more established companies, she did have the locale working in her favor. Nature, quaint shops and casual cuisine combined to pack a triple combination hard to resist.

"Hi, Sierra." Lucie wove her way around the long line before arriving at the table Sierra had snagged. Her eyes widened at the beverage and muffin placed at what was presumably her seat. "You didn't have to buy me anything."

Sierra laughed and waved her hand. "Mom insisted. She said if you're thinking of hiring me and keeping me in town, the least she could do is buy you breakfast." Her expression suddenly turned serious. "It's not a bribe, though. I only want the job if I'm qualified and if you want me on your staff."

"This interview's a two-way street. You'll have to determine if you want to be a member of my staff." Sweat broke out on Lucie's forehead at the thought of signing payroll checks for an entire staff.

This dream of running a training and wellness center was coming together so fast. Maybe too fast as she'd be responsible for a staff who'd depend on her for their financial welfare.

The thought terrified her. She wasn't someone everyone in Hollydale looked up to, not like Caleb. Maybe she should have stuck to running her parents' wedding destination lodge, where she'd worked as a teenager. However, she sure wasn't a role model for a successful marriage, or an observant wife.

And she certainly wasn't a hypocrite.

Not that marriage was bad for everyone. For her friends Georgie and Mike, who'd married a few months ago, true love helped them weather storms that would have scuttled other couples. In Lucie's case? One trip to the altar was enough.

Love was fine for other people, but it wasn't for her.

"Let me pull up your résumé on my phone." Lucie settled into her seat and kept from digging into the apple-cinnamon-crumb muffin. *Thank you, Sierra's mom.* For all of their sakes, she hoped Sierra would accept the job. "Your credentials are impeccable, and we graduated from the same college."

They launched into a discussion of professors before Lucie steered the conversation toward the job duties.

Young and personable, Sierra would bring energy and excitement for clients embarking on a day of white-water rafting or hiking. Her upcoming certification as a yoga teacher was an added plus, as Lucie would love to expand her list of offerings beyond team building and spa days. When it came time to talk salary, Sierra examined the measly sum Lucie printed on a notepad and picked apart her croissant. "Any chance of a raise, say...before the first paycheck?"

Lucie blew across the top of her coffee, the steam tickling her nose. "I was worried someone with your qualifications probably wouldn't be able to come on board. That's as high as I can go for now. But if the business is a success..." Lucie stopped and shook her head. Positive thinking for her venture began with her. "Let me rephrase that. *When* the business is a success, I'll look into increasing salaries."

"That's just not what I expected. Student loan debt is a real bummer. Opening a yoga studio in the old dance studio is my best bet to stay in Hollydale at this point."

An inspiration came out of nowhere. "I have an idea. It might take some initiative on your part, but we'd both benefit. Here's a rough layout so you can see what I mean." Lucie snagged a napkin and drew the main-level floor plan of the event center, then sketched out a nearby field she'd planned to use for outdoor lunches and the like. "You could use this extra conference room for your studio—" she pointed to it on her sketch "—and this field would provide space for something like a sunrise class or anything else you want to take outdoors. If I get the all-clear from my insurance carrier, I'd let you use those free of charge. You'd work for me and organize the outdoor excursions, but you can pocket any money from your yoga classes. We'll work out a schedule for you to use my facilities. Everyone wins."

"That makes a lot more sense than my starting from scratch and shelling out money that could go toward my loan. I wouldn't need much, just some mats and a couple yoga blocks. I might be able to stay in Hollydale after all." The positivity in Sierra's voice was clear, and Lucie clenched her fists, hoping for a decision in her favor.

The bell jingled and Lucie glanced toward the door. Connie Witherspoon walked in, her face dour. When she met Lucie's gaze, she popped her hands on her hips before heading over. Connie wasn't supposed to arrive for another half hour, well after Lucie's interview with Sierra would have ended. Not that she'd been sure Connie would show up. The bookstore owner always held her nose high in the air when she passed Lucie at the grocery store. From the expression on Connie's face, this conversation wouldn't be as pleasant as her time with Sierra.

Lucie jumped up and extended her hand. "Hi, Connie. Thanks for coming. You know Sierra, right?"

With a humph, Connie sat and folded her arms before sending a polite nod Sierra's way. Lucie counted to ten in her head. If she had a dollar for every time someone gave her the cold shoulder, she'd have enough to buy dog food for Ladybug and Pita this week.

Ramping up the enthusiasm she wasn't feeling, Lucie pasted on a smile. "I have a business proposition." She reached for her purse. "How about you buy something on me while I conclude this interview? Then we can talk."

Connie pursed her lips together. "You have some nerve asking me to do any business with you. Your husband stole my best friend's life savings."

Join the club. Lucie stayed silent, as that response would only invite further disdain. Trust didn't blossom overnight like a dogwood. Time and action were what counted. Maybe after Lucie brought in needed revenue to some of the local Hollydale coffers and stayed the course, people would start to trust her again.

Until then, she'd have to fake enthusiasm to start bridging the gap. No, not fake it. That would be dishonest. While the old Lucie had cajoled to get what she'd wanted, this new Lucie recognized begging. If she had to beg to get her business off the ground, so be it.

"My *ex*-husband stole from your friend." Lucie raised her chin and then calmed down. Groveling required more humility and a tone a shade less fierce. An image of Ethan and Mattie popped into her head, and she started over. "I'd like to talk to you about my business plan. My offer stands about a coffee on me."

"I'll buy my own." Connie raised her eyebrows and grabbed a book from her purse. "I'd think you were the last person who should be asking people to do business with you. Why Mitzi roped herself with the likes of you, I don't understand."

Connie stood and strode to the end of the line.

Lucie returned her attention to Sierra, hoping she hadn't already lost a potential staff member. "Sorry about that."

"Go ahead and talk to Connie. That'll give me enough time to finish my croissant."

More than ever, Lucie wanted Sierra on staff. Smiling, she rose and made her way behind Connie. While there was something to be said for humility in the proper context, Lucie didn't deserve to be the scourge of Hollydale for the rest of her life. All she wanted was to provide a home for her family, with meals and clothing and love, on top of building a business she believed in. Converting Connie to her corner would be proof she was creating a path worth treading.

Lucie tapped Connie's shoulder. "Mitzi gave me a job when some wanted to run me out of town on a rail. She's been a true friend. Hollydale used to care for those in trouble. My ex-husband—" Lucie made sure she stressed the *ex* "—caused too much trouble, and while some have a point in saying I didn't help matters, I want to make the lives of those who visit the Hollydale Training and Wellness Center better. I'd like to talk to you about a way to do that while benefiting both of us. I hope your friend would tell you to at least hear me out."

They'd reached the front of the line and Connie remained silent, her nose stuck in her book, despite customers chattering all around them, a sign of the warm atmosphere the owner, Deb, cultivated. Speaking of Connie's best friend, there was Deb herself, manning the cash register, her short gray hair matching the pretty infinity scarf looped around her neck. "Connie, what can I get you?"

Connie laid her book on the counter and jerked her thumb at Lucie. "You can get rid of her, for starters. How can you stand there and smile at her when her husband cheated you out of your life savings?"

Lucie gasped and stopped short of kicking the counter. This was never going to stop. She had been blind not to see that earlier. All she'd wanted was to rebuild a life for her and Mattie and Ethan. Now? She didn't know where home was anymore, something she never thought she'd say about Hollydale.

"Ex-husband." Deb kept her smile intact and reached for Lucie's hand, giving it a firm squeeze and a pat before letting go. "Justin is Lucie's *ex*-husband. I started The Busy Bean after I divorced my no-good ex-husband and

I had to support my family. I'm not turning away a customer who's going through the same predicament. Lucie and I cleared the air a long time ago. If I've come to peace with what happened, why shouldn't you?"

"Because I'm…I'm your friend. That's what friends do," Connie sputtered. "They look out for each other."

"That's a wonderful attitude, Mrs. Witherspoon, and a commendable one." A harsh masculine voice came from behind, and Lucie glanced over her shoulder to find Franklin Garrity. The banker's long face and cold, dark eyes resembled those of a weasel. "Community members should look out for each other. Mrs. Decker, have you given more thought to my suggestion you do the right thing and sell your parents' property and donate the proceeds to the innocent victims of your husband's crimes?"

"Ex-husband." Lucie clenched her teeth, the atmosphere growing icier every moment. Her light jacket wasn't enough to ward off the chill. "And I believe the best way to thrive is by supporting my family and my staff. That's the right thing to do with my land."

She had to keep her focus on that, or people like Franklin Garrity would distract her. If that happened, there wouldn't be much point in staying in the town she loved so much.

Someone tapped her shoulder, and Lucie nearly jumped out of her skin. Heartbeat racing, she turned and found Sierra. What must she think of Lucie now? Sierra smiled and handed Lucie her cup of coffee. "If that offer is still open, I accept the job. I'll be at the lodge this afternoon. I have to run."

Speechless, Lucie stood rooted to the ground while Sierra headed for the exit. No sooner had she left than Caleb entered. He locked his gaze on Lucie and headed straight for her. She dismissed the sweet burst of exhilaration from his mere presence.

"Lucie, hope you haven't been waiting too long for me." Caleb shrugged out of his jacket and threw it over his arm.

"The Hero of Hollydale. Welcome home, Caleb." Franklin extended his hand and pumped Caleb's. "Anytime you want to come to the bank for a chat, I'm sure we can work out manageable terms for one of Hollydale's own."

Her stomach twisted. Caleb deserved every accolade for finding those three boys. Didn't she deserve a chance to rebuild her life? Was that too much to ask? Caleb kept his gaze fixed on hers, as if he could see she was fighting tears.

"If you're treating my friend well—" Caleb came over and looped his arm around her shoulder "—and if she vouches for you, I look forward to doing business with you."

She'd have expected his arm to feel like deadweight, but it didn't. Something about the casual nature and the way his flannel shirt curved along her shoulders felt right. Too right. Having her heart shredded once for the town's viewing pleasure was enough.

All eyes were trained on her. She might as well use the attention to her benefit. However, she wanted to stand on her own merits, so she ducked out from under Caleb's arm. "Connie, I want to discuss a means to promote your bookstore inside the lodge, especially since the volumes in my parents' attic veer more toward encyclopedias and anthologies. If you'd like to talk shop, I'll be at the lodge all afternoon." Lucie reached into her purse. "Here's my business card."

Then, with her head held high, Lucie scooted toward the door. Making a quick getaway was her best chance of leaving The Busy Bean with some dignity intact.

And leaving before her problems tarnished Caleb's image was best for both of them.

"LUCIE! WAIT UP!" Caleb yelled across the town green before catching up to her. Her slight sniffles brought out his instinct to guard and protect. With Lucie, however, that innate feeling wasn't associated with his career, rather it had everything to do with her caring nature. "What's wrong?"

"Hollydale hay fever. I get it every spring." Lucie stopped and sniffled before shrugging it off. "Okay, that's only a half truth, but I have a full day of work ahead and no one else is going to do it for me."

"I thought we were going to talk. Five minutes in The Busy Bean would do wonders for me." His day wouldn't be complete without seeing her smile at least once. She'd clearly gone through quite a beating in there. He tried out his goofiest smile, the one that had made Vanessa giggle for a good five minutes. "Have mercy on me. I haven't had anything to eat or drink yet. You wouldn't deprive a starving man a bite of food, would you?"

"What kept you from eating breakfast?"

"A visit to the doctor." He rolled up his sleeve and showed off the bandage covering the spot where they'd extracted tube after tube of blood. "See?"

"Did you have to see the doctor as part of your transfer?"

"Yes." A pang of guilt almost prevented him from saying any more. When she found out about the woodpecker habitat, she'd be hurt he hadn't come to her house last night and confided in her. But he had to know something for certain before he gave her the bad news. "Is it always like this?"

Her eyebrows lowered, almost touching each other. "Running here and there most days? I guess so."

That wasn't what he'd meant. Despite the inviting décor and the heater doing its job, the atmosphere in The Busy Bean had been downright frosty.

He'd just witnessed firsthand the impact Justin Decker's actions were having on his ex-wife and children. Although Justin had committed the crimes, Lucie was forced to deal with the consequences, facing Hollydale's residents day after day. Taking the easy way out and moving would have appealed to many others. However, she remained in town, forging a new life out of the ashes. How did she do it?

"The way people treat you. Is it always like this?"

"You yourself asked questions about where I came up with the money for the renovations. Imagine two years of some people concluding I must have known what Justin was doing when I didn't." She let her hair cascade over the left side of her face, hiding one eye, her most expressive feature.

An attractive feature, too.

If she managed to handle this with grace, there must be a way for him to balance his duty as a son with the needs of an old friend. He owed it to her to try.

"I know you didn't know about his lies." A little time to reflect made a world of difference.

"Why do you believe me all of a sudden?"

"First of all, you can't lie. You never could."

"I guess you remembered that from the hospital." She kept looking down, as if she wasn't used to compliments. Maybe for the past two years, she hadn't received many.

"It took me a while. I finally let myself remember, too. Everything, including what you meant to me then."

"I knew I'd stayed friends with you for a reason." She pushed her hair away from her face, laughter replacing some of the sadness lingering in her eyes. One curly section stayed loose, and he restrained himself from putting it back in place.

"Why have you stayed in Hollydale? Why didn't you move?"

"The government had the deeds to my house and the lodge property. They only returned them at the end of last year." She shrugged. "I really have to get to work."

He fell into step beside her. "But you have the deeds now. Why not start over somewhere else?"

Silence settled, but it wasn't disagreeable. Their friendship of old was beginning to blossom again—it was one of the few he cherished, one of the few he didn't want to lose. They passed through her fence and headed up her sidewalk.

"This is Mattie and Ethan's home and the last link to my parents. Besides, some people in town are worth the hassle. They've supported me through everything. Georgie and Mike Harrison, Mitzi, Deb."

She reached into the front section of her purse and pulled out a set of keys with a thousand and one of those loyalty shopper tags attached, along with a picture of Mattie and

Ethan. "You need to go eat something substantial for breakfast before you report to work. Let's say goodbye now before you get dog slobber all over you."

While he could call Robin and visit more properties today, that paled in comparison to spending more time with Lucie. *No one else is going to do it for me.* She didn't trust other people would come to her aid. He could help change that. Besides, one day in her presence before he dropped his bombshell was better than nothing, and the idea of sitting idle didn't suit him.

"Owen doesn't want me reporting until next week, so I'm yours today." Spending time with Lucie was the jalapeños on a plate of nachos.

"I'm sure you have somewhere else you need to be." She unlocked the door but kept it closed. "I'll be fine."

Her hesitancy made him pause. Myriad activities came to mind. Finding a place to live. Hiking the trails on this beautiful day. Setting up that goalpost in the backyard like he'd promised Izzy. But the way Lucie's shoulders stiffened, as if she expected him to back out, threw those plans out the window. Someone needed to look out for her. Make her laugh.

Give her a reason to trust people could be there for her again.

Since there was no one else lined up outside the gate, he might as well apply for the job. At least for today. "Maybe the place I need to be is with someone who needs a friend."

He needed his friend back. Staying with Jonathan and his daughters reminded him what it was like to spend time with interesting people, people he liked and who cared about him.

While in Yellowstone, he'd kept busy, volunteering for any extra shifts and working on holidays so his coworkers could spend time with their families. The one time he'd lowered his guard and surrounded himself with new friends, an attractive brunette in particular, things had ended in disaster.

The whining from inside became louder and more frequent. Ladybug knew Lucie was out there and wanted to be with her. Caleb couldn't blame the dog—she had good taste.

"Hold that thought."

As soon as Lucie opened the door, Ladybug waddled their way, her snout in the air. She came over to him and wagged her curly stub of a tail while shooting Lucie a loving glance to let her know she was still number one in the bulldog's book. With Ethan and Ladybug now on his side, it was just a matter of time until he could convince Mattie and Lucie he was trustworthy. Then he'd tell Lucie everything and hope she didn't hold the revelations against him. For now, he wanted to loosen the tension around her shoulders by helping out.

Caleb squatted, ignoring the protest in his lower back. "Glad to see I have a new female conquest." He kept his tone light, although he wouldn't mind if Lucie gave the slightest hint at jealousy.

"Don't get too overconfident. Ladybug likes the mail carrier and her vet. English bulldogs are good natured."

So much for any jealousy. "How long have you had her?" He lavished some affection on the dog, whose stubby face rose in appreciation.

Lucie shut the door behind them. "A couple years. She's a sad story with a happy ending. A truck threw a burlap bag out the window near the picnic table where Mattie, Ethan and I were having lunch, and Ladybug was inside. We rescued her, and Mattie named her, and she's been a part of the family ever since. Residents know I have a soft heart for animals, and they see if I have room before taking a stranded animal to the shelter."

Interesting they could hold a grudge against her at the same time.

"Do you have room?" The rhetorical question slipped out of his mouth, the answer obvious.

"Always. Animals deserve a good home and love, just like everyone else." A streak of black fur shot down the stairs and darted toward the kitchen, almost as if the cat knew they were discussing Lucie's pet menagerie and chose not to be ignored. "That's Midnight. She and Ladybug live inside, as do the rabbits, whose hutch is in one of the guest rooms. My border collie mix, Pita, wanders in and out. Sometimes she stays outside with Fred and Ethel and sometimes she stays in Ethan's room."

Caleb needed a chart for all of her animals. "How do you keep track of everything?"

Lucie crooked her finger and he followed her into the kitchen, where she opened the pantry and pulled out a can of cat food. "I love them, so it's become second nature to me. I can only guess what you must think of the chaos that has become my life."

Chaos. That was one description of her life, but happiness radiated from her as she dumped the contents into Midnight's dish.

The cat curled its lithe body around Lucie's feet in appreciation.

While Caleb had been away, Lucie had gone from the town sweetheart to the town pariah who housed unwanted animals while starting a business to support this household. In that same time, Caleb had gone from the town no-name whose surgery sidelined him to the town hero who worked around the clock to make sure he was never without sufficient eggs in different baskets.

He couldn't help but wonder if Lucie had gained more.

"It suits you." The two times he'd visited this house in the distant past, it had been exactly that—a house. A cold residence with impeccable interior design highlighting good bones.

Lucie had created a home.

What would it be like to find his way home every night to this?

While he'd love nothing more, this couldn't be his. Not when his parents had lost everything.

He couldn't pursue anything with Lucie with a clear conscience.

Her gaze met his, and her cheeks flushed a sweet pink, the same hue of his favorite flowering Carolina dogwood petals, yet he could only admire them from afar. "This has always been a part of me. It just took me a while to grow into myself."

Midnight abandoned her weaving ways for her cat dish while Lucie scooped out dog kibble for Ladybug, whose grunts signaled impatience. The pellets dinged against the metal of her bowl, and Ladybug licked Lucie's hand before turning her attention to the more important issue of a full stomach.

"Do you mind if I run back to Jonathan's and eat breakfast? Then I'll drive to the lodge. Once I have something substantial, I'll give you the benefit of free labor for the whole day."

Her shoulders stiffened and the bloom faded from her cheeks. "If you show up, I'll put you to work."

"I'll be there. You can count on it."

Her entire demeanor screamed disbelief that he'd follow through. While returning to Hollydale reminded him what he loved about it, he'd also witnessed the downside this morning. The town's attitude toward Lucie had to change. She had to believe in people again. Friends helped friends. If he could only be her friend, so be it. He'd find a way to help her believe people were trustworthy without betraying his parents.

And he'd find a way to be around her without that feeling of home catching up to him and complicating everything.

If such ways existed, that was.

CHAPTER FOUR

CALEB LAY DOWN the wrench and took a long swig of water, glancing around the utility room in the heart of the wellness center basement. While the water heater and the industrial washers looked new, this ancient furnace was about ready for the junkyard. From his perspective, Lucie should have already called a repair company. The pilot light worked, and he'd performed common troubleshooting procedures. Out of ideas, he replaced the air filter, shut the door and wiped his hands.

A head popped around the corner and, not even a second later, Ethan came into full view. "Hey, Mr. Caleb. I'm all done with school for the day. Can I help?"

"Depending on how you look at it, you have perfect timing since there's nothing more I can do. I'm putting my tools back in the box." Caleb set his wrench and pliers in the top section and snapped the lid shut.

"Miss Georgie taught me and Mattie all

about tools. She says a good worker cleans up after him or herself." Ethan closed the distance between them, his gaze not leaving Caleb's toolbox. "Do adults talk in riddles a lot?"

Caleb drank another sip of water and then wiped his mouth dry with his sleeve. "Depends on the adult. I try to say it like it is, so go ahead and tell me what's on your mind. I might be able to help you figure out the answer."

Ethan tapped his chin and scrunched his nose. "Miss Georgie also says it's important to stay true to yourself and not let anyone change you."

"Miss Georgie's right." Caleb lifted his water for another sip.

"Well, my friend Noah's mom and dad change his little brother's diapers all the time, and Noah says he stinks up the room. Is that because he's letting someone else change him?"

Caleb sputtered his water every which way, as he couldn't hold back his laughter. Walking away, Ethan jammed his hands in his pockets. Caleb placed his water bottle on his toolbox and rose. "Hold up. I laughed because you're funny, not at you."

Ethan stopped and turned back around, his grin slowly widening. "You really think I'm funny? Mattie tells me all the time I'm not as funny as I think I am."

Speaking of Mattie, she entered the room, her arms folded, her foot tapping. "You shouldn't be down here. Mommy said we weren't supposed to bother him. I'm telling Mom you're bugging Mr. Spindler."

So this was sibling rivalry in action. He'd grown up an only child, so he'd never experienced it. "He's not bugging me. I was about to come upstairs anyway."

"And Mr. Caleb was going to show me his tools. I was here first." Ethan scrambled to Caleb's side.

"So? Miss Georgie's tools are better." Mattie popped her hands on her hips and faced Ethan with fire in her deep blue eyes, the mirror image of Lucie's.

Later he'd have to ask Lucie how she navigated this constant tug-of-war. For now, he was on his own. Before he opened his mouth, another young girl entered, her long braids the same color as her large brown eyes. While she looked like she was a few years older than the twins, she didn't appear old enough to be a full-fledged babysitter. "Here you are. I've been counting forever."

How long was forever? Caleb blinked. "And you are?"

"I'm Rachel Harrison. Mattie and Ethan have told me all about you. How do you do?" Rachel threw back her braids and extended her hand, shaking his with a firm grip. "Are you in need of a matchmaker? I'm really good at getting couples together. I got my dad together with my stepmom, and she didn't even want any money to marry him or anything."

There was a story there, and he'd have to ask Lucie to explain later.

Caleb thoughtfully scratched his chin and swigged the last sip of water, wishing the bottle contained something stronger. Then again, if he'd been drinking spirits, he wouldn't be able to keep up with these three—a person had to be on his toes around this crew. "Nice to meet you." Caleb hesitated, unsure of how best to answer Rachel's questions.

She stared at him with brown eyes, her fingers with purple polish tapping the wall as if indicating she was waiting for his answer about possibly hiring her. He thought he'd better clear the air.

"Thank you for your offer, but I'm happy

with my bachelor status. I have no plans for getting married, and I'm definitely not in need of a matchmaker."

Lucie rounded the corner and he stemmed back his groan. It was one thing to admit his relationship status to a young girl, but he hadn't meant to do so in front of Lucie.

"Why is everyone gathered down here?" Lucie rubbed her arms together. "Is it that cold upstairs?"

He might as well start with the easiest part. "It's not the pilot light or anything obvious. You'll need to call your repair service."

"Already did that. He can't come out until tomorrow, although I was hoping against hope you'd tell me you'd fixed it and I could cancel that appointment." She sighed and he could almost see her running calculations in her head. "I hope it wasn't that blasted bird pecking at my chimney that caused this."

"No chance of any furnace wires being located in your chimney. But about that blasted bird…" Caleb hesitated, the kids gathering around like he was the Pied Piper. It must be what Lucie felt like all the time. How animals and children could be so at home around her while the townspeople withheld their forgiveness was something he couldn't grasp. "If you see it, take a picture of it. My boss wants confirmation it's in the area. We'd like to start documenting the Timber River woodpecker's whereabouts."

"My dad's talked about that bird." Rachel tugged on the sleeve of her puffy pink coat. "My new grandma bought him and Georgie tickets for a fancy dinner. Miss Georgie said she'll go on account of some of the proceeds protecting animals. Dad told her he can't wait to see her in the dress Miss Lucie picked out for her." Rachel tucked her hand into Lucie's. "It's a pretty dress."

"Thank you. I had fun picking it out with her." She and Rachel looked at each other and burst out laughing at their inside joke. In the time he worked at Yellowstone, he'd never formed a friendship close enough to rate inside jokes, and he and Leah hadn't progressed to that stage of their relationship.

Someday he wanted a relationship with inside jokes.

"The bird that's making all that noise on our chimney is special? It's really loud." Ethan's scowl was plenty evidence of his taking his mother's side.

Caleb stepped toward Ethan and knelt so their gazes met. "The Timber River woodpecker is endangered. If people don't come together and help the bird, we could lose its beauty forever. If we protect the bird and its environment, it might not become extinct."

"What's extinct?" Ethan tilted his head to one side.

"It means there'll be no more of them, silly." Mattie moved next to her brother and nudged his ribs.

"Don't call your brother silly. It's not polite. Please apologize." Lucie's firm tone brooked no argument.

"Sorry," Mattie muttered, tapping her sneakered foot against the cement floor.

Ethan leaned forward and tugged on the bottom of Caleb's brown flannel shirt. "I know where the bird's nest is. Can you keep the nest safe so there can be more of them?"

Better yet, Caleb would take a picture and send it to Owen for verification. Then he'd look for more and map out the habitat area. "I'd like to see it." Caleb nodded before glancing at Lucie.

"Let's go find that nest." Lucie laughed. "Besides, it's warmer outside than inside."

The slight edge to her voice conveyed some of the pressure she must be feeling. Pressure to make this venture a success. Not enough for her to toss and turn all night, but enough for someone who knew her well to worry about her. He'd do everything he could to ease her burden.

Caleb picked up the toolbox and headed for the stairs, waving the others ahead of him. "Lead the way, Ethan."

"Yesss." Ethan clenched his fist in victory. "Hey, Mattie, you have to follow me."

Caleb didn't miss the way Lucie rolled her eyes before moving forward. Maybe it was time for him to do the same. While his heart liked that idea, his head thought of his parents and the money they'd lost. If he stayed in the past, though, he'd lose out on something that could be real and lasting, something that could bring laughter and inside jokes and the home he'd dreamed of in that hospital bed so long ago.

THEY PASSED THE ropes course, and Lucie pulled herself together. An impossible morning had turned into a catastrophic afternoon. She'd arrived to a freezing lodge only to discover the furnace system had stopped working and the technician couldn't show up until tomorrow to give her an estimate for the repair. Caleb's arrival shouldn't have come as a surprise—he'd come when he'd said he would—but she'd been surprised nonetheless. Now the quintet was traveling deep into the woods, past the labeled nature trails, to find the nest of an endangered woodpecker, much farther than seven-year-old Ethan was supposed to venture out on his own without adult supervision.

"Ethan Christopher Decker. What were you thinking hiking this far away from the lodge? You could have gotten lost." She kept her voice terse, hiding her fear of something having happened to him.

"I wasn't alone, Mommy. Miss Natalie was with me and Mattie. We were 'sploring for treasure."

Lucie would need to have a talk with her friend about exploring closer to home. As a kindergarten teacher, Natalie sometimes got carried away with using the world around her as a canvas for learning. "If an adult was with you, that's okay, but don't wander this far again, and especially not on your own."

"Yes, Mommy." Ethan sounded chastised, but then his body quaked with nervous energy and his finger pointed toward a decaying tree. "In the hollow over there. That's where Miss Natalie said the treasure was. Bird eggs."

They all peered into the hollow where the trunk of the tree had split in two. A round bundle of sticks and twigs formed a nest with three eggs safe inside. Lucie stepped back at the same time everyone else did, the beauty of the scene settling in. "Why isn't the nest higher up?"

Caleb clicked several photos with his phone and nodded. "Woodpeckers look for tree hollows and other types of holes. They're what are known as cavity nesters."

"How do you know so much about birds?" Mattie leaned back and folded her arms.

"I'm a park ranger, and I'm about to start a new job at the Timber River Park." Caleb smiled and placed his phone in his back pocket. "I love drawing birds and nature. When I knew your mommy a long time ago, sometimes I gave her the drawings from my sketchbook."

Until now, Lucie had forgotten those rare presents, all the more precious given what she'd been through since those carefree days. She loved coming out here, free of the pretensions of the rich girl, and soaking up everything around her, reveling in the greenery surrounding her. Come to think of it, those moments were part of the bond to this area that made her so reluctant to leave. Even now, in the busyness of her world, moments like these renewed her and reminded her why she'd committed to this path.

Mattie reached for Lucie's hand and gave a light squeeze. "Do you still have any of Mr. Caleb's sketches, Mommy?"

"I don't know." The plain unvarnished truth sometimes hurt.

Caleb's drawings had leaped off the pages—the birds often appeared lifelike and in flight rather than stationary two-dimensional images. "Time to go back to the lodge."

"But it's cold inside." Mattie released Lucie's hand.

"Then run like me." Ethan jogged circles around a log.

Lucie shook her head. "I think I have the ingredients for hot chocolate."

"Yippee!" Ethan cheered and started ahead on the trail before turning around. "What about marshmallows? Hot chocolate's not the same without marshmallows."

"I think there's a package in the pantry."

The girls let out a whoop and caught up with Ethan.

Lucie raised her voice. "Stay in our sight. I don't want to lose anyone."

"Including me?" Caleb's voice sounded from behind. "Ethan's a boy after my own heart. Marshmallows make everything better."

She smiled, appreciating the lightness in his tone.

"I take my hot chocolate straight. Unless there happens to be some whipped cream around." Lucie had never cared for marshmallows, although she kept a supply on hand for Ethan and Mattie.

"More's the pity and more for me, then." Caleb's boots crunched in the leafy vegetation. "That is, if I'm invited. For hot chocolate, I'll even come back and help you tomorrow."

This was getting too cozy. She'd fallen for one man's quips and look where that had gotten her. Investigated by the government. Almost arrested. Broke with no safety net. She'd best put the brakes on, and fast. With the twins and Rachel out of hearing range but still within line of sight, Lucie needed to ask that favor of him. Then whether he'd want to stay would be another question.

"Sierra came by for her paperwork while you were in the basement. She can't start until next Monday since she's finishing her yoga certification this week, and I could use your assistance with the installation of the audio-visual equipment tomorrow morning. Hot chocolate's the least I can do, considering…"

"I'm not another obligation. As a matter of fact—"

Lucie held up her hand, cutting him off. "Before you go any further, let me get something off my chest." Lucie hated keeping anything back, and she'd contacted him for a specific reason. She needed to lay it on the line. "You're welcome to stay, no matter what. The hot chocolate is a thank-you, not a condition."

"I'm more and more intrigued, but then, you always were the most interesting girl in our class."

With that pronouncement, Lucie lost her footing and stumbled, his arms reaching out and steadying her before she fell face-first into the dense pile of leaves surrounding them. His warm hands, strong and secure, kept her upright, and his sense of steadiness permeated deep, almost as intense as the smell of leaves and his citrusy cologne. Attraction flooded her. There was something solid about Caleb, as enduring as the forest on her property, which bordered the Park Service's land.

If she didn't watch out, she could find herself trusting him…

And he'd already said he had no intention of getting married or letting anyone play matchmaker for him. So it wasn't like he was available, even if she intended to date again, which didn't figure into her plans.

"I wasn't the most interesting girl. Not by a long shot. Georgie Harrison is much more together and independent." She bounded two steps away from Caleb. With much-needed distance between them, she set her shoulders in an effort to appear as cool as the weather.

"Georgie who? I remember Georgie Bennett, but you two weren't close." Caleb caught up with her. She seized the moment to take a good look at him and liked the way he carried his broad shoulders with authority. He tapped his stubble, an attractive addition for him.

"She moved away for a while, but she came back and married Mike Harrison, who's now the sheriff. When they were going through some issues, we mended our fences. She's my best friend, and Rachel is her stepdaughter." Lucie kept an eye on the group ahead before scanning the ground so she wouldn't trip again.

And so she wouldn't lose her nerve by

searching those hazel depths of his. Any way she could stem this growing attraction to him had to be done and fast.

"Good to know."

"Georgie is now a co-owner of Max's Auto Repair. She and Mitzi Mayfield, the owner of A New You, the salon downtown, helped me create a business plan. Mitzi and my aunt, who lives in California, decided this was a good opportunity." Her voice wobbled, betraying too much. She didn't take others' investments lightly. More than that, she cared about Caleb's perception of her as a business owner.

"Hey, you don't have to be nervous around me."

She glanced at him, the same guy who she'd spent more time with than anyone else in high school, someone who'd always treated her as an equal, even when others dismissed her as a rich debutante. She felt at ease around Caleb; that came when someone accepted you and let you be yourself. She breathed out, happy to be around someone who didn't judge her and find her wanting.

"I know. It's funny how there are people who, no matter how long since you were last together, it's like no time has passed when you see them again. You're one of those." While she wanted to fight this warm acceptance and guard herself against it, today wasn't the day to pick a battle she didn't believe in.

"But Luce…"

They arrived in the clearing where the forest ended and the low ropes course began. He kept walking and she cleared her throat. He glanced over his shoulder, and she mustered her courage. At the most, he'd leave.

"Somehow being around you makes me talk about everything and nothing." This wasn't coming out right. "I leave happier but then realize I've never cleared up why I contacted you in the first place."

He nodded, and she walked in the blue gravel of the alligator pit, taking care not to bump her shin against the treated lumber.

"I had an ulterior motive when I emailed you. I wanted to take advantage of our former friendship."

His hand reached out and touched her sleeve. His warmth sank in, a tease of spring after a cold winter, and she wanted to lean into that, but she halted and met his gaze.

"Former friendship? You're revoking my friendship card?" His eyes twinkled.

In spite of everything that had gone wrong that day, laughter bubbled up. "I guess I have to tape it back together and make sure it has a safe place in your wallet."

"Ha. You need to laugh more often. Your laugh lines are rusty. See, there's a bit of rust coming off now."

She marveled at how he'd always kept his sense of humor, even back when the infection set in after his surgery and she and his parents had huddled together, scared he wouldn't live. She remembered the first time she'd made him laugh after he'd recovered, and now he was returning the favor.

He stepped toward her. For a second, she thought he was going to kiss her. Of course, he wasn't. He wasn't looking for a relationship.

"That might be the result of how much WD-40 you used on the utility room door this morning." Lucie blinked and pulled herself together. Although she sensed chemistry between them, she was out of practice when it came to men, and her sense of someone being attracted to her was definitely off. He'd called her his friend. Sure, friends joked around, but she couldn't wander off topic again. "Anyway, Georgie and Mitzi went through every room of the lodge, from the ballroom to the conference rooms, with me. Then they helped me create a budget."

"How we went from friendship cards back to business, I'm not quite sure, but I'll go along with you." He scrambled onto the balance log, the chains jingling.

She could have sworn he'd felt the attraction as strongly as she had. That awareness she had wasn't her imagination, but she shrugged it off nonetheless.

"Once I had a business plan with the start-up costs on a spreadsheet, and I took into account everything from the construction of the ropes courses to lodge updates to employee costs, including insurance—"

"And Mitzi had enough money to finance all of that?" Any traces of his earlier humor faded when he jumped off the log and wiped his hands on his jeans.

"Along with my father's sister, Rosemary." She nodded and kept a close eye on the kids as they ran around the clearing, playing tag. "I sold every asset that had been in my name only, other than my house, and raised a good deal of the money myself." It had about killed her to part with her mother's engagement ring, but she'd had no alternative.

"After a long legal battle, around Christmas the government returned anything that could be traced back to me from before my marriage as my private asset. When I approached Aunt Rosemary and Mitzi, I asked them if they'd either become partners and share the profits or loan me the money with the lodge and cabin as collateral. Aunt Rosemary had her lawyer draw up a repayment contract. Everything is recorded, and the limited liability corporation's funds are in an account they also own and can monitor. I made sure everything is out in the open."

Caleb's shoulders relaxed, but he remained standing. In the stillness of the clearing, she heard the calls of the cardinals and even the soothing whisper of the Timber River. "You've done a lot of work."

Lucie inhaled a deep breath. While she didn't like asking for help, it had become easier in the past two years. "That's only half the battle. You see, twenty percent of small businesses fail in the first year, and half fail within five years." She rubbed the bark of an oak, the solidity and roughness reminding her she'd endure because she had to. "That's where you come in."

And hence the vague email to the Hero of Hollydale in the first place, reminding him of their past connection and asking him to contact her. She was sure he'd respond, but she hadn't thought he'd answer in person. She glanced at him, at home in the natural elements surrounding him, his broad shoulders filling out his brown flannel shirt. How far Caleb had come since he'd left Hollydale.

He came over and leaned on a tree, his weight sagging against the trunk. "You mentioned something about the outdoors. I assumed you wanted my advice about a nature walk or something like that."

Now that he mentioned it, that idea made sense. Who better than a park ranger to make sure the paths were in order, and possibly even lead tours in his spare time?

"When I emailed you, you lived in Montana. It would have been hard to hire you long-distance. But now that you live here, can you take a second job? You'd be a great asset for ensuring I'm doing everything I can for the environment, and you could help with nature walks. I'll have to check the budget to see if I can afford another staff member..." She shook her head, determined to stay on track. "The reason for my email was to ask you for a reference, a banner quote for our website, supporting my business."

Saying it aloud made it seem silly. How had she expected him to tour her business all the way from Montana to promote her North Carolina venture?

"I'll have to check with Owen about that. As a government employee, I don't know if I can endorse a private business in my capacity as a park ranger." To her surprise, he sounded genuinely disappointed he couldn't help her out.

"I understand." Another setback for today. She'd have to figure out another way to market her corporate retreat and fill her calendar with bookings beyond the first three weeks.

Caleb's hand reached over and covered hers. "I'll find out. And when I talk to Owen, I'll ask about moonlighting as a nature trail expert, too."

"Mommy! My tummy is waiting for you to finish talking and it can't wait anymore!" Ethan ran over and yanked on Lucie's coat before turning to Caleb. "Sorry. Mommy says I shouldn't interrupt, but we've been waiting soooo long."

Lucie glanced over to find Mattie sticking out her tongue and panting like she was a nomad seeking water and Rachel grinning from ear to ear. "Okay, I get the hint."

In no time, she'd be in the comfort of her

kitchen with three kids clamoring to stir the cocoa powder and sugar into the milk.

Caleb removed his hand from hers, and she missed the contact.

"I'll let you enjoy your cocoa," he said.

"Did you forget about the marshmallows, Mr. Caleb?" Ethan licked his lips and patted his belly. "Marsh. Mall. Ows. Yum."

Caleb met her gaze. "Is the invitation still open?"

"Of course." She remembered his earlier words to Rachel about not needing a matchmaker and wished he wasn't the type who always said what he meant. Then again, it was refreshing to be around someone who was honest and above reproach.

Another flutter of awareness of the new Caleb surfaced like the gentle breeze stirring the tops of the nearby pines. With neither of them looking for anything more than friendship, what could mere hospitality hurt? "No strings attached."

"Friends, then." He extended his hand to Lucie and she gripped it with a tight hold.

"Friends."

CHAPTER FIVE

CALEB STOPPED AT the gate in front of Lucie's home. If there was a prettier spot within the city limits of Hollydale, he'd like to see it. From here the Great Smoky Mountains were in full display, their green rounded tops a sign of constancy and awe. The light scent of Lucie's azaleas, their blooms a rainbow of red, yellow and orange, tickled his nose.

He glanced into the backyard. This time no grunts or barking sounds greeted him. The pigs weren't outside, and neither was the border collie. He hadn't considered Lucie would be anywhere else this evening. Maybe he should have called first. Then again, her house was on the way from Jonathan's house to the Whitley Community Center where Izzy's soccer game was set to begin in half an hour. He'd promised to be there but had taken a chance Lucie would be home.

So much had happened this afternoon.

He'd stopped at the park station to show

Owen the pictures and, as a result, he wanted to share his news in person with Lucie. He opened the gate and passed through.

Now that he was here, though, he hesitated at the top of her porch steps. Ten minutes wasn't enough time for all he had to say. He thought back to telling Rachel he wasn't interested in a matchmaker—or any type of relationship for that matter—one beautiful blonde whose life was pulling herself out of her own personal crevice wouldn't leave his thoughts.

Tomorrow it was. Lucie deserved a full explanation, not a rushed statement.

At that moment, the creak of the door sounded and a black-and-white blur on four legs tackled him. Then someone else followed the dog and catapulted into him with a loud "Oof." A plastic trash bag rolled down the stairs and thudded to a stop at the bottom, the contents spilling everywhere. Caleb steadied himself before making sure the small bundle of energy was okay.

"I didn't see you out here." Mattie's voice held a note of accusation as Ladybug found her way through the open door, sat on her haunches and barked. Mattie glanced at

Ladybug, and began petting her. "I made a big mess."

Caleb clucked softly, and Pita responded by circling him twice before sitting at his feet.

"It was an accident. You weren't expecting anyone to be out here." Caleb smiled and scratched Pita behind the ears, earning a small groan of happiness for his effort. Mattie's lip quivered while Ladybug settled on the porch. "We can clean it up before Ladybug starts a nap."

The front porch light flickered on and Lucie appeared at the threshold. "Why is the front door open? Oh, Caleb, hello." Her voice rose an octave on the last syllable. "Make sure the dogs don't escape. Neither one is wearing her leash."

The thought of slow, steady Ladybug making a getaway brought a laugh to Caleb's lips. He pointed to the trash below. "Do you have a broom and dustpan handy?"

Lucie's gaze wandered toward the mess. She groaned. "Watch Mattie and the dogs, will you?"

In no time at all, Lucie returned with the necessary supplies, and the three of them picked up the trash dotting the bottom of her porch stairs. Lucie's hand brushed Caleb's and a shiver of awareness traveled down his spine.

"I know today's been busy, but did I forget you were coming over? We just finished dinner and it was Mattie's turn to take out the trash before family game night."

"I stopped over before going on to Izzy's soccer game." Almost on cue, thunder boomed in the background. Caleb reached for his phone at the same time as he received a text from his cousin. "Well, the game was canceled due to the storm." Caleb kept reading the flurry of texts and started laughing. "They're going out for hot chocolate."

Lucie laid her hand on Caleb's arm. "It would be nice if you could stay, but I know you have a family obligation. Family should come first."

While Caleb wanted to reconnect with Jonathan and his daughters, he wanted some time with Lucie, too. "I've already had my fill of hot chocolate for the day. I'll take a rain check and plan something with them this weekend."

Mattie giggled. "*Rain* check! That's funny."

That giggle made his whole day. When he glanced Mattie's way, she gathered the rest of the trash and then scurried off with Pita on her heels while Lucie held on to Ladybug's collar. Caleb rose, and the metal rod in his back thanked him.

"Thanks for helping. What brought you by?" Lucie released the bulldog, stood and wiped her hands on her yoga pants.

"Game night, of course. What's on tap?" He kept an eye on Ladybug, who came over and sat near him. "I'm excellent at Scrabble and darts."

"Both of which are well suited for seven-year-olds." Through Lucie's wryness, he detected and appreciated the note of humor. "Since Mattie had trash duty, she'll get to choose between Chutes and Ladders or Candy Land. Hot time in the Decker household tonight."

Warm and cozy was more like it. A far cry from the sophisticated dates he and Leah had shared before he'd discovered the real reason she'd dated him. "How about I be the judge of that?"

Lucie squinted her eyes and folded her arms. "You don't have anything else to do? Look at you, all dressed up in that blue chambray shirt and nowhere to go. This is the first time I haven't seen you in flannel since you've been back. Were you expecting to find a hot date at the soccer game?"

"Hardly." Although the fact that she noticed little details about him did feel good. What else had she noticed about him? "Did you hear what I said to Rachel this afternoon?"

She shrugged. "Yeah."

While he knew about Justin, Lucie didn't know about Leah. "About three months ago, I started dating Leah Lundgren, who had just broken up with her artist boyfriend of five years. What I didn't know was Leah wanted a ready-made date to her sister's wedding, someone her parents would approve of. A respectable someone so her parents would release her trust fund to her. At the rehearsal dinner, I heard her talking to a bridesmaid about my rescuing those kids, only endearing me all the more to her parents, who were now discussing car colors with her for her new Cadillac. I confronted her and she told me the whole truth, including the revelation about the trust fund and her reunion with her exboyfriend, who she was still involved with."

"Ouch. That's cold." She bumped her forehead with the palm of her hand. "What must you think of me emailing you for a huge favor after you rescued those three boys, especially since we hadn't seen each other for years?"

She stopped and drew in a deep breath, her hand trembling in the rays of the porch light.

He moved closer and chucked her chin. "Hey, this is different. You didn't lie and deceive me." Although Leah's lies and deception didn't rise anywhere near the level of Justin's, it had hurt. If anything, he could relate somewhat to Lucie for the experience.

"If you no longer have any plans, you're welcome to stay."

As if to signal her agreement, Ladybug settled on his foot.

She moved inside and he and the dog followed.

Mattie skipped down the stairs, photos of her and Ethan at various ages dotting the wall, and held out her hand to Lucie. "Come on, Mommy. I chose Candy Land. Good night, Mr. Caleb."

"Actually, I've invited Caleb to join us." Lucie ruffled Mattie's hair.

Mattie batted Lucie's hand away. "But it's only supposed to be the three of us."

Mattie's reaction to him was perplexing. At work, in his khaki uniform, most kids loved him, their eyes glowing as they drank in the wonders of Yellowstone. Was she just protective of her mother, or did she truly not like him?

"There's always room in our house for one more." Lucie raised an eyebrow but smiled at her daughter anyway. "Mr. Caleb moved back and he's an old friend. I think we should be nice to our friends, don't you?"

Caleb hesitated. While he wanted to stay, he also wanted Mattie to accept him and lose the scowl she always wore when he approached. Having Lucie force him on Mattie probably wasn't how to make that happen. "Thanks for the invite, but it's okay. I should get going—Jonathan and the girls will be arriving back in town soon. I'll see you tomorrow."

Caleb nudged his foot enough for Ladybug to get the message. He started to walk away. While he now had an excuse to put off talking to Lucie, he would have preferred getting this out in the open.

"Wait." Mattie's voice caused him to stop.

He turned around, caution keeping him rooted in place.

"Ladybug wants her footrest back. You can stay."

Mattie ran inside and Ladybug tottered after her. The door swung shut behind them, and Lucie started up the stairs before turning to wait for him. "You never answered my question. Why did you stop by tonight?"

"Have you dated much since your divorce?"

The porch light illuminated the bewilderment written on Lucie's face. "Huh? Did you stop by tonight to ask me about whether I've been on a date since my divorce? I could have saved you a trip with a short answer."

"Actually, I had another reason."

"What is it?" She folded her arms and remained still. "I can't leave them by themselves for long. And I should warn you now, the twins are competitive about games that involve no skill whatsoever." Lucie closed the distance to the door and rested her hand on the knob.

"I talked to Owen." He paused, the details of both of his conversations where she was the main topic too long and too involved for a casual porch chat. A night like this with a faint cool breeze invited two people to sit on a front porch and cuddle to stay warm. Too bad that couldn't happen tonight. Not with a possible storm coming as well as his parents and Mattie presenting real reasons why, even if he wanted to, he couldn't invite her to sit next to him on her glider.

"What did he say?"

Quite a bit. "There's good and bad news." Those words slipped out of his mouth and he winced. He hated it when people started like that.

"The bad news first." Lucie's shoulders stiffened and her chin went up.

"Hmm. This could take a while. Maybe we should just enjoy game night. Make a happy memory. Then we'll decide whether to talk tonight or tomorrow." He joined her at the door and longed to tuck that stray lock of curly blond hair behind her ear. There was never a good time for them to find out if there could even be a them.

"You're avoiding the subject. You could have just told me the bad news by now." She was so close he could make out her long eyelashes setting off the violet glint in her blue eyes, the exact color of a morning glory flower.

Okay, then. He rubbed his stubble, now a beard. It was taking some time to come in, but he liked the solidity of it, same as he liked the solidity of Lucie's home. She deserved the truth. "Owen had qualms about my giving you an online recommendation. He's worried that might sound like I'm using my official capacity to endorse your business. A part-time job is okay, but he drew the line at the other." He leaned against the house, her light floral scent making it especially hard to keep his distance.

"So I can hire you as a nature consultant to lead hikes and tours, but you can't publicly promote my business while you're a park ranger? I guess there are worse things than seeing your mug on a regular basis." Her lightness came through, and good humor brought a twinkle to those morning glories before it faded and disappointment lurked there instead. "You won't endorse my company. It's not that big of a deal."

"*Can't*. There's a difference."

Her stiff shoulders argued otherwise, and her hand tightened on the knob.

Before she could open the door, he laid his hand over hers, an ice block to say the least. "Your hands are freezing."

He rubbed the tips of her fingers, wanting to transfer some of his warmth to her.

"I only came outside to check on Mattie. And speaking of Mattie, she and Ethan are scariest when they're quiet, unless they're fast asleep. Is that everything?"

The warning about hurrying wasn't wasted.

"No. How much do you know about last month's rescue?"

Her cheeks flushed two pretty spots of pink, an exact match for the carnations dotting her long-sleeved T-shirt. "You sure are jumping around a lot tonight, but I can keep up. I know what every news outlet reported." She glanced at her socked feet, from which two woolly llamas stared up at him. "And the Hollydale papers. And social media accounts."

Hmm. She'd read about him? In spite of everything standing between them, he couldn't help but feel flattered and appreciated. "Then you know the father of one of the boys used to play for the Carolina Cannons and was MVP when they won the championship. Now he's their manager, and he's the reason the story was such a big deal in the news. I called Jared and asked if he would endorse you. He's right in the middle of spring training, but when the team returns to North Carolina, he's going to contact you about setting up a visit." For Lucie, Caleb had broken his rule about calling in a favor.

"On the one hand, you should have consulted me. It is my business, you know." She arched an eyebrow and untangled his hand from hers, folding her arms.

"I know. I should have asked you first."

"But I'm so glad you did it." A smile lit up her expression, and she hugged him.

The door flew open and there stood Ethan, who turned around. "Hey, Mattie, you're wrong. Mommy isn't sending Mr. Caleb away. She's hugging him."

Ladybug trotted to the front door, while Pita escaped again.

"Mommy, Pita wants in on the fun."

"Mattie, set up Candy Land, please." Lucie turned to Caleb, her smile a little shakier now. The silence extended for a long beat then she started for the kitchen. "I'll be right back. Make yourself comfortable."

"Wait a second. Does the family like pita bread or how did Pita earn his name?" Caleb extended his hand for Pita to sniff, the dog's tail wagging faster than an oscillating fan.

"*Her* name." Lucie's nervous laugh gave nothing away as she slipped on some fuzzy boots. "I'll let you figure it out."

The challenge was there, almost like she was daring him to decide whether he was brave enough to take on the Decker household.

Pita sat on her haunches, her tail continuing its back-and-forth trajectory. She waited for Caleb to pet her while Ladybug came over and claimed her spot on Caleb's foot, her tongue lolling, her low grunts hopefully those of approval.

Mattie threw her hair back and stomped off toward the dining room, her stance on his decision to stay very clear. Ethan tapped his foot, his wide grin giving Caleb confidence he fit right in.

Fitting in wasn't something Caleb did well. Coming to Lucie's house with its blended family of animals and humans felt like finding his way home. Felt like...but couldn't be—not with all the obstacles between them.

He petted Pita with one hand and used the other to lavish attention on Ladybug, all the while smiling at Ethan. Looking around, he smiled at how Lucie blended the old with the new in an eclectic style that matched her personality. After the game was finished, Caleb would have to open up to Lucie about the woodpeckers and Owen's pronouncement about possible legal action to protect their habitat. Caleb had no idea how Lucie would take all of that. For a few more minutes, Caleb would enjoy the time in Lucie's presence.

Someone needed to look out for her and

be her beacon in the midst of all this. While he'd love to apply for that position, he worried more about being the next resident of Hollydale to hurt her again.

TEN MINUTES LATER, Lucie shut the shed door behind her, Fred and Ethel content in their pen, which gave them access to the sheltered run adjacent to the building. She'd come back and turn off the infrared heater before she went to sleep. For now, the miniature pigs were snuggled together with water and clean bedding.

No more excuses separated her from game night and Caleb. Her cell phone rang and she glanced at the screen. She'd gotten a visit from the furnace repair service this afternoon—they'd had a cancellation at the last minute and had sent the technician out to look at her furnace. A call in the early evening did not bode well. She listened as the owner of the furnace company confirmed her suspicions that the whole air-conditioning and heating system needed replacing. She leaned against the shed for support before thanking the man for the personal call.

Twenty thousand dollars for a new unit. Where would she get that kind of money? That and the cost of Caleb's salary, if she hired him, were not in her current budget. Tablets for the staff had maxed out her last reserves. Her business account only held enough for the salaries of the staff she'd already hired and little else. She'd be running on fumes until the companies that had already signed up as clients forked over the remainder of the amount owed after their retreats were over.

The outline of her Victorian house glowed in the evening dusk, the yellow fading to a soft cream. If her business failed, Aunt Rosemary could swoop in and lay claim to the lodge and cabin, and Lucie would have to go back to odd jobs to make a living. When all was said and done, her aunt could sell everything associated with the business if Lucie didn't pay her back. Then she'd have to start all over again.

At least she hadn't mortgaged the house. If she had done that and failed, she and the twins could be homeless, not to mention Fred and Ethel, Midnight, Ladybug and Pita, and the bunnies.

Without a working heating and cooling system, though, her business would definitely fail. The lodge and surrounding land would be sold to pay back what she owed Mitzi and Aunt Rosemary, and who knew what developer would purchase the property and for what reason.

Selling her assets and leaving town was the option the bank president, Franklin Garrity, had wanted from the beginning—and he wanted the proceeds to go to Justin's victims, herself and the twins excluded—but that was never under consideration in her book. There'd have been no way to support herself or to try to win back the town's respect.

Had she been a fool to even think she could win back Hollydale's respect?

She looked at her phone. One phone call to her partners would clear up whether they'd be willing to shell out more money. After all, this was a legitimate business expense, and she couldn't open without a working furnace. Protecting their investment would be prudent. Giving them that option was her best choice.

Might as well get the more difficult call over with first. She called Aunt Rosemary and tried to get a word in edgewise.

When would that first repayment check be transferred to her account? When would she see a return on her money? If Lucie listened to her more…

Finally, the opening she'd been waiting for came. "The furnace gave out."

Stony silence fell over the line. "I have a buyer lined up." Her aunt's words sent a chill down her spine.

"I'll figure something out."

The call ended within seconds, and Lucie stared at her phone. How could she rope Mitzi into extending her any more money?

Her stomach roiled at the last-ditch option she'd been keeping in her pocket. She saw no other choice but to march into the bank, swallow the remnants of her pride and apply for a mortgage so she could buy a new furnace. Better to mortgage the house than to sell everything she'd worked for over the past few months.

Somehow, in the walk between the shed and the house, she'd have to paste on a fake smile that would convince Caleb nothing was wrong. That might prove impossible considering the gaping ache that dulled her stomach. Caleb had always been able to read her like a geological terrain map.

Reaching the door, she flung it open and put aside her feelings. She couldn't wait to lose herself in a round of Candy Land.

SOMETHING HAD HAPPENED out in the shed. Caleb was sure of it. While the dining room's crystal chandelier bathed its occupants and the antique mahogany table with a golden glow, Lucie's smile hadn't reached her eyes since she'd come inside. Sure, she had laughed at Ethan's puns and ribbed Mattie about her bad luck, but she'd also held back.

Her vitality had buoyed up Caleb since his return. Before he left tonight, he'd ask if she'd share with him whatever had happened earlier. Maybe together they could work out a solution.

"One more game," Ethan pleaded when Caleb moved his piece into the winner's circle.

"It's bedtime, and it's a school night." Lucie reached for the last kernel of popcorn and popped it in her mouth.

"I demand a rematch."

Lucie shook her head at Mattie's demand.

"Then winner has to clean up." Mattie pushed her chair away from the table with a stare in Caleb's direction before she turned to Ethan. "Bet I'm done getting ready for bed first." Mattie ran for the stairs, Pita bounding after her while Ladybug snored and snuffled on Caleb's foot. The bulldog must sleep through anything.

"No fair. You have a head start." Ethan scrambled out of his seat in the dining room and followed his sister.

Caleb reached for the game box with a shrug. "I was rooting for Mattie, but I couldn't figure out a way to let her win."

Lucie shook her head while collapsing the board. "That's called cheating and you'd also be taking sides. I started family game night with them so they'd learn how to win or lose with grace. On the whole, everyone's wins and losses balance out."

Since he'd left Hollydale, it seemed as though more losses had added up in Lucie's column while the wins had factored more in his. At least, most people would sum up their present situations like that. Then again, contented animals and happy twins proved them wrong. While he'd succeeded in his job, she'd succeeded in rebuilding her life.

"I thought for a couple minutes it would be family fight night, but they seemed to take defeat well." He handed her an errant token, and electricity zapped his fingertips at her touch. From the way her eyes widened, she'd experienced it, too. He jerked his hand away, remembering he had no right to reach out for her warmth. "And that might be the first time I've ever heard kids bet about who'll be ready for bed first. Jonathan's daughter Vanessa always wants to stay up later than her sister Izzy."

"I made a deal with them a long time ago." Lucie placed the lid on the box and rose. "Whoever's ready and in bed first gets stories and tucked in after the other twin, thereby staying up for a whopping ten extra minutes. Bragging rights are a great motivator. I'll be right back."

She climbed the stairs and he debated moving, but Ladybug was a definite deterrent, her snuffled snores endearing. When he returned to Jonathan's house tonight, he'd miss all of this.

And when he moved out of Jonathan's?

He wouldn't think about resuming his life as a bachelor. By then, his work schedule would be full and he'd lose himself in learning his new job. Work had always kept him busy in the past.

Why did that not seem enough anymore?

Pulling out his phone, he checked the real-estate listings the agent had forwarded. Nothing caught his eye. The best properties were too far from the station, and the close ones needed too much work for a rental. He typed his thanks, along with a request to keep looking.

"More bad news? The look on your face

is quite intense." Lucie hesitated at the doorway of the dining room, her laptop in hand.

"Nothing dire." He laughed and held up his phone. "It's Robin, my real-estate agent. No luck yet."

"Guess all your luck tonight went toward winning the game." And yet again, that smile didn't light up her eyes.

"Lucie…" How did he begin to get her to trust him when he himself withheld information from her?

As much as he'd wanted to explore something more with her, to find something more to life than just work, she needed him to listen right now as a friend, nothing more.

"I'd ask if you want decaf or something, but I've got a couple hours of hard work in front of me." She crossed the room and reached for the dimmer switch on the wall, increasing the intensity of the lighting from a soft glow to blaring incandescence. "I'll let you know if and when I hear from the baseball player."

While he recognized the brush-off, he couldn't leave. Not yet. "What happened when you checked on Fred and Ethel?"

Her soft sigh filled the room. "I almost forgot about them. Do you want to walk out with me? We can say good-night before I turn off the infrared heater."

Her message was clear. The evening had come to an end, as all good evenings did. For a few hours, though, the Decker family had included him, and he was the better for it. "I'd like to meet the infamous Fred and Ethel before I go." Rising brought a muffled moan of discontent from Ladybug. "Sorry, girl."

Ladybug licked the denim of his jeans, as though accepting his apology for dislodging her from a contented nap, before shuffling toward the stairs.

"Don't be alarmed if they don't accept you. It takes a while for miniature pigs to accept anyone. I think they're worth the time and effort."

They stopped in the foyer while he gathered his coat. Then he followed her to the kitchen. Lucie grabbed her jacket from a hook on the back door, picked up the bin of scraps, and flicked on the patio light. She opened the door. The blast of cold air took him by surprise. One thing he had missed about the Great Smoky Mountains was the unpredictability of the seasons. In Yellowstone, the seasons were simple—three winters and a week of summer. Here, spring turned back to winter before coming through in all its splendor.

"Be careful on the path. There's some loose gravel."

Lucie wedged the shed door open enough for him to go into the enclosure, more like a small barn inside than a typical shed. Caleb wandered in, and a motion-sensor light flickered on, illuminating the area, which was warm from the infrared heater in the corner next to a dilapidated couch on one side and a pen on the other. The sweet smell of hay filled the air. One of the miniature pigs, that description misleading as it probably weighed a good hundred and fifty pounds, grunted its hello and came over to them, nudging his hand.

Caleb glanced at Lucie.

"Wow, Ethel likes you. She doesn't normally take to new people so fast. Sit down on the couch. I'll wager Fred comes out of the pen, too." Lucie pulled a carrot from the top of the bin and handed it to Caleb. "This one's for Ethel."

A slight twinkle returned to Lucie's eyes as they dared him to follow her instructions. Caleb was game for anything. Once. He settled on the couch. Ethel followed him and jumped up next to him. His eyes widened, and every muscle in his body went on full alert. "Is she allowed up here?"

Lucie laughed, the sound music to his ears. "Are you going to tell her different?"

Good point. "What do I do now?"

"Give her the carrot. Miniature pigs are slow to bond with people, but, for some reason, she liked you on sight." Almost on cue, Fred peeked over the edge of the pen, and Lucie patted his head. "Fred is more of a ladies' man. Nothing personal."

"No offense taken." Caleb held out the carrot and Ethel munched it with glee. "Now what?"

"You're the park ranger. You should know."

Forestry school had prepared him for integrating forestland with community needs, analyzing soil samples and adapting plans for wildlife to exist in nature with encroaching settlements. Nothing had prepared him for Ethel.

And yet there was nowhere else he wanted to be than on a couch in a shed with a pig who thought she was a lapdog.

Ethel climbed on him and nuzzled his cheek, her short fur grazing his stubble. If miniature pigs didn't accept people right away, he'd hate to see what happened when they bonded with someone.

"Now, Ethel. Caleb's not used to you yet." Lucie clucked her tongue and Ethel retreated to her side of the couch. "You can scratch behind her ears or in the area between her eyes. Miniature pigs are quite affectionate. Here, watch me with Fred."

She demonstrated, and Fred grunted his appreciation. After feeding him his carrot, Lucie went over and dumped the contents of the bin into a trough. When Ethel remained on the couch, Caleb followed Lucie's lead and scratched her head, her pig grunts her sign of gratitude.

"How do you feed all the animals?" And how did she make each of them feel loved and wanted? Like each was special in a unique way. The same way she was making him feel.

Lucie came over and sat on the edge of the couch that had probably been rejected by a thrift store. Blowing out a breath, she tucked that errant strand of curly hair behind her ear. "Some people drop off bags of dog and cat food on my porch knowing I take in any animal that comes my way. Others drop off non-clumping kitty litter, which I can also use for the bunnies that live in the guest room.

Whether people leave supplies out of guilt or gratitude, I don't care. They get put to good use."

"Owen knows about the woodpeckers. I showed him the picture of the nest." As much as he didn't want to put any more frowns on her face, Caleb couldn't hold it in any longer. "He's talking to the local environmental law attorney who works in conjunction with the Park Service."

Only Ethel's grunts broke the silence. For some reason, this pig liked him and wanted his attention. Here Lucie was, collecting strays all around her, animals that people in Hollydale didn't want, and he couldn't tell whether he was another stray or not. While he longed for a place in her life, he couldn't settle for simply being part of her collection.

Then again, the longer her silence stretched out, the more he became convinced she didn't want him around. With friends like him, who needed enemies?

Ethel tired of him and jumped off the couch. Maybe he'd overstayed his welcome.

"That's why I respect you. You tell the truth even when it's hard to do." Lucie remained perched on the edge of the couch, her open face stormy but serene. "I knew when you snapped those pictures why you were doing it. Is everything settled? Am I losing the center?"

"No, he's waiting for my final report."

She reached over and patted his hand. Then her eyes narrowed. "I'm not upset at you."

Her ability to read him and his moods was astonishing. After several months of dating, Leah had compared him to a rock, unyielding in both emotion and facial expression.

"This is the first time someone has spotted a nest in the wild for a couple years."

"And of all the places, it graciously chose my land and my chimney." Lucie moved her hand away, and he regretted losing the tender touch. She rose and clicked off the heater. "Good night, Fred and Ethel. Sleep well."

That was his cue to rise and return to his temporary home at Jonathan's. He approached her by the door. "I'll come to the center tomorrow. Since it'll be a Friday night, why don't I take you and the twins to the Holly Days Diner afterward?"

He moved closer, and it was as if the air stilled. He reached out and stroked her cheek.

She pulled back and toed the dirt of the shed with her suede boot. "I don't think I can accept the dinner invitation…or anything else."

"I'm sorry if I overstepped there."

She lifted her chin and met his gaze. "No. That's not it."

While he should cut his losses and bide his time, he couldn't walk away like this. "What's going on?"

Lucie took a deep breath and offered a slight smile. "When Justin was arrested, I visited him and believed every word until the authorities laid out the entire case for me." Her voice broke, the last syllables husky and breathless.

"I'm not Justin. I came over tonight to tell you everything." *I have to tell her about my parents.* His mouth didn't move, though.

"I know." She ran her hand through her hair. "Around here, some want me to fail, while others let me lean on them. Until I can prove I can stand on my two feet, I'm not sure I'm ready for anything more than friends."

"Whatever's happening, you don't have to go through it alone. I'm here." Did she believe he'd hurt her on purpose? That he would place himself above the needs and well-being of others? "You haven't had enough time yet to see I'm different. I won't go against my principles or turn my back on what's right."

"I've done everything I can in the past cou-

ple of years to try to show people *I'm different*, I'm worth something. I need time to
believe that about myself. I need time to trust
again."

"Lucie." He rubbed his chin. He wanted to
stand out from her collection of animals and
from the residents who judged her. Having
her notice the real him rather than his accom-
plishments would be a first step toward something lasting. He understood she wanted to
show people she was different, but he needed
her to see the same about him. "You're the
best friend I have in the world. I'm here for
good, and if there's one thing that hospital
bed taught me, it was patience."

Conflict warred on her face. "That first
night, you asked to turn back time for a fresh
start. Now I'm asking for time. Please."

She opened the shed door, the blast of
mountain air downright freezing. It seemed to
wake him to the reality of what she was really
saying. Leaving her, leaving such a nice family, pigs and all, was harder than he'd imag-
ined, but he nodded. She was worth the wait.

CHAPTER SIX

"GOOD MORNING, SLEEPYHEAD. Izzy and Vanessa are already at school on this rainy but otherwise gorgeous Friday morning." Jonathan stood near the pantry in his kitchen, searching for something on the top shelf. "Aha. Found my poison."

Jonathan rattled a box of sugary cereal as Caleb made a beeline for the coffeepot. He selected a plain black mug and filled it to the brim before settling onto one of the benches in the breakfast nook. Wrapping his hands around the mug, Caleb breathed in the rich aroma, willing the caffeine to enter his bloodstream.

Jonathan sat on the opposite bench and poured cereal into his bowl. He then shook the box in Caleb's face. "Breakfast. It's the most important meal of the day. That's why I get up early before my shift starts and make Izzy and Vanessa oatmeal. After they board the bus, I save the bad stuff for me. Sure you won't have some? Only the finest of artificial flavors for us cousins."

Caleb lifted his cup of coffee and shook his head. "I gave up that stuff when I was a teenager."

His cousin walked to the refrigerator and pulled out a carton of milk before returning to the breakfast nook. "Hey, where's your sense of adventure, your sense of childhood?"

"My common sense, you mean?" They laughed as Jonathan settled in front of his breakfast.

"You don't know what you're missing." Jonathan held up a spoonful of chocolate corn puffs and smacked his lips. "Chocolaty goodness in every bite."

"I'll take my chances without it, thanks." Caleb shrugged. "You know I'm looking at rental properties, right? How did you get along without me for so long? What are you going to do without me when I move out?"

"Have time in the bathroom again?" Jonathan munched, contentment written in his smile. "How's the house hunt going?"

Caleb's phone rang. Was it Owen reconsidering his decision and calling to say he needed Caleb to report early? Or perhaps it was Lucie? She might have awakened and decided they could save the world one stray at a time before working their way to protecting the woodpeckers together. The screen flashed a picture of his mother, and he sent a longing glance at his cup before answering.

"Hi, Mom."

"Hi, Aunt Tina!" Jonathan's mouth was full of cereal as he yelled his greeting and Caleb had to wipe off the small spittle of milk that landed on his arm.

"Don't you love knowing who it is before you answer? Say hello to Jonathan for me, Caleb. I miss those girls of his." Tina Spindler's voice came over the line, cheerful as always. "You know you could have sent me to voice mail if it's too early to talk."

"Figured it must be important to call this early." He ran his finger along the rim of the mug.

"Your father's employer is transferring him back to Hollydale. He applied to be a manager of environmental services at one of their closer facilities and got the job. Isn't it marvelous?" The joy in his mother's voice woke him up faster than caffeine could. "We've already started packing and should be back before the pink and yellow lady's slippers begin blooming."

Lady's slippers. He'd almost forgotten his mother's favorite flower. Every April during high school, Caleb searched the mountains for them and presented her with a huge bouquet, the lone exception being his senior year. That year, his mother had brought him the flowers.

"If you'll be in town in April, guess I'll have to see if they still grow in the field behind Miller's Pond over by Lake Pine Falls."

Jonathan stilled his spoon halfway to his mouth. "Your parents are coming for a visit? Do they have somewhere to stay?"

Caleb shook his head and placed his hand over the receiver. "Not for a visit. They're moving back permanently."

And when they did in a few weeks' time, they'd find out Lucie was now the owner of the Hollydale Training and Wellness Center and that she'd invested a good deal of money in it. While he wanted Lucie to succeed, he didn't want his mother hurting. After all, it wasn't possible to live in Hollydale without running into everyone from your third-grade teacher to your dentist on a weekly basis.

"Did Jonathan just ask if we'd like to stay there? That's such a wonderful offer. Your father and I accept." His mother must have tucked the phone between her shoulder and her ear as she clapped her happiness, unless…

"Am I on speaker, Mom?"

"Of course. Your father didn't want to miss your reaction. Say hello, Drew."

"Hello, Drew." His father laughed heartily at his joke. "Hi, Caleb. Will we recognize Hollydale?"

"Will we recognize those beautiful girls of Jonathan's?" his mom chimed in, her smile evident without her even being in the same room.

Jonathan lowered his spoon back into the bowl. "I'm going to need to buy more cereal and a bigger house with all of my guests."

Nothing was going as planned for Caleb. For so long in Yellowstone, he'd traversed his own trail as a lone wolf. Now everyone was converging on his path.

It was best he told his parents before they heard it from someone else. "Hollydale hasn't grown that much, but there have been some changes."

"For the better, from what I've heard from my friends. I can't wait to hike to the falls again," Tina said.

"It's still rather treacherous this time of year, Mom." He took a sip of coffee for courage. "Mom and Dad, there's something I need to tell you."

"Sounds serious, so I'll leave you to talk to them without me. I have to get ready for work anyway." Jonathan rose and carried his bowl to the sink. "Don't forget you're picking up Izzy and Vanessa from school. I added you to the authorized list yesterday. You'll have to show your ID when you get there." Jonathan exited the kitchen muttering something about having a bathroom to himself when his daughters started college.

Caleb turned his attention back to his mother. "Lucie Decker still lives in Hollydale."

Silence settled, and it wasn't hard to imagine the long look his parents were exchanging.

Caleb should have demanded they consult an attorney and go after restitution rather than offering to report whether the retainer fee would be worth it. "Are you still there?"

"I intend to have a long talk with Lucie Decker when I arrive in town. Don't worry." Tina clucked her tongue.

That was exactly what worried him—it could destroy any chance he had of Lucie trusting him. Somehow, he'd have to make sure his parents' paths and Lucie's didn't intersect until he could tell Lucie for himself. The vise kept a tight clench.

"We wanted to tell you the good news before we hired movers." His father's hearty voice took over. "Busy day ahead. The real-estate agent is coming over to list the house. We'll call this weekend with our expected arrival day. Your mother can't wait to see you."

"Love you, Caleb," she sing-songed before the click ended the call.

He exhaled the breath he hadn't even realized he'd been holding. The phone rang again. His mother always did like to hear him echo her sentiment. He pressed Accept without even looking at the screen. "I love you, too."

"Um, thanks," a strange masculine voice replied.

Caleb lowered the screen and groaned.

Dr. Keane. Caleb closed his eyes and clenched his jaw. He'd told his new doctor he loved him. "My mother was just on the phone."

"That explains that. Do you have some time this morning to come to my office?"

"I can, but wouldn't it be easier to discuss whatever it is over the phone?"

"Does ten thirty work for you?" In not so

many words, the doctor hammered home his point, and that spot in Caleb's back acted up.

"I'll be there."

THE MUSTINESS OF the lodge basement made Lucie's nose twitch. With the exception of the finishing touches for the spa area, which awaited Mitzi's help, and the three closed rooms on the upper level, which were scheduled to become guest lodging next summer, the rest of the center was almost ready for the staff and their pre-opening orientation in two weeks. Then this place would bustle with activity.

She flicked on the light switch, and Georgie followed her down the stairs—together they were determined to eliminate the stale smell and replace it with freshness.

A little like her life in the past few months. Before the government contacted her and reverted the land back to her, she'd been juggling three jobs and getting nowhere. Eventually, she was able to give her notice at each place. Working until her time was up and creating a business plan had kept her busy while the contractors installed updates. Now she was doing something about the stagnancy that had settled over her since her divorce.

Standing on her own two feet had taken a long time, and she'd thrive from here on out. Mattie and Ethan would be proud of her someday.

Georgie waved at the stale air, and Lucie amended that to thriving with the help of her friends. "Wish there were windows we could open."

"Not to mention it's freezing down here without a working furnace." Lucie winced at her words, a reminder of the deposit the service company required this morning, which had maxed out her business credit card. They'd require the balance upon completion of the services in two weeks. "Thanks for giving up your Friday afternoon for me."

"For the person who stopped me from leaving Hollydale? Anything. Do you want me to look at the furnace? If it's anything like a car's engine, I'll have it repaired and running in no time." Georgie lowered her bucket of cleaning supplies and stepped toward the utility room.

"Thanks for the offer." Lucie dragged the vacuum cleaner behind her and then unlocked the office door opposite the utility room. "But the technician said the compressor is broken, the control board is shot, and the whole system needs replacing to bring it up to code."

"Sounds expensive." Georgie picked up her supplies and followed Lucie into the small office.

Expensive was an understatement. "It's a major purchase for a lodge as big as this one." Around three this morning, Lucie had awakened to a line of drool running from the corner of her mouth to her laptop, the mortgage application only half done. Since her home was independent of the limited liability corporation, cashing out a portion of the equity seemed the best way to raise the remaining funds. Between the twins and completing her morning to-do list, she still hadn't finished the paperwork. She'd have to submit it on Monday if she was going to have enough money for the new furnace.

Pride, however, kept her from mentioning any of that to Georgie.

Instead, she plugged in the vacuum. "This morning, I cleaned the walls in the sister office next door. If you do the same in here, I'll scrape the peeling paint off in the other room and then stick the painter's tape to the toe molding."

Georgie held up her hand. "I've painted before. I know the drill."

Lucie pulled out an extra bandanna from one of her overall pockets. "I borrowed one of Ethan's red ones as I know you're allergic to anything pink."

Georgie snatched it out of Lucie's hand and scoffed. "Thanks to my stepdaughter, I have a new appreciation for the color." She wrapped the bright red cloth around her head. "But I'll take this one anyway."

"Knock on the wall if you need anything." Lucie moved to the office next door.

Walking in, she leaned against the wall for a second, letting a wave of dizziness subside before she turned on the light. Come to think of it, she hadn't eaten breakfast or lunch. If she didn't eat something soon, she wouldn't be of much use for the rest of the day. Even though she hated the thought of Georgie working while she frittered away her time, a banana and a peanut butter sandwich would go a long way until dinner.

Her mind made up, she asked Georgie if she wanted anything before heading to the kitchen. Lucie had a peeled banana halfway to her mouth when the doorbell buzzed.

After a longing look at her hasty lunch,

Lucie hurried to the front door and found Caleb. Last night she'd asked for patience and yet here he was, standing before her. Had he volunteered to help and she'd forgotten? No, she would have remembered if she'd accepted his offer. Regret at how she'd left things last night roiled through her. He'd been trying to help and she'd made it seem like he'd committed a crime.

His voice brought her out of her thoughts. "Can I come in? It's starting to rain." Caleb shook water drops off his windbreaker, taking care to send them in the opposite direction of Lucie and her clean floors.

"Of course." Since they'd established they'd remain friends and nothing more, she should be able to concentrate on substantive issues rather than pay attention to what her heart was telling her. "I'm glad you came by today. Any updates about the woodpecker? I'd like to know what Owen said." Every detail, in fact.

"Nothing new to report. Park Service is still compiling the information needed for a thorough report." He crossed the threshold and water droplets landed on her overalls. "I came because I needed to talk to someone."

"That's what friends do. Listen." Her chest tightened at the word *friend*.

Awareness of the real reason for her dismissal of him last night dawned on her. She wasn't upset with him for getting close. Her concern was really directed at herself. After her divorce, she'd promised herself she'd stay far away from any romantic entanglements.

The first man who turned her head in all this time would have to be Caleb, an attractive man who didn't want a matchmaker, was content to be a confirmed bachelor.

And why would he think of her as anything more than a friend? Lucie was no longer the high school homecoming queen, and it was time to remember how much was riding on the success of this center. She'd best take the reins and act in an appropriate fashion, and cooperating with the local Park Service in the interests of an endangered species was her smart choice. If the final report showed her property was the primary habitat of the woodpecker and she lost her entire livelihood, it would be better to hear the news from Caleb than someone else.

Then again, that made it sound as if she wanted him to give her inside information.

She shuddered. She'd never take advantage of their friendship in that way.

Nor would she ever have him risk being accused of any impropriety that could jeopardize his professional reputation. She had to keep her distance.

She and Caleb would be friends and nothing more. Like they'd agreed.

"Caleb—"

"Lucie," he interrupted while he crossed the threshold into the lobby of her new world. "If I rushed you, I'm sorry."

What? In the few times she'd met with Justin after his arrest, not once had he ever offered an explanation or an apology. She blinked and let out a deep, cleansing breath. Justin was her past. This business was her future. And what safer friend than a park ranger? The confident air he projected came from doing his work well and loving what he did. Lessons she could use in her life.

Keeping Caleb as a friend would prove she could trust people, trust men, again. "I thought I might have felt…"

Footfalls sounded behind her and recognition lit Caleb's eyes. "Georgie Bennett?"

"Georgie Harrison now." Her friend headed toward them, her red bandanna still covering her hair. "I always think I should break into 'Here Comes the Sun' when I say that. Good to see you again, Caleb. Grab a brush. There's nothing like spending your day off painting with friends."

Hesitation hovered in the air as Lucie situated herself between them. She turned to Caleb. "You're not obligated to stay. And you don't have to apologize when I'm the one who asked for time."

"Okay, then—" Georgie interjected, jerking her thumb toward the basement. "The two of you need to talk. Without me. I'll start painting. Take your time. I'm good."

Georgie disappeared and more guilt threaded through Lucie at someone doing her work for her. Her business, her sweat and blood. "I really should be painting." Her stomach grumbled loud enough for Caleb—and downtown Hollydale—to hear. Her cheeks flushed. "After I eat a banana."

"Where do we go from here?"

Lucie motioned for him to follow her into the kitchen. "We tell each other the truth and keep everything, including our friendship, out in the open."

She grabbed her banana from the counter and bit off a hunk.

"I have a herniated disk in my lower back."

The large piece of banana went down too fast, and she sputtered before reaching for her water bottle situated next to her peanut butter sandwich. Coughing and clearing her throat, she waited a second before chugging down the water. "When did it happen? Will that impact your job? Will it go away on its own or…?"

She settled on a stool. He followed suit and rubbed his new beard, not scraggly like some beards when they were starting out. "From best as Dr. Keane can figure, it's a result of the rescue. Aggravated by one thing and another since I got back to town."

She kept listening while he talked about the possibility of physical therapy, hanging on his every word. He seemed to be taking that to heart and was determined to play by the book. Their easy camaraderie wasn't lost on her. It had always been like this with Caleb, this gentle banter, this being there for each other. Now, however, there was something else. Maybe it was the beard, or his solid presence, or the concern he projected.

There was something about this Caleb that made her want to spend more time with him. To show him her favorite vista from the porch of the small cabin or to pop popcorn and sit alongside him and Ladybug on the couch, talking about everything and nothing.

There was something about this Caleb that made her long to throw caution to the wind and trust someone again. However, her first go-round showed how unreliable a judge of character she was. Thank goodness, she and Caleb had settled on friendship.

Friends, especially friends who went back a long time, could shoot the breeze and care for one another. A relationship might spoil all of that.

"I heard what you want, but what does Dr. Keane recommend?" She bit off more banana and pushed the rest of the bunch toward him.

He broke off one and peeled it back. "Six weeks of limited activity."

"Then what?" She polished off her fruit and picked up her sandwich. Seeing the dismay on his face, she offered him half. His smile was more than enough thanks.

That smile faded, though. "Another MRI, followed by a consultation about whether I'll need surgery."

His expressive eyes gave away more than his flat tone. The man who could sit on a couch with a one-hundred-and-fifty-pound miniature pig without being fazed was concerned about his future.

Friends helped friends, and it was clear Caleb needed someone in his corner. Maybe part of his concern was having all this fall in his lap here in his hometown with only her and his cousin on his side.

Helping others was what she did best. Dwelling on what might happen would set him back. Moving forward was the answer.

"No more sitting around feeling sorry for yourself. I'm taking you on the deluxe grand tour."

"And that differs from the grand tour how?" A flicker of life in his hazel eyes encouraged her.

"I'll show you the cabin and tell you about my plan for it. Let me just tell Georgie where I'm going first."

In no time, she was back. She caught Caleb staring out the window at the magnificent view. Too much time for contemplative thought wouldn't help him right now. Sometimes action was the best remedy. She pulled on his arm.

"Let me grab my raincoat and umbrella, and we'll walk over to the cabin. If it wasn't raining, I'd show you the new and improved fire pit area and the volleyball court." She smiled and they headed for the front door.

The rain came in a steady rhythm, bouncing off the golf umbrella at a fair clip. Rain washed away everything. Spring was a season of rebirth, and maybe she should claim that for herself.

She considered picking up the pace, but the fine sheen of sweat on Caleb's forehead made her wonder if she'd chosen wisely. Instead of taking him through her center, she should have sent him home to Jonathan's.

They reached the cabin and he ran his hand over the front porch railing, sheltered from the rain. "This old place is still part of your property?"

"Yes, and since we no longer have brides staying here overnight before their weddings, I hope to incorporate it into the center next year. For now, I have an arrangement with the local bed-and-breakfast to provide a special rate for companies who sign up for the deluxe package with lodging, transportation and team building included in the cost. My business plan counts on enough capital to purchase furniture next year. Then I can provide overnight lodging."

"Have you thought about bringing in

speakers like Howard Otto, the keynote for the Sunset Soiree? They might attract some business."

Caleb made a good point. "I'm more focused on getting the word out, but that's a good idea to implement down the road. I'll talk to Mitzi and my aunt to see if we want to add that to phase two."

She reached into her raincoat for the keys and opened the front door.

Mustiness surrounded her as she stepped inside.

Caleb followed and coughed, the air dry. "It's smaller than I remember from the time when I worked here."

"That's surprising considering there's nothing in here." She'd sold anything that wasn't pinned down or necessary for the first few months just to pay her share of the ropes course and other updates.

Lucie closed the door behind them and pointed to the stairs. "That leads to the loft, which is a storage area for now, but I'd like to put a pair of twin beds up there. Then behind that wall is a bedroom, where I hope to install two sets of bunk beds so the cabin can comfortably sleep six."

He followed her as she led him to the luxurious bathroom, still fitted with quality fixtures. She just hadn't been able to bring herself to sell those. "The plumber said everything still works in here. Now I'm just hoping for more clients so I can upgrade the cabin. When I think of all the happy couples this lodge served in the past, I'm hopeful for a successful tomorrow."

"Your parents always treated their guests well. Same with their employees."

It hadn't been that long ago when she'd run into Caleb mowing lawns while she'd toted champagne and orange blossoms to this cabin. Love and happiness happened for other people, like Georgie and Mike.

Why not for me?

She ignored that little voice. Creating a corporate training and wellness center for fostering communication and honesty would serve people better than orange blossoms and gold bands. She flipped off the light switch and motioned for Caleb to follow her.

"Why do you have electricity running in here if you don't plan to use this right away?"

"Business codes and regulations." She kept her pace slow. Now that she knew his diagnosis, the little cues of fine lines on his forehead standing out and the hand on his back to steady himself were all the more obvious. The herniated disk was bothering him, and he hadn't mentioned it once.

Of all the people he could have turned to after talking to Dr. Keane, he'd turned to her. Somehow, they were intertwining their lives once more. For Mattie and Ethan's sake, she had to make sure they didn't rush into anything. No matter how strong the growing attraction was within her, committing with her heart wasn't the way she'd ever live again.

From the bathroom, she headed to the cabin's tiny kitchen, which would be the last stop on her tour, and a good thing, too. Caleb needed rest. She led the way to the galley area.

"Let me get this straight." Caleb ran his hand over the granite countertop above the dishwasher. "You have all this space and you're not using it."

Frustration uncorked within her at his tone of voice. "Well, I had to make a choice. It was upgrade the lodge or the cabin. I chose the lodge to be phase one. It seemed the most responsible way not to lose my shirt in this project, especially since I'm responsible for the twins, three rabbits, one cat, two dogs and a pair of miniature pigs."

"You aren't going to lose your shirt. You have a great setup." His encouragement came with a ready smile. He leaned against the counter, relief etched in his face. "Would an extra thousand a month come in handy?"

"I'm not accepting any more partners."

While another investor might help subsidize the new furnace and air-conditioning system, she'd already had several of Justin's victims level looks at her. She'd heard mutters about Mitzi's investment being a lost cause, as well. There was no way she'd have anyone insinuate she was taking advantage of the Hero of Hollydale.

"I'll walk you to your car so you can go home and rest. I have a full afternoon of painting and getting the offices in order. My staff arrives in a few weeks and the first clients shortly thereafter." And this weekend, she'd have to fill out the mortgage paperwork, new priority number one.

"Who's watching Mattie and Ethan after school today? I have to pick up Vanessa and Izzy. It's no problem if the twins join us." Caleb folded his arms and stood still, giving no sign he was going anywhere anytime soon. "You can include me on your list of people in case you need a helping hand with them when you have to work late."

"You don't need to do that. They're enrolled in the after-school program. Natalie Harrison watches over them and brings them home when she's done teaching for the day."

Natalie loved kids and, even better, she was an identical twin so she knew the inside tricks to watching multiples. However, Caleb might have hit on another idea she might have to explore for phase three, child care. She'd reach more families and a wider group of potential clients if she had child care available.

"And I already have a lead on a permanent babysitter." That defensive edge she'd heard too often in the past couple of years lined her voice. She should have thought of these ideas herself.

"I think you misunderstood me earlier. What I was getting at is, I'd like to rent the cabin from you. And I'd *like* to spend time with Mattie and Ethan on my days off."

Having Caleb in such close proximity wasn't a good idea. But she needed a better reason. One that didn't sound like she was blowing him off. "There's no furniture."

"I'm a bachelor. I don't need a lot. My park ranger cabin at Yellowstone only came with the bare basics." Caleb volleyed back and the ball was now in her court.

"No dishes, no pots or pans, no linens." How much would all of this cost? Money was already tight. Then again, if the mortgage came through, she could furnish this place and offer more services. "I have to apply for a mortgage for my house to pay for the new furnace system. Depending on how much of a loan the bank is willing to give me, I could go ahead with furnishing this place a year early."

"But my renting the cabin would come with a built-in babysitter whenever my schedule allows, and I wouldn't ask you to furnish anything. The stove and fridge still work, right?"

"Why would you agree to that?" Cynicism hadn't been in her vocabulary before Justin, but now she looked at people's ulterior motives. "There are other places to rent in Hollydale. Certainly ones that wouldn't have you doing any babysitting."

"This one is close to the park ranger station." He shoved his hands into his pockets. "And I'm on desk duty for the next six weeks. I can't stop working, Lucie. I can't."

"But taking it easy for six weeks might keep you from needing surgery."

She tapped her fingers against the cold

stove. Rent money from him would help off-set the mortgage. Better yet, it was an excuse to keep distance between them—she couldn't get involved with a tenant, especially one who wasn't looking for a relationship.

She nodded. "Deal."

"What made you change your mind?"

You. How could she be honest while not giving anything away? "Ethan likes you."

He laughed. "And this will give me a chance to work on Mattie."

But not on Lucie. She was determined to keep their relationship strictly on a landlord and tenant level from now on.

CHAPTER SEVEN

CALEB KNOCKED ON Lucie's front door for the second time. There was still no human answer, although Ladybug and Pita were barking up a storm. Lucie's car was parked in the driveway, so wherever she'd gone with Mattie and Ethan, it couldn't be far. He tapped his foot.

A key to the cabin would be nice so he could measure the bedroom and the loft area— The door flew open. "Hey, Mr. Caleb. Mommy says not to open the door to strangers, but you're not a stranger, so I s'pose it's okay."

Caleb warmed at Ethan grinning a broad smile. Something was different. "Did you lose a tooth?"

"Yep. Mattie's so mad. She says 'cause she's older she should have been first."

Ethan waved Caleb inside as Ladybug trotted outside and Pita bounded toward him. "Mommy's out back feeding Fred and Ethel."

Pita jumped on Caleb, causing him to stumble before he steadied himself. "Down." He stuck out one finger and kept a level tone.

Pita obeyed, though her tail wagged with the speed of a cheetah.

Caleb petted her head. "Good girl."

Ladybug pressed her snout against Caleb's leg and he switched his attention to her. "And you're a good dog, too."

Caleb moved for the doorway, but neither dog made an effort to join them, instead sunning themselves on the porch, today's warm temperature a contrast to yesterday's rainy weather. He whistled and he could almost hear the dogs' sighs before they followed him and Ethan inside.

"Mattie and me are kicking the soccer ball in the backyard. I was soooo thirsty that I took a break. Wanna join us?" Ethan's face brightened even more.

Caleb shuffled his feet. Dr. Keane wouldn't approve of soccer, but someone Ethan's age might not understand the logistics of a herniated disc. Then another idea came to mind. "I need to talk to your mom first. Then I might have a surprise."

"I love s'prises." Ethan ran for the back

door. "Hey, Mattie, Mr. Caleb has a s'prise for us."

The dogs followed Caleb as he waved to Mattie before heading to the shed. "Lucie?"

"Back here."

He walked in the direction of her voice and found her lifting a fifty-pound sack of pig feed. "Here, let me help."

"I can manage."

"I know, but it's always nice to have a partner."

Together, they tilted the bag and the contents emptied into the feeder.

"Thanks." Lucie wiped her forehead with the side of her arm, pushing back that curly strand that liked to escape. "Did I forget a meeting?"

"I stopped by to see if you have an extra key to the cabin." He accepted a wet wipe and cleaned his hands as Ethel bounded over to him. She jumped onto the couch, taking her place with a majestic air. He joined her and she nudged him with her pig snout, making appreciative grunts.

Now that he'd converted Lucie's pets, he'd have to find some way of endearing himself to their owner.

Until he told her about his parents. *Just tell*

her and be done with it. Yet, seeing her covered with hay and pig feed pellets, he wanted to make her life easier, not be another voice of dissent.

"I'll stop by Farr's Hardware and have one made for you after I grab lunch. Have you eaten yet?" Lucie glanced at him like she hoped he'd turn her down.

"It's almost dinnertime."

"That late?" She cleaned her hands, checked her phone on the ledge, and groaned. "It is that late and I still haven't even started on the mortgage paperwork. Mattie and Ethan haven't complained once."

"Then how about I kick the ball around with them while you—" *You can't play soccer with them.* "I'll figure out something for us to do indoors while you finish up. Then after we stop at Farr's, I'll treat the three of you to dinner as a thank-you."

"Really, dinner out?" Mattie's voice came from behind. "Say yes, Mommy. We haven't eaten out in the longest time."

Lucie bit her lip and let that veil of hair hide her expressive morning glories. "I can fix something for dinner in no time."

"But this is a celebration." Caleb smiled

and continued scratching behind Ethel's ear. "Ethan lost a tooth today."

Mattie kicked the dirt and her lower lip jutted out. "Why does this have to be about him? Everything's always about him."

"Anything good happen in school this week?"

Mattie met his gaze and shrugged. "I read a whole book by myself."

"Then we're celebrating that, too. Right, Ethel?" On cue, the pig grunted, eliciting a small lift of the lips from Mattie.

"I'll tell Ethan." Mattie ran out of the shed and Lucie sighed.

"This isn't a good idea."

Caleb patted Ethel's head one last time and rose, crossing over to where Lucie stood. He longed to reach out and hold her hand, but he was intent on developing trust first. "My treat. How's that bad?"

Lucie's shoulders slumped. "I don't mind if people aren't comfortable around me. I do mind when they take Justin's actions out on Mattie and Ethan. That's why we don't go out to eat more often."

But they were kids, young kids. Before he could form any words, one look at Lucie's pursed lips told him all he needed to know. "Then we go in with our heads held high."

She met his gaze and gave a slight nod. "Fifteen minutes, then." She tilted her head toward Ethel. "If I can drag you away from your newest fan."

Lucie left the shed and Caleb settled next to Ethel once more. "Tonight. I'll tell her tonight."

Ethel's grunt sounded like she didn't believe him, either.

LUCIE TRIED TO settle the rhinoceros stomping around her stomach. If every gaze hadn't been trained on her and Caleb when they entered the Holly Days Diner, she might have been able to relax. As it was, the letters on the menu blurred and jumbled around before she decided on the fried chicken. No matter how hard she tried, hers never came out as well as her mother's or Miss Joanne's.

"Thank you. This is a real treat."

Even Mattie and Ethan were on their best behavior as they studied the children's menus.

With no dinner cleanup tonight, she'd have enough time to fill out the mortgage application. No, she wouldn't think of business now. This was a rare night out.

Lucie sank into the plush red leather of the booth and luxuriated in having Mattie by her side while Caleb and Ethan sat across from them.

"What's that?" Ethan pointed to the jukebox at the back of the diner.

Caleb dug into his jeans' pocket and pulled out quarters. "It's a jukebox. You and Mattie can go pick out a few songs to play."

"Bet I beat you there." Ethan grabbed his two coins and scooted out of the booth before Mattie could even react.

"Thank you, Mr. Caleb." Mattie palmed her quarters and rushed to Ethan's side.

"One dollar and I have you to myself. Not a bad bargain." Caleb smiled as the waitress delivered a basket of corn bread and biscuits to their table.

After Lucie ordered for the twins and herself, Caleb chose the meat loaf special. When the waitress left, Caleb leaned back and patted his stomach. "I didn't realize I missed the diner until now. I especially missed Miss Joanne's meat loaf."

Lucie felt the same way. On a Saturday night, the diner vibrated with energy and purpose, feeding half of Hollydale. "I should help Mattie and Ethan. They won't be able to read all the selections." Lucie placed her hand on the table so she could scoot out more easily.

Caleb covered hers with his. "It's not so important what they choose. You can see them. They're okay. It's the small taste of freedom."

He glanced at their hands, and the attraction sizzled. Then he pulled away and reached for a corn bread square.

Lucie had just selected a biscuit when the owner of The Book Nook, Connie Witherspoon, headed toward their table. Lucie froze like a fawn in the headlights on a foggy mountain morning. Nowhere to go. She stiffened and drew in a deep breath, while many in the restaurant turned to stare at her. Lucie steadied herself. She'd done nothing wrong. People would have to get used to her showing her face around here more often.

"Lucie," Connie said, stopping at the edge of the booth.

Lucie glanced at Mattie and Ethan, who were still deciding on songs at the jukebox. She'd protect them come what may, even if she had to eat humble pie. "Good evening, Connie. Beautiful night."

"I've been talking with some people and there's something I have to say about you and your husband." Connie's strident voice echoed through the restaurant, the noise around them fading.

Complete quiet descended on the patrons. "My *ex*-husband, you mean. The man who happens to be the father of my children, who are over there at the jukebox. If you have something to say to me, you can make an appointment with me and come out to the Hollydale Training and Wellness Center on Monday morning." Her heart beat so fast she was sure it would explode out of her chest.

Connie's frown caused a furrow in her brows. "I wouldn't say anything untoward in front of your children." She sent a glance at the jukebox and her cheeks softened. "Your mama would be real proud of how well behaved they are in public."

Patsy Appleby would have loved the twins and spoiled them rotten. "Yes, she would be proud." Despite all her contradictions and complexities, Lucie's mother had worn her heart on her sleeve. The apple hadn't fallen far from the Appleby tree. For the longest time since her parents' fatal car accident, she'd lost her way. Forgotten the strength and resiliency they'd practiced every day. The center helped her remember those attributes. She'd do her best to raise Mattie and Ethan with the same ideals and give them a rosy future. And for herself, as well. "Thank you. Now, if you'll excuse me."

"You were right, Lucie Appleby." Connie stood there and folded her arms across her chest.

Lucie was right about a lot of things but, for the life of her, she didn't know what Connie was talking about. "Lucie Appleby *Decker.*" Using the last name that went along with her lapse in character judgment reminded her not to fall into the same trap again. She quickly glanced at the twins, who were entranced by the lever that flipped the pages of music lists.

"I'll call you on Monday about placing my books in your library." Connie lifted her chin, swiveled on her red pumps and tottered away.

Lucie blinked. Someone in Hollydale had acknowledged she had a good idea when it came to business. It was only a small start, but she'd take it on a silver platter, preferably alongside Miss Joanne's fried chicken and biscuits.

Enjoying her dinner had just become that much easier.

CALEB STROLLED ALONG the sidewalk near the center of downtown Hollydale, taking care not to move too fast or too slow, his herniated disk now at the forefront of every decision. How would he work if surgery was part of his future?

Mattie and Ethan sprinted for the gazebo, the true center of life in the town—the surrounding twinkling white lights provided illumination so they wouldn't trip or fall. As much as he'd like to be there if either of them, or their mother, stumbled, it wasn't his place. Not with an uncertain future, clouded by his parents' arrival.

"I'm going to let them run off those chocolate sundaes before we walk the rest of the way home." Lucie climbed the steps to the interior of the structure and leaned against the railing, her gaze tracking Mattie and Ethan's game of tag. "If you have somewhere else you need to be, I understand. This is Hollydale. We'll be fine walking home without you."

Jonathan and the girls were attending a women's soccer game in Asheville. While they'd offered to scrounge up one more ticket, Caleb had urged them to go without him. They wouldn't be home until later, and Caleb didn't fancy returning to a dark house. Not when Lucie's home was full of life, literally and figuratively.

"I still need that key, remember?" He settled next to her on the railing and watched the townspeople go by, some hurrying to dinner, some enjoying the spring air, others probably on their way to shoot pool at the new bar that made great nachos. One of these days, he and Jonathan would have to break a rack.

Lucie tapped her forehead with her fingers. "I forgot. We better check to see if Farr's Hardware is still open."

The soft scent of roses tickled his nose and he reached out for her hand. "The kids are having fun. Can't they have one more minute to play? Lucie…"

"You promised me more time."

Her admission exhilarated him and frustrated him at the same time. "Then you feel whatever's between us."

Her cheeks flushed, and the evening was too cool to be the cause. "Why else would I ask for your patience?"

"That's not a direct answer."

"Isn't it?" She fidgeted and picked at the edge of her pink jacket. "It's hard to resist a man who swoops into town and plays Candy Land with my kids, pets my pig without judging me, and tries to fix my furnace."

"Then why resist? I'll admit it right here

and now. I'd like to explore what's between us. You just have to say the word, and we can take our time to see where these feelings will take us."

He'd have all the patience in the world if she thought he was special and worth the wait.

"But if I lose your friendship?"

"What if we gain more? Maybe we should invest our patience in seeing where this could go."

"You are a persuasive man, Caleb Spindler. That's what I like about you."

"Then first, one kiss."

He met her gaze, and she licked her lips, giving enough of a nod for him to proceed. Lowering his lips to hers, he tasted the hot fudge from her dessert, the softness of her lips against his.

"Hey, Mr. Caleb, does my mommy have a boo-boo on her mouth? Is that why you're kissing her?"

People on the sidewalk stopped at Ethan's announcement, which Jonathan and the girls had probably heard all the way in Asheville.

"Caleb? The Hero of Hollydale?" An older man stopped and waved. "You made us proud, son. Keep up the great work."

The woman next to him nudged the man's

ribs and whispered something in his ear before the two hurried along.

Lucie backed away, sheer horror coming into her eyes. Why? Was it from kissing him in front of her children?

"I'll get the key next week." Caleb didn't want to stay to find out what caused her to look so aghast.

Especially considering how much he'd enjoyed the moment—he wouldn't have minded asking for another before he left for Jonathan's place.

He waved goodbye and almost sprinted down the stairs, ignoring the twinge in his back. For once, an empty house was just what he needed.

CHAPTER EIGHT

THE COLD RAIN was back on Sunday afternoon. Lucie huddled under Mitzi's canopy, waiting for her friend to open the salon door. Mattie and Ethan were spending the afternoon with Natalie, welcoming her college roommate and young son to town, and Lucie was looking forward to inventorying Mitzi's supplies for the spa section of the wellness center. That had to be why she was brimming with nervous energy.

There was no way it had anything to do with Caleb's kiss last night. Her first kiss since the divorce. A beautiful kiss under the stars, with fairy lights bathing the gazebo in a magical glow. That romantic atmosphere must have been what led her overboard and into deep trouble. Why else would she have kissed Caleb? At that thought, she was reminded of the teenager who'd made her laugh when everyone else expected her to be a frilly debutante, a girl who might giggle but never belly laugh. She thought of Caleb now, the man who accepted her hectic life without judgment.

It didn't matter that the kiss had made her toes wiggle and her spine tingle. When the man passing by had acknowledged Caleb as the Hero of Hollydale, Caleb had fled the scene, embarrassed at having been caught kissing the town pariah, especially when he had no intention of settling down.

A blur in a yellow rain poncho whizzed into view. Mitzi stopped at the front door, a disposable cup in each hand. "Sorry, Lucie. The line at The Busy Bean is out the door. I thought I'd have enough time to grab us cappuccinos before you arrived. Hold these while I find the key, okay?"

"I can't argue with that." Lucie used care not to burn her fingers, having already been burned once in the past twenty-four hours.

Mitzi unlocked the door, and Lucie followed her inside. Little puddles of water accumulated wherever Mitzi stepped, and Lucie wiped her feet on the big mat.

"Ah, honey," Mitzi said, "a little water never hurt nobody. Besides, my floors are drip dry, same as me."

For the first time since last night, Lucie

cracked a genuine smile, although Pita had tried her best to coax one by running in circles trying to catch her tail, as if she'd instinctively known Lucie had needed a dose of cheer. "Don't tell Mattie and Ethan that or they'll bring the outdoors in every time it rains."

Mitzi dropped her keys at her station, the clang echoing through the empty salon. "I'll sure be glad when all the extra inventory's out of my storeroom and at the center. I can't even get to my trusty old coffeepot." She opened the lid of the cappuccino and inhaled. "But Deb makes it better than me, so I don't mind springing for this."

"The spa suggestion has already brought business my way. A couple real-estate offices have been in touch and have signed up for the spa getaway retreat." Lucie walked toward the rear of the shop. "I'll bring my car around tonight and load whatever's ready to go."

"That's why we make a good team." Mitzi sipped her coffee and squinted. "Are you sure you don't need a cucumber mask? Those dark circles under them pretty eyes of yours haven't disappeared yet."

If only a cucumber mask could take away her problems. "Didn't sleep well."

"Then let's test out two new complimentary masks I got in the mail from someone who wants me to buy their products."

"Shouldn't we work on the inventory?"

"Oh, honey, we are the living embodiment of our inventory. Half of being a success is projecting confidence and authority. Lucie Appleby walked around like she owned the town. You've gotta connect with that old part of you, the part that danced in the rain and spoke of moonbeams with stars in your eyes." Mitzi rummaged through the big drawer at her workstation. "You want lavender cucumber or orange lemongrass? There's nothing like a good mud mask to make you feel all fresh and ready to take on the world."

The old part of her? Was her romantic side really gone forever? After Caleb had kissed her, that dewy feeling had returned and, for one minute, she'd seen the gazebo with rose-colored glasses. Caleb made her feel beautiful. Too bad she embarrassed him so much.

"Lucie Appleby was a spoiled debutante." The truth hurt, but she'd gone around Hollydale without a care in the world. That young girl had expected people to keep their word and their promises.

Mitzi came over and grabbed both of

Lucie's hands, shaking them. "You were not spoiled. You worked at your parents' wedding destination lodge and you promoted that business with spirit, same as you love and care deeply for life. Repeat after me. 'I am a caring person who throws all of me into whatever I do. I *will not* let Justin Decker take away the rest of my life.'"

"I won't let Justin Decker take away the rest of my life." That was the easy part. "Caleb Spindler kissed me last night."

Mitzi laughed and squeezed Lucie's hands before releasing them. "Honey, no one talked about anything else in that line today. I was wondering when I was gonna hear it from you. We are so doing these mud masks before you leave. When are you seeing that handsome hunk again?"

"Last time I went near a mud mask, the police invaded Georgie's house and my best friend was arrested. No mud masks." Lucie shuddered at the memory. "And I have no plans to 'see' Caleb anytime soon."

A rap on the front window stopped her, and she glanced at Mitzi, who shrugged. They swiveled toward the glass and found none other than Caleb there, pointing at a cup in his hand and then tilting his head at the rain and pretending to shiver.

"You're closed." Lucie turned to Mitzi, her eyes wide as she tried to telepathically urge her friend to agree with her. Avoiding Caleb might be the most honest way of dealing with this for now.

Mitzi started for the entrance. "I'm going to at least see what the man wants."

Probably the key. Lucie thumped her forehead. "I forgot to stop by Farr's Hardware again."

"Not the usual first stop after a kiss, but if that works for you, honey." Mitzi threw the dead bolts and opened the front door. "Caleb, as I live and breathe, come inside where it's nice and warm. You're in need of a haircut. I'm closed on Sundays, but, for the Hero of Hollydale, I'm sure Lucie won't mind if I take scissors to that shaggy hair of yours. A little bit off the ends and she'll find you all the more attractive. There might even be a second kiss—"

"Caleb—" Lucie strode to the front of the shop before Mitzi could have them married and expecting a child "—the closed sign is front and center. Why are you here?"

She popped her hands on her hips and

waited. She was done apologizing for herself. She didn't need anyone in her life who was embarrassed to have her nearby. Her gaze met his, and that was a mistake. Sincerity poured out of his eyes, and she wanted to hold the connection between them for a little longer.

He held out a disposable cup. "I remembered you like hot chocolate with whipped cream on cold days. I overheard Mitzi at The Busy Bean saying you were working here this afternoon."

Mitzi turned to Lucie and then back to Caleb before fanning her face. "Is it hot in here? I'll adjust the thermostat before starting that inventory. Caleb, honey, you just say the word and your first haircut will be on the house."

She bustled away and Lucie pursed her lips. *Traitor.* Lucie simmered until the squeak of the door let her know Mitzi had reached the storeroom. She traced the outline of the nearest chair with her finger. "I understand, and I don't blame you one bit."

"That's good, but if you want to let me in on whatever you're talking about, I'd appreciate it. In the meantime, this is yours. You don't want the whipped cream to melt. That was always your favorite part." He removed the lid and handed her the cup, the white mound still fluffy.

She'd never told anyone that before, or at least she thought she hadn't. "How did you know that?"

"You never said it in words, but you're expressive." He shrugged and stepped back. "Or you used to be."

Was it possible to bridge the past with the present? Or was it preferable to be done with the past and make the present and future better for Mattie and Ethan? She blinked and her world came back into focus. "You're observant. I imagine that's a good trait for your job."

She wound her hands around the cup, appreciating the warmth. Mitzi's offering sat on her workstation, and more warmth filled her that not one but two people had gone out of their way today to make sure she had a spot of happiness. "By the way, thank you for the hot chocolate."

"You're welcome." He moved forward, lines creasing his forehead. "About last night…"

With the cup halfway to her mouth, she halted her progress and held up her hand to stop him. "You'll be renting the cabin from me. I'm your landlady. We shouldn't do anything to damage that professional bond between us."

"You want to keep this on a professional level only?" Disappointment flickered in his eyes.

I'm happy with my bachelor status. I have no plans for getting married. Caleb's words echoed in her mind, and how he'd sprinted for the hills last night only confirmed what she already knew. A mother with active seven-year-old twins and a houseful of pets would be a bit much for most men. Add into that a depleted bank account?

She forgave him for running. She'd have done the same. "I think that's best."

He searched her eyes as though he expected some sort of nonverbal cue that she thought otherwise. He wouldn't find it. Keeping him at arm's length was the right choice.

"No more kisses?"

"I can't speak for Ladybug or Pita, but I have no plans to kiss any of my tenants." Lucie sipped the hot chocolate, the sweetness teasing her tongue.

"Good to know." He turned and walked toward the door.

"Wait a second." She placed her cup on the welcome counter as he halted. "Can you come by tonight to sign the lease and pick up the key?"

He glanced over his shoulder. "Tomorrow afternoon at the center would work better for me. I'm doing something with Jonathan and the girls tonight."

She gave a quick nod.

"I'll drop by the center after work. Gotta confess, I already miss Ladybug and Ethel."

His smile didn't quite reach his eyes. He departed, leaving the bells jangling. The storeroom door opened and Lucie reached for her hot cocoa before facing Mitzi, who was shaking her head. "You heard everything, didn't you?"

"I heard enough to know that man is smitten with you." Mitzi shook out two different capes. "Which would work better for your spa? This basic black cape or the gray robe?"

"The gray robe. I think men would like that better, and it's still feminine enough to appeal to women." Lucie licked a dollop of the whipped cream. "He told Rachel Harrison he's a confirmed bachelor who doesn't want to get married."

"Like he said, verbal and nonverbal don't always go together. It's like when someone says she loves her haircut, but her eyes scream she hates it. I've seen it all, and I know when words don't say everything. You're not saying everything, Lucie Decker."

"Huh? Whenever you say my name like that, you call me Lucie Appleby. Why the change?"

Mitzi held up the gray robe and nodded approvingly. "Lucie Appleby may have prattled on sometimes, but she saw more than she let on. That's the girl I know and love."

But that was the point. She always used to say too much, and everyone wrote her off—first as a silly debutante, then as a possible accomplice. She'd have to reassess her image to win back the town's acceptance.

It wasn't just for her. Mattie and Ethan were depending on her. Family came first. Always.

CHAPTER NINE

ON MONDAY MORNING, Caleb emerged from his car and stretched his back. The gray drizzly day caused a twinge near his tailbone, but it didn't rise to the same level of pain he'd experienced the morning after he'd arrived in Hollydale. He'd take that as progress. With some physical therapy, rest and luck, surgery might not be in his immediate future.

He reached into the rear of his SUV for his hat and plopped it on his head, whistling as he prepared to start his new job, even if he was limited to desk duty. Butterflies fluttered about his stomach but, compared to the buffalo stampede that had marked his first day on the job at Yellowstone, he could handle this.

"Caleb!" Marcie Williams, one of his mother's best friends, adjusted the glasses framing her ebony face when he entered the building. "You're a sight for sore eyes, and your mother called me to tell me her good news. All the Spindlers returning at once. I'm happy y'all are back."

Last night his parents had called and said to expect them next Monday night. This afternoon Caleb would have to sway Lucie into letting him move in as soon as he could get a decent mattress delivered. Jonathan's house was too small for six people. "Vanessa and Izzy are also looking forward to it."

"I keep forgetting you and Jonathan are cousins. Tina will love spending time with her great-nieces." Marcie's computer started making noise and she squinted at the screen. "Owen's expecting you. We'll catch up later. Go on back."

"Thanks."

Caleb hurried to Owen's office. While desk duty wasn't his favorite, he wouldn't mind any assignment that brought him back to serving visitors again.

The deputy director held up his hand and pointed to the phone at his ear. "Be with you in a sec."

Just as Caleb took a seat in front of the desk, Owen finished his call and lowered the phone facedown on his desk. "Caleb."

"My first day here at last." Caleb smiled. "What's my assignment?"

"A week off and then desk duty for the next five weeks until your next doctor's assessment."

He searched his boss's face for any sign that was a joke. Seeing none, Caleb leaned forward, his elbows on his knees. "I must have heard you wrong. Every time I report to you, you keep giving me time off."

Owen frowned. "I had no alternative. You failed your physical. After two days of desk duty, you'll see Dr. Keane again so he can make sure that working won't do you more harm in the long run. I can't have you endangering yourself, let alone our visitors."

"Should I be worried?" His herniated disk flared up. "Do I need to update my résumé?"

Caleb couldn't go back to Yellowstone—his position had been filled the second his transfer had gone through. A premium spot like that had more than its share of takers. The Park Service had been his life since graduation, and Caleb had gloried in having nature all around him. What would he do if he had to work somewhere without these trails and paths, without the Great Smoky Mountains? What would he do if surgery cut his career short? An office cubicle would seem cramped and stifling after life as a park ranger.

"Not yet, but you know about the high turnover in our profession. We have to deal with the physical demands of the job, the unpredictability of the visitors and their remarks and actions, not to mention that rangers are assaulted at a rate not found in many other government jobs. It's a fact of our lives that many who start out in this profession don't retire from it." Owen sighed and reached for his coffee mug, taking a long swallow.

After his surgery, Caleb had dreamed of this—guiding visitors, working on forestry projects, sketching the wildlife. His paycheck was a fringe benefit of the job. "But everyone hopes they're the exception to the rule. Desk duty isn't that strenuous."

"The doctor says you need more time off." Owen tapped the edge of his desk.

"How can I change your mind? Isn't there anything I can do to make myself useful around here?"

"Hmm. There is a project you could do from home this week."

"Name it." Anything to show Owen he could be a team player who'd make a difference at the station. And while he'd loved going to the movies with Jonathan, Izzy and Vanessa last night, he could start becoming more involved in the community on his own. He'd seen a bulletin board of activities at the Busy Bean, and there was always the bar Jonathan mentioned.

"Marcie's been handling the details of the Sunset Soiree, but I need her for a grant proposal. If anything about the soiree comes up in the next week, you can handle it from home." The deputy director's intercom buzzed. "Hold on a minute." Caleb jerked his finger toward the hallway and Owen shook his head. "You don't have to leave."

"Are you sitting down?" Marcie's voice sounded a great deal more strained than mere minutes ago.

"Yes, Marcie."

"Howard Otto, the keynote for the Sunset Soiree, is in the hospital. Alligator bit him. Couple hundred stitches and a full leg cast."

Caleb winced, the picture not pretty. He glanced at Owen, whose face had lost all traces of humor.

"Can he travel by the weekend? The soiree is this Saturday," said Owen.

"He'll be lucky to be out of the hospital by then." Sarcasm dripped from her voice, even over the intercom.

Owen exhaled and flipped his phone over. "I'm checking our backup list now."

Caleb pulled out his phone. "I have contacts out in Yellowstone who might be able to fly in on a minute's notice."

"Are you thinking what I'm thinking?" Marcie's voice crackled even though she was only in the next room.

"Yes. I'll get back to you in a few." Owen switched off the intercom and stared at Caleb so pointedly that the temperature in the room seemed to escalate by a couple degrees.

Caleb tugged at his beige collar. "Something wrong with my uniform?"

"Have you unpacked your tuxedo yet?" Owen's gray hair glinted under the fluorescent lights.

"I didn't realize we were that formal here."

Owen scattered the papers on his desk and pulled out a red manila file folder. "How's the Hero of Hollydale at public speaking?"

Caleb wished he could unbutton the top of his shirt for some much-needed air. "I dropped my college speech class twice before I finally passed."

"Surely your experience as a trail guide and in front of the media has paid off, and your fee can't be beat. Since you're a public employee, we won't have to pay you, which means more money for the woodpecker defense fund and the new conservancy Frederick Whitley is planning. With your imposed vacation, you'll have that much more time to rest and work on your keynote. A win-win, if you ask me."

"I won't have to shave my beard, right?" Caleb scrubbed his facial hair. All those years shaving every morning, yet he liked his new look.

"No, don't worry about that. And there is one perk—a table at the soiree."

Owen opened the file and studied the paperwork.

"The seats go for fifty dollars each," Owen continued, "and each table seats eight. Having his own table was one of the original speaker's requests, and we okayed it. Now, if you want us to sell the other seven seats, we'll be able to raise even more money."

Four hundred dollars for a table? In Yellowstone he had no doubt the price would be double, but in Hollydale? The figure seemed pretty high. Then again, most of the people attending were probably business people. Business people who might benefit from team building at the new Hollydale Training and

Wellness Center. "I only have one condition to become the new keynote."

Owen raised his eyebrows. "I can't, and won't, go against doctor's orders."

Caleb shook his head. "This has nothing to do with my herniated disk. Are the programs printed yet?"

Owen clicked on the intercom. "Marcie, have the programs gone to the printers?"

"I was about to hit Send when I got the news, but the copy has to go this afternoon. We can always add an insert with the new speaker's info." The question was in Marcie's voice even if she hadn't said it aloud.

"Hold that thought." Owen flicked off the switch and turned to Caleb. "What's your condition?"

"I'd like for you to add the Hollydale Training and Wellness Center as a guest." Caleb held his breath. While he couldn't officially endorse her business on its website, he could help it get off the ground in other ways. If he were able to procure a ticket for her, she'd have to do the rest of the PR work herself.

Owen tapped his desk, a wistful look coming into his eyes. "Isn't the owner of A New You one of Lucie's partners?"

"Mitzi Mayfield? I think so."

"What do you know about Ms. Mayfield? I've seen her around town. She speaks her mind and defends her friends. Pretty, too." While Owen tried to sound casual, there was a definite undercurrent of interest in his voice. "My daughter wants to apply for a job at the salon. Just making sure my first impression is accurate and it's a good place for Ashleigh to work."

Caleb searched his mind for what he knew about Mitzi. "I know she was close to Lucie's mom. The two of them grew up together. Patsy married into the Appleby family, which was the closest thing to royalty around here. After her divorce, Mitzi started working at the salon and then bought the owner out before I moved away." Caleb laughed. "I only know all that because of Lucie. It was a big story way back when, so much so, even a teenager like me knew all about it."

Owen's phone pinged and he looked at the screen. "Mondays. Can't live with them, can't live without them. Get Marcie to include the training and wellness center on the brochure list of businesses attending. She'll also need your bio for the section about the keynote by this afternoon. And you've got my okay to do any community outreach you can from home."

Caleb recognized the dismissal and waved goodbye. Now he had a reason to talk to Lucie as soon as possible. A great reason.

LUCIE SMILED TO HERSELF as she stacked printer paper in the basement storage room, the last task on her list for this Monday. True to her word, Connie had brought surplus paperbacks, and the library looked downright cozy now with the wingback chairs and shelves of books and games.

She glanced around the storage area with everything labeled and organized to help the staff. Now she had no reason to postpone the inevitable. It was time to head downtown and turn in the mortgage application. For four generations, the Appleby family owned the land and house free and clear of any debts. Her father had nailed the importance of a person's good name and good credit into Lucie at a young age, and her aunt Rosemary had invested in the center so Lucie wouldn't have to sell any of the property.

She'd warned Aunt Rosemary of the latest development last night, finding comfort in petting Ladybug during the entire painful conversation. Even though Aunt Rosemary hadn't chided her, she hadn't sounded happy about Lucie's decision, either. News of the extra income Lucie would be receiving from Caleb's rental of the cabin had placated her aunt and provided a more stable repayment policy so Lucie could get out from under these obligations sooner rather than later.

After Caleb signed the standard rental lease, she'd fill out the rest of the mortgage application and drop it off before the close of the business day. The money should be in her account by the end of the week, and next week the new furnace would be installed and paid for.

Her phone pinged and she glanced at the screen. Caleb was outside? She hurried upstairs and opened the front door. Sure enough, he was on the porch, sitting on the wooden swing connected to the eaves by metal chains, clanging in the wind.

"Want to join me?" Caleb patted the spot next to him and she laughed.

"In case you haven't noticed, it's raining." She pulled her jacket close.

"Your fingers are already blue. Come on over."

A few minutes couldn't hurt. "They do need to warm up so we can sign the lease."

She settled in next to him, his warmth emanating like a space heater, and it took all of her willpower to stay on her side of the swing. "We never negotiated the final amount." Although he'd batted around a thousand per month, she needed a number for the income section of her mortgage application.

"I'm still willing to pay a thousand a month."

"Then it's only fair I provide some of the furnishings. So I'll feel better about charging that amount. How soon were you looking to move in?"

"As soon as possible. This week even."

Her legs stilled and she turned to him. "You're joking, right?"

The musty smell alone would take a couple days of fresh air to overcome, and she couldn't get everything done at the wellness center if she had to concentrate on the cabin, as well.

"I'm not high-maintenance. Besides, all the utilities are already turned on. That's the important part. And don't worry about the furnishings. I left a message with Dr. Keane to ask if a special mattress would help my back.

I should hear something by the end of the day. I'd rather buy what I need than have it come with the place. I'll stay at Jonathan's until the mattress is delivered, but then I should be good to go." Caleb kept the swing moving under his power.

"Pardon me, but I haven't met many people who are low-maintenance." She regretted the words as soon as they left her mouth.

He stilled the swing and placed his hand over hers. "I am. I love the outdoors. Once I find something special, I hold on to it and don't need much else."

"I know."

"Thank you for understanding."

The more she connected with Caleb, the more she recognized the truth in his words. He didn't need much more than the outdoors, friends and family. "Nothing to it, actually, since you live what you speak."

"I'll go ahead and ask. Why Justin? When I introduced the two of you, I never thought you'd marry him."

Everyone in her sorority had told her what a good match they were—the golden boy with a bright stockbroker background and the golden girl whose family connections could help him live up to his full potential. Then came the freak car accident that had claimed her beloved parents. Vulnerable after their deaths, she'd listened to her friends and to Justin's parents, who had proclaimed they'd love her forever.

"According to his family, who has disowned me as well as my children, I ended up being the worst thing to ever happen to him." A pang of hurt traveled through her. She didn't care so much that she'd lost the Decker family, but she minded for Mattie and Ethan. "They justified his actions by saying he was obviously trying to fulfill my need to live in the lap of luxury. They said I was as much to blame for his crimes as he was."

She gripped the wooden railing, her knuckles turning white. No one except Justin was responsible for his actions. Still, she'd married him...

"You don't believe that, do you?" he asked, his incredulity evident.

"Of course not." She shuffled her feet and kept her gaze trained on the steady rain, eager to change the subject away from her ex-husband. She wanted to look forward. "The cabin is rather small, and since you'll be bringing your own furniture, I don't feel right charging more than six hundred. I'm paying for utilities, but I can understand if you only want to pay five hundred a month."

"You undervalue yourself." Caleb started swinging again, the metal melody keeping time with the staccato rhythm of the rain. "Did he ever tell you why he stole the money?"

Many people in Hollydale only asked the question with their eyes. "At first he denied everything. He was already in prison and everyone believed I must have known, but I didn't. I even believed him until the feds sat down with the evidence and I had to hire an attorney to protect myself and the kids. They kept insisting I helped Justin hide information about more possible victims, but they couldn't prove anything because I wasn't involved.

"For the longest time every cent I had that didn't go toward utility bills went toward paying the lawyer. There were times I had to work three jobs to cover all the costs and put food on the table."

"You didn't answer my question."

Lucie shrugged and traced the outline of the metal links. "Justin said his family expected him to succeed and he saw dollar signs in my eyes rather than love. He made it about everyone except himself. Not once did he ever bring up Mattie and Ethan." Her throat clogged at how he'd signed away all custodial rights without even blinking an eye as he entered prison. She was their only family now.

Caleb stretched out his legs and shook his head. "Are you happy?"

Of all the follow-up questions he could have asked, that wasn't the one she'd expected.

She cleared her throat, trying to find her voice, something she'd been doing for some time now. "No one's asked me that in forever."

"The answer's important to me."

Lucie folded her hands in her lap, trying to move forward with the present. Her home was full of love and laughter, something to be grateful for. "I think I'm finally coming into my own. My life is full with my pets, the twins and my business. That has to be enough for now."

Enough so she wouldn't cause trouble for Caleb by having anyone turn on him. Besides, Mattie and Ethan needed a mother who would protect them, would provide stability for them, would surround them with people they could depend on. They'd finally turned a corner over the last six months. Maintaining stability was everything.

"Where's the Lucie with happy stories and daydreams in her eyes?" The steady downpour of rain almost drowned his words—his voice was that low.

That Lucie had returned before their kiss. It would be so easy to believe in twinkling lights, moonbeams and happy endings. Part of her yearned for that idealism again. Yet the memory of jumping for joy after a police officer had dropped groceries on her porch because she couldn't afford food held her back. She had to stand on her own two feet for the sake of Mattie and Ethan.

And she had to prove something to herself, as well.

"That Lucie grew up fast. Without my parents or money in the bank, I have to make this business work."

"It's not an either/or situation, you know. You can be a successful businesswoman while still reaching for the stars. Mitzi believes you can make a go of this, and so do I. Today I arranged a deal with my boss, Owen, so you can attend. You're not a corporate sponsor, but you can still publicize your company all you like."

Lucie rubbed her ear. Those tickets cost a fortune. "Say that again?" Between the metal chains and the soft rain falling to the earth, she'd missed something. "You were able to make a deal on my behalf?"

Caleb's hand still rested on hers and she kept it that way, his presence flooding her with happiness. "Only with the best of intentions. This morning the keynote speaker had to back out. When Owen asked me to step in, the only thing I asked in return was that the Hollydale Training and Wellness Center come as my guest. Owen agreed."

She blinked. She would love to support a great cause and promote herself, but there had been no wiggle room in her budget for a ticket. "I don't know how to thank you, especially since Jared Engel followed up with me and I sent him the cost and program information he requested."

"Why don't we go to the soiree together?" He smiled and her gaze landed on his mouth, which made her think of their kiss at the gazebo.

A kiss implied a relationship, something Caleb himself had said he didn't want, something she knew she couldn't have for so many reasons. For one thing, she was his landlady. The rent money would come in handy toward her future mortgage and starting to repay

Aunt Rosemary. For another, whenever she was near him, she didn't get much work done. That wasn't the way to run a business.

"I have a better idea. You can move in anytime you want." She scooted back to her side of the swing.

"That's not as much fun."

No, it wasn't, but it was much easier and safer for her heart. "How about a handshake, then, to seal the rental agreement and as a thank-you for the invite?"

"I'm a patient man, so a handshake it is." He slipped his hand into hers, providing sparks of electricity made all the more romantic by the misty rain. She'd have to stoke her control and keep a strong head.

Staying true to her present course required vigilance. His endearing eyes showed the challenge in that.

But thanks to his gaining a spot for her at the Sunset Soiree and a celebrity endorsement possibly on her horizon, life might finally be falling into place.

SOMETHING WAS WRONG. Work had been Caleb's lifeblood for the past eleven years. He shouldn't be strolling downtown on a Monday afternoon with Lucie at his side. Not since he'd battled that infection had he missed this much time away from a job. The urge to march to Dr. Keane's office for another evaluation made his hand itch. He scratched his left palm, but the irritation continued.

"The sun is finally peeking out from the clouds, yet you look on the outside like I feel on the inside. What's bothering you?" Lucie broke through his reverie, and he blinked, regaining his bearings.

This was a day for a walk. A red cardinal alit on the branches of one of the maples in full color on Timber Road. The cooler air lent itself to a cup of decaf, but The Busy Bean had closed a few hours ago. A customer emerged from The Book Nook with a full tote bag and a disposable cup. Smart move on Connie's part if she offered drinks to her buyers and browsers. The customer smiled and dipped his head in passing before sipping from his cup.

Pleasantries like that had engrained themselves in Caleb's memory about his hometown. Sharing his problems might not seem like a way to spread cheer, but he'd take the chance. "Owen placed me on temporary leave for yet another week due to my back. And when I report next Monday, I'll officially be on desk duty for five weeks until Dr. Keane clears me."

"I was wondering why you weren't working today, but I didn't know if I should ask." Lucie laid her hand on Caleb's forearm, and he leaned into her touch. The world seemed happier for it. "Look at the bright side. You have extra time to write your keynote speech and to furnish the cabin. It'll be a real home by the time we're done with it."

Whether she realized it or not, Lucie's true nature couldn't stay hidden forever. Seasons came and went—the ice and snow of winter always melted into a verdant and vibrant spring. He steered her away from a puddle and they strolled along.

"Before I lose my nerve, thank you for coming with me to drop off my mortgage application. Having you here—" Her voice cracked, and she exhaled while moving her hand away from his arm. "It means everything to me. I'm taking a heavy risk with this mortgage. I need a working furnace to open the center. This is a step forward, not a step back, and I'm doing it on my terms."

They stopped in front of the bank. He already had the rental agreement in his pocket, so he should leave her here, hike over to

Bryant's Furniture on Oak Street and check out their selection. His father had graduated with the owner and had always spoken highly of Todd Bryant whenever they passed the store. If Caleb found what he needed, he could arrange for delivery as soon as possible.

But first, he wanted a memory of this day. Something to put into a frame on his mantel. A picture of this Lucie, professional in a blazer and matching pants, her curly hair shining in the afternoon sun. Caleb whipped his phone out of his rear pocket. "Before you go in, let me take a picture of you."

Lucie laughed and crinkled her nose. "I'm hardly presentable."

"One or two quick pictures, that's all." He opened the camera app on his cell phone. "Someday, when you pay this loan off, you'll look back at this and feel a huge sense of relief."

"Oh, I need a photo for that? I would think submitting the last payment would be relief in and of itself." Lucie shrugged and looked toward the entrance. "Besides, they're about to close."

"Hold up the application. That way you can see how far you've come when you pay it off." Caleb lined up the shot. "The quicker you let me do this, the sooner you can go inside. And today's a day to celebrate. It's not every day you score a ticket to the Sunset Soiree."

"Hurry up." She raised the paperwork and kept her face scrunched.

"Come on. A real smile."

"For you." Her cheeks softened and her eyes glowed.

He snapped the picture, and she walked toward the entrance. "Wait. Let me get one of the paperwork really fast."

"Caleb. They close in ten minutes, and I have to pick up the twins at the salon after that." She rolled her eyes, but her smile reassured him that he'd helped her relax even a little.

He situated her hands and took a close-up of the paperwork. "There, all done. I'll run over and tell Mitzi you'll be there soon." Her salon was on the way to Bryant's, so he wouldn't lose much time.

"Thanks." She came closer, reached up on her tiptoes and kissed his cheek, his beard scrunching under the softness of her lips. "Thanks for believing in me and for being honest with me."

Lucie scurried inside, and her kiss seared into his skin. Believing in her? Always. Being totally honest with her? He'd have to tell her about his parents before they moved back. Taking a chance on her understanding his slight delay was much better than facing the consequences down the road.

LUCIE ENTERED A New You, unsure of whether the weight had been lifted from her shoulders or was heavier than ever. All four chairs in the salon were occupied, each stylist taking care with a customer. Including Mattie, her wet blond hair receiving a trim from Mitzi, and Ethan, across from her, his shoulders hunched as Wendy snipped away at his bird's nest of hair. Lucie winced. She'd only meant for them to hang out in the break room with Sadie the teenager who helped sweep up hair and did the other thousand and one tasks Lucie used to do.

With her credit cards maxed out, she wasn't sure how she was going to pay for this. "Mitzi! I didn't expect you to cut their hair."

Mitzi waved her over to where another surprise awaited. There stood Caleb, acting like the casual observer but staying close enough to keep an eye on Mattie and Ethan. "Hi again. I decided to take Mitzi up on her offer of a free haircut before I start shopping for furniture. I'm next."

Mitzi kept her trained eye on Mattie's hair. "They couldn't stay in the break room, darlin'. Sadie's grades are tanking, so her parents and I persuaded her to take some time off to devote to her studies. Caleb arrived while they were getting their hair washed. I should have called you first, but this girl of yours needs to make sure to rinse all the shampoo out of her curly hair, which is absolutely gorgeous. I'll give you some spray that will help tame the frizzies while keeping the curl." Mitzi gripped her scissors and trimmed the ends. "Don't worry, sweet girl. I know how to cut curly hair. It'll be more beautiful than ever with a couple inches off. And Ethan needs to discover water and shampoo won't hurt him. How's that looking? Okay with you?"

Mitzi had somehow said all of that without taking a single breath. Lucie met Caleb's gaze and bit back the giggle threatening to escape, but the thought of paying for two haircuts quickly tamed those stray giggles. "Of course. You're as close to a grandmother as they come. I know you wouldn't do anything bad…" Would her business partner accept a payment plan? Or a chocolate-chip pound cake in trade? That familiar coppery tang of failing her kids flooded her mouth.

"Lucie!" A customer in a hot pink cape with perm rollers in her hair shouted over the din of the hair dryer at the front of the salon.

At the realization she was about to face off with Belinda Chastain, the Pie Queen of Hollydale, Lucie wished the floor would open up and swallow her whole. No, that's what the Lucie of last December would think. Her nostrils flared and her shoulders stiffened. The new Lucie had painted and renovated a training and wellness center, fought a bat battle and won, and steeled herself to do what was best for her business so she could keep food on the table and in the pet bowls. She was a survivor, and she wasn't going to let anyone make her feel otherwise.

"Mrs. Chastain." Lucie nodded but kept her resolve firm. "I'm so glad Alicia and her family moved back to town. You must be ecstatic to have your grandchildren nearby. Tell her to give me a call sometime."

If Belinda's daughter would talk to her, that was. Alicia's in-laws had been two of Justin's victims. Hopefully, by reaching out an olive branch, she'd at least be able to look Alicia in the eyes and not have to skulk around the Piggly Wiggly if they were shopping at the same time.

"I know you know about what happened to Austin's parents," Belinda said, arching her newly plucked eyebrows. "But I also know someone left a chocolate-chip pound cake on Alicia's front porch and the first bite took me straight back to your mama's kitchen. Your mama could bake."

"Yes, ma'am. Thank you." And Lucie was fortunate to still have her recipes. The government hadn't confiscated that precious recipe box. Lucie gazed around the shop, all eyes glued to the exchange. Even Luanne, who'd been using the blow dryer, had switched it off to listen in.

"I'm not saying one cake will clear the air between the two of you, but Alicia and Austin know you didn't have anything to do with what your husband did to Susan and Herb."

"My *ex*-husband." Lucie inched closer to Mattie. "And Mattie and Ethan don't need constant reminders. They should grow up like your grandchildren, free of reminders of the past."

Belinda pursed her lips but nodded. "You're right. Little ones are real precious, and I admire what you're trying to do with your new business. I think that pound cake was more than worth two children's haircuts. Mitzi, just add those to my tab."

Lucie inhaled and shook her head. "I'm not taking charity. I pay my way in Hollydale." With a little bit of luck, her credit card wouldn't be declined. "I don't ever want anyone to think I don't put in an honest day's work."

"It's not charity, Lucie." The Pie Queen squinted and pulled out a pair of glasses from beneath the cape, placing them on the bridge of her hawklike nose. "My Alicia's going through a rough time right now. That's why they moved back. That chocolate cake is the only thing she's enjoyed in a while. She needs a friend right now." She sighed and removed her glasses again. "I'll say this about you—you're always there when someone, or some animal, needs you."

Mitzi nodded. "That's my Lucie. And in this salon, she's *our* Lucie. Got it?" She glanced at every person in the room, all of whom were nodding. "Back to work."

No sooner was the hair dryer buzzing than the bells on the front door jangled and a man with thinning gray hair walked in alongside a teenage girl with long, straight, black hair and perfectly manicured black nails. Her dark brown eyes lit up when she drank in the atmosphere around her.

"Be right with you," Mitzi called out. "Take a seat."

"That's my boss. I think he's here to see Mitzi." Caleb stayed in the shadows where he wasn't visible from the front of the store.

So, this was Owen Thompson, the man who'd made Caleb take some much-needed time off. It was all Lucie could do not to run over and hug him for making Caleb rest so his back had a chance to recover.

Mitzi eyed the ends of Mattie's hair and used a towel to blot out the extra moisture before applying some spritz and scrunching it into the curls. "Now, sweet girl, I'm going to use something called a diffuser on my hair dryer because that's the best way to blow-dry curly hair." When she finished, Wendy was almost done with Ethan's hair.

Lucie accompanied Mattie and Mitzi to the front, where Mitzi smiled at Owen and his daughter. "Your hairstyles both look good to me, and that's saying something since I like to eat and turning away customers doesn't help pay the bills." She eyed the length of Owen's hair. "You could use a trim, but I think the extra half an inch suits your bone structure."

"Pardon me, Mrs. Mayfield." The teenager spoke up, her voice lower than Lucie had expected. "My dad brought me here so he could check you out while I applied for a job."

Owen turned a mottled red and jumped to his feet. "That didn't quite come out as Ashleigh intended."

"Ashleigh doesn't want to work here, then? And you are?" Mitzi rumbled with laughter and she wiped the corners of her eyes.

"Owen Thompson. I came to check out your fair establishment, not you." If anything, he blushed an even deeper red. "Not that you're unattractive, Mrs. Mayfield. You're very attractive."

He groaned, and Caleb came up to the front, holding Ethan's hand. "Owen's the head ranger at the Timber River Park. He's also one of the people in charge of the Sunset Soiree. I hope you and Lucie will be joining me at my table on Friday night."

"How did a woman get so lucky as to have two such handsome males in my establishment talking about my favorite night of the year? Formal dancing with men in tuxedos?" Mitzi fanned herself, her grin stretching across her face. She turned to the girl in black. "And to have a real go-getter applying for a position that just opened up today? I should play the lottery tonight."

Ashleigh shuffled her feet. "Sadie told me she's on leave. I'm taking advantage of my inside knowledge."

"Honesty. I like that." Mitzi reached into a drawer and pulled out an application. "Honey, you fill this out and I'll let you know tonight. This is Hollydale, so y'all call me Mitzi. Owen, since you're in charge, I gather you'll be at the soiree?"

Lucie glanced at Owen, who was tugging at his collar, and then back to Mitzi, whose eyes sparkled as she smoothed her sleek silver-gray hair and adjusted her scarf. *Good.* Mitzi hadn't been seriously involved with anyone since her divorce, her husband's infidelity cutting deep and causing a lasting scar.

"I'll be at Caleb's table, as well," said Owen.

If Mitzi could move on and trust again, Lucie should find a way to do the same.

Lucie turned toward Mattie and Ethan, who were leafing through the pages of a popular children's magazine. Mitzi didn't have seven-year-olds depending on her. Lucie wouldn't stop living her life for them, but she did have to consider them in everything she did, including any future relationships. Love her, love her kids…and her cat and her dogs and her pigs and her bunnies. Most men would run at the very thought of getting involved with her past, let alone an entire menagerie.

Yet Caleb was still around.

Speaking of Mattie and Ethan, however, Lucie had to decline attending the soiree. Mitzi would carry the Hollydale Training and Wellness Center banner with pride. "While it sounds like a great evening, Mitzi will be representing our business."

Mitzi turned to her and frowned. "If it's about your hair or those nails…"

"Not at all." Lucie shook her head and examined her nails for the first time in forever. When her business was on the upswing, she'd try to reward herself with a manicure. In the meantime, she'd have to spare some time for self-care. Somewhere along the line, she gave up the ghost of her debutante past. After Mattie and Ethan retired for the night, it might be time to pull out her buffer and favorite nail polish. "I don't have a babysitter and can't afford one."

"I'm certified in first aid and CPR," Ashleigh chimed in. "And I have reasonable rates."

Caleb motioned to Lucie, and she closed the gap between them. "I'd like to hire Ashleigh, if that's okay with you." He kept his voice low enough for her ears only.

Lucie hesitated. "I don't know. I've never met her before."

"Didn't mean to eavesdrop, but Ashleigh's responsible," Owen said.

"I've never burned anyone's dinner, and I have references." Ashleigh waved at the twins. "I have cousins their age."

"It's Lucie's call, but it's only fair I pay your fee since I arranged this," Caleb said.

"I'd like those references, but I'll agree for now." Lucie glanced at Mattie and Ethan, who nodded their approval. "Thank you." She wasn't sure who she was thanking, but one time ought to cover everyone.

Caleb reached into his jeans' pocket and pulled out his phone. "If you could program your number in, I'll start a group text with Lucie. Then we'll be on the same page."

The Sunset Soiree was the hottest ticket in town, and it might give Lucie's business a needed boost. Still, she'd have to be on her guard. Twinkling lights and a gazebo had triggered her long-buried romantic side.

After her life became stable, same as Mitzi's, she'd consider merging her romantic side and her business professionalism. Until then?

Ladybug kept her company at night. That was more than enough. *Honesty, Lucie. Always honesty.* Okay, it might not be enough, but it would have to do. She'd been wrong about Belinda Chastain just now, more proof than ever that her character assessment radar needed a lot of maintenance. And if she was wrong about Caleb and he wasn't one of the good guys?

It would take her a lifetime to get over that.

CHAPTER TEN

THANK GOODNESS Odalie Musgrove had come through for Lucie, letting her have this blush-pink lace cocktail dress at cost with a rolling payment plan, especially considering Lucie had served out a two-week notice and quit on her earlier this year.

Working for Odalie had been her favorite of her odd jobs, a dream really, handling the delicate material of the cocktail dresses and evening gowns. So often she'd remember the fun comments she made with her mom after seeing each bride emerge in the clearing. Patsy Appleby had sworn she could tell the minute she glanced at the groom whether the couple would last or not. When the groom only had eyes for the bride, her mother knew they would make it through anything.

The doorbell rang and Lucie hurried downstairs. Considering the keynote speaker for tonight's Sunset Soiree was picking her up, no one could start the show until they arrived, but it was never nice to keep anyone waiting. Besides, she'd have to work the room, a throwback to her homecoming queen days.

Lucie picked up the gold antique clutch from the foyer table, the sequin swirl of roses complementing her dress. Ladybug and Pita barked and danced almost as if they knew tonight was a festive occasion.

"Mommy, you're beautiful." The awe in Mattie's voice took Lucie's breath away, the love in each syllable meaning more than any compliment she'd ever received.

It didn't matter if she rumpled anything. Lucie hugged Mattie and caressed her cheek. "And you grow more and more beautiful every day."

"Ooh, girl talk." Ethan stopped halfway down the stairs and scrunched his nose before delivering a fake sneeze. "It smells like a rose garden in here."

The door to the kitchen opened and Ashleigh ran in, oven mitts on both hands. "Sorry, Mrs. Decker. The dogs were sniffing, and I was worried they would steal the chicken, so I closed the door. I should have let them outside instead."

The doorbell rang again, and her tension slipped away. For a few hours on a Saturday night, she'd be wearing glass slippers and dancing. Unlike Cinderella, however, she wouldn't mind when the clock struck midnight. It was nice to have a night away, but she loved returning home to her family.

Ethan catapulted down the rest of the stairs and stopped an inch short of colliding with the door. "Geez, if it weren't for me, nothing would ever get done around here."

"Ethan," Lucie cautioned, and hurried toward him. "Don't open the door if you don't know who it is."

"It's Mr. Caleb." Mattie lowered the curtain in the parlor into place. "He's not as pretty as you are. He didn't even shave his beard."

Ethan threw open the door and frowned. "Of course no one's as pretty as Mommy, but he doesn't look that bad. I like the beard. I want one someday."

Pita leaped forward and jumped on Caleb's tuxedo, bringing cries of alarm from everyone inside the Decker household.

"Pita!" Lucie lunged and caught her border collie's collar. "I'm so sorry, Caleb. Wait a second and I'll get the dogs into the mudroom."

Ashleigh helped her corral the dogs, then Lucie returned, wiping her hands while fur still flew everywhere. She sent an apologetic smile toward Caleb, who stood there with his mouth ajar. She didn't blame him, as she should have made sure the dogs were out of striking distance of his impeccable black tuxedo pants. The whole picture of him stunned her. Even without shaving off his beard, Caleb cleaned up well, his broad shoulders filling the jacket with authority, a far cry from his days as a teenager.

Yet, deep down, the two were one and the same. Digging beneath the surface, she conceded the kind, funny boy from her past was still a kind, funny soul.

Lucie stepped toward Caleb and waved her hand in front of his face. "Earth to Caleb. The fur will brush off, if that's what you're worried about. Or is it your speech? You'll do great. You care about your subject and everyone in the audience will be better off for listening to you. Your enthusiasm will carry the night."

Caleb blinked, the amber glints in his hazel eyes all the darker tonight, the black of his tuxedo bringing out the energy within. "It wasn't any of that. I lost sight of everything else with you standing there in that dress." He thrust a box toward her. "It's probably corny, but I brought you a wrist corsage."

"I didn't expect this." Lucie snapped open the plastic container and stroked the soft petal. "It's beautiful. Thank you."

"It's a rare beauty that can eclipse an orchid." His gaze didn't leave her as he transferred the corsage to her wrist, his large hand taking an extra second to linger on hers, the warmth of him imprinting on her cold skin.

If her mother were here, she'd tell Lucie she was in deep trouble.

And she'd be absolutely right.

"IN CONCLUSION, THE environment surrounds us and supports us with its life force. By making small changes in our driving habits, by taking reusable bags with us, and by drinking out of our own water containers rather than plastic bottles, that force will continue to bless future generations down the line. Thank you."

Caleb backed away from the podium but remained on the dais, uncomfortable with the applause surrounding him.

The organizers had outdone themselves, turning the Hollydale Town Hall Pavilion into a wonderland, the glass windows highlighting the gorgeous sunset that marked the occasion. Crisp white tablecloths dotted each circular table, and now that Caleb had delivered his address, he'd be able to eat his vegetable risotto with local herbs with gusto. Yet no one in the audience matched Lucie, her bright eyes shining with appreciation, applauding the loudest of all. That made every minute writing the speech worthwhile.

Owen came over and waited for the noise to die down before moving in front of the microphone. "Does anyone have any questions for Caleb?"

One woman in the back shot her hand up. "Are you single?"

The crowd erupted in good-natured laughter, and Owen even joined in before stepping over to the microphone. "Let me clarify. Does anyone have any park ranger- or ecosystem-related questions?"

Another woman raised her hand and Caleb braced himself. "Were you scared you wouldn't be able to find those boys in time?"

Owen's gaze made clear he'd field this one as well, if Caleb wished. Caleb stepped up to the mic and Owen moved aside.

Caleb cleared his throat and rubbed his hands against his black tuxedo pants. "I'll start with the easier of the two questions. It's complicated, and I'm not fielding any outside offers at the moment." He waited for the chuckles to die down, although there was nothing funny about the feelings he was developing for Lucie. Whether she wore a lacy pink slip of a dress or overalls didn't matter. She was beautiful inside and out. Before his parents arrived tomorrow night, he'd lay everything on the line and see whether they could ever move forward.

He stepped closer to the microphone, wanting to get rid of the elephant in the room, or to aid the woodpecker on the chimney as the case might be. "As far as the incident in Yellowstone last month, it was part of my job. Yes, I was scared something had already happened to the three boys, but it wasn't one person working in isolation. Park rangers aren't superheroes. Instead, we work as a team, relying on technology and our training, and we sometimes do it in the worst of weather conditions and the most stressful situations.

"It was a joint effort, from the people who were mapping out where we'd already searched, to the K-9s and handlers, to the volunteers who willingly gave of themselves to bring those boys home. While I found them, I only did what anyone else would do. I stayed behind with the one who had broken his leg until the helicopter came, but each person working toward the same end deserves the credit. I just photograph well."

Owen reached for the mic and tapped the tip, resulting in a high-pitched squeal that brought a wince to most of the audience. "Be generous with the silent auction. We've had a few last-minute surprise additions that didn't make it into the program, so look out for those and open those pocketbooks. We'll be making some announcements in a few weeks about the Timber River woodpecker and the conservancy station coming next year through the generosity of Frederick and Agnes Whitley, so stay tuned and enjoy the rest of your evening."

Caleb made his way off the dais. Tonight, he'd have a dance with Lucie. With his back as an excuse, it would have to be a slow one. He wasn't complaining, though. Not one bit.

LUCIE SNIFFED AND dabbed a tissue to her eyes. Strolling through the pavilion's gardens and talking up her center before the dinner had done a number on her hay fever.

She'd stopped in front of a gorgeous framed

charcoal sketch of the Great Smokies that would look perfect in the conference room where she met with prospective clients. Even though the artist had only used charcoal, his choice was the right one, as the scenery spoke for itself. There was something about the land around here that spoke to her soul—the gentle slope of the mountains, the soft whisper of Timber River, the wildflowers blooming as spring returned to Hollydale.

Apart from her children, her ties to the land and her pets were the main reasons she endured the hard times. Handing out her business card to some of the sponsors tonight brought her hope those times would ease once the center was open and operational.

Of course, there would have to be one more glitch before she could move forward. Yesterday the bank let her know there was a holdup with her application. Her pride went by the wayside when she called her aunt Rosemary to cover the cost of the furnace until the mortgage money came through. Fortunately, she'd planned ahead and taken her aunt on a virtual tour. After grudgingly admitting Lucie had exceeded her expectations, she agreed to loan her enough until the mortgage came through.

Once that happened and people booked

events, she'd be doing what she loved, helping people and spending time in the natural setting of the lodge. It didn't get much better than walking the trails around the center or enjoying a cool evening at the fire pit.

Sharing that with someone would be that much better, especially someone who felt the same connection to the outdoors.

After all, the Great Smoky Mountains sustained her, and this sketch spoke to her in the same way as that one spot on her property where an old log provided the perfect perch for contemplating life while watching the river flow by. Even without a signature to identify the artist, she knew Caleb had sketched it.

She wanted to share her life with him.

"Lucie." Natalie placed her hand on Lucie's shoulder. "Are you okay?"

Her friend moved in such a way as to shield Lucie from the rest of the room, and Lucie loved her for it. "Just hay fever." Another sneeze backed her up, and Lucie shrugged. "The pollen is getting to me, but that's okay. This should be a happy night, and I'm out of the house for a few hours. I refuse to let my problems taint this evening."

"There's something else, isn't there? You're

the one who always says it's not good to hold things in." Natalie sipped some of her champagne and glanced around the room. "I might not be Georgie or Mitzi, but I'm a halfway decent listener."

"Why do you always do that?" Lucie picked up her own flute of ginger ale and sipped.

"Do what?" Natalie tapped her fingers on the edge of a table that held envelopes for the bids.

"Compare yourself to others." Lucie wished she could bid on Caleb's sketch, but the minimum bid was high and there were several envelopes already in the bid box.

Natalie shrugged and examined the sketch. "Most likely because I'm a twin, but you're also very good at deflecting from yourself. Half my kindergarten students seek the limelight, and the other half don't. Funny thing, though—back in high school, you were always front and center, and you seemed to thrive there."

Lucie sipped her ginger ale, wishing she'd picked something that wasn't quite so dry. "When you have the whole town's attention on you for something you didn't do, it's easy to seek a quiet corner."

Then again, even in high school, she hadn't

craved the notoriety. Why she'd put on a false front for appearances' sake was beyond her. She was much more comfortable in the background. Visiting Caleb had been something she'd started doing to escape the constant attention and it had turned into her favorite time of the day. Caleb's easygoing manner, even when he was at the end of his rope, made the visits fun.

He still made normal tasks more fun just from his steady presence.

"You know you're one of my heroes, right?" Natalie waved off Lucie's protests. "I know you don't see yourself that way, but, like that orchid on your wrist, you're strong and elegant."

"What do you mean?" Lucie brought the orchid to eye level and frowned. "What does strength and elegance have to do with orchids?"

"I worked in the floral shop in high school. Each flower has a different code, so to speak, and sometimes the color also adds meaning. Yellow roses represent friendship while red ones, of course, indicate love. Violets represent modesty, and orchids have a few meanings, a couple of which are elegance and strength." Natalie paused and tapped the ribbon on Lucie's wrist. "I see those traits in you, more so now that the center is almost ready for business."

Had the florist told Caleb any of that? Was that why he'd purchased an orchid? She felt the petals, his gift touching her all the more.

"Thanks. Wasn't that risotto delicious? I didn't see your table." Deflecting questions was par for the course for Lucie, so one more time couldn't hurt. "Are you here with a hot date?"

Natalie laughed and waggled her finger. "Hardly. I came with my former roommate Shelby, the one who just moved to town. She's in search of some aspirin for her headache, but you'll have to try her new lunch café, Snickerdoodles, when it opens in the summer."

Lucie searched the crowd. "There has to be some eligible attractive man in town for you. Jeremy from Timber River Outfitters? Caleb's cousin Jonathan? He's single."

"I'm quite content with my life for the first time in a long time." Natalie's eyes held a touch of sadness, which was odd for her bubbly friend who usually loved everything about life. Lucie made a note to ask more about that at a later date. "I notice you didn't include Caleb on that list. While you couldn't see me, I saw you at his table."

Lucie's heart sputtered as she gripped the crystal flute. She did care about Caleb, that infuriating, handsome man who'd dug around the foundation of everything she'd built in the past few months and turned it upside down.

Once she'd been content with a future where her character radar didn't have to be on full alert all the time. A future where her pets and children kept her happy.

But could she have more? Her thoughts landed on that charcoal sketch, which brought the mountains she loved so much to life and made her think that anything was possible.

"So, is he your date?" Natalie asked.

"Is who her date?" Caleb emerged, his deep voice like whiskey on a cold night, welcome and warming.

"You, of course!" Natalie saluted him with her flute. "To the Hero of Hollydale." Then she held it up to Lucie. "And to an unrecognized hero who shows me day by day how to be a better person." She winked at them both. "Why, yes, with this amazing toast, I am putting in my shameless plug to be Lucie's maid of honor when the two of you end up together. You don't even need to answer my question.

If anyone ever looks at me again like you're looking at Lucie, then Lucie can be my matron of honor."

"If I ever marry again, Mattie, Ladybug and Ethel would beat you to the punch." Lucie tried to keep the moment light. "My money's on Ethel."

Natalie fake shuddered. "I'm losing my best friend status to a pig. A miniature one, but a pig nonetheless. Only in Hollydale." She spotted someone and waved. "At last, there's Shelby, so I bid you adieu. By the way, the other meaning is love and fertility."

Lucie sputtered out her last sip of ginger ale and tried to compose herself. She didn't dare look at Caleb.

"Something makes me think I missed quite the conversation." He sipped his champagne. "I take it Natalie wasn't talking about the Timber River woodpecker when she ended on 'love and fertility.'"

His light tone gave away too much, but she was willing to play along with the easy exchange. Before Lucie could come up with a clever retort, an older couple in their sixties stopped in front of the bid table. "That would be perfect in the lobby of the new nature conservancy, dear." The woman hooked her arm around his, a loving gesture, pulling the man closer to her. "Look at how the artist captured the perspective. It's like the mountains are right here in front of us."

"The conservancy won't be ready for another year. The architects are only now completing the plans." The man laughed and patted her hand. "You really want it for our new dining room, don't you?"

She laughed, the black taffeta of her long evening gown rustling against the cherry hardwood floor. "You know me so well."

The older man squinted at Caleb through his black-rimmed glasses and nudged his wife's side. "You're Caleb Spindler. Nice speech."

Lucie racked her mind, trying to remember where she'd seen the couple before. The man's white hair was distinguished and his stature proud, the woman's cropped silver hair simple yet refined. The man extended his hand to Caleb before stopping short of shaking Lucie's. "If I'm not mistaken, you're Lucie Decker."

She'd heard the tone before, his instant recognition of her unmistakable, and she remembered where she'd seen the two of them. The courtroom during Justin's sentencing. They'd held hands then, as well.

"Mr. Whitley." She gave a polite nod. "Mrs. Whitley."

The couple owned a successful furniture manufacturing plant less than an hour's drive from Hollydale and were known for their philanthropy. Lucie had sent their human resources manager several emails regarding the importance of team building for managers and staff, but the emails had gone unanswered.

"Mrs. Decker." Frederick Whitley's voice dripped ice, but Lucie refused to melt into the woodwork.

She would not spend the rest of her life answering for her ex-husband's crimes.

He turned to Caleb, the slight tick in his jaw flaring. "As I was saying, excellent speech, Caleb. You have a bright future ahead of you. I'd just make sure you limit your acquaintances to those who are good judges of character."

Caleb's arm wound around her shoulders. "My friends are my friends, and Lucie here—"

Has had enough. "Is more than capable of standing up for herself." Lucie placed her crystal flute on the bidding table. "Hollydale is my home, and those who are my friends know I didn't have the slightest idea what Justin was up to. Now, to some like yourself, I'm automatically guilty by association. I'm rebuilding my life and my home, thanks to the loyalty of people like Caleb. I value honesty and communication. If you want to make sure your employees have that same truthfulness and candor, send them to the Hollydale Training and Wellness Center. The best way I can ensure no one ever turns a blind eye to what's wrong is to provide training that will build people up rather than tear them down."

Lucie reached into her purse and pulled out a card, laying it next to the bid box. "Caleb's sketch is my favorite, and I'd recognize his work anywhere. While I regret not having enough money to buy it, I know it will make whoever does buy it happy. I hope it gives them the same peace it makes me feel."

While she respected Caleb and didn't want her being with him to put him in a negative light, she was tired of still having to defend herself. She extricated herself from under his arm and walked away.

Tears threatened to come, but she wouldn't let them. Not here at a happy event. Her heart ached at how hard she was fighting two years down the road from when Justin had committed his crimes. All this time she'd thought Hollydale was her home and that even the most critical of naysayers would come around. She'd believed that with all her heart.

But while many kind souls had helped her move on, others were determined she pay a steep price for Justin's behavior.

Outside, the cool night air kissed her skin, and she hurried toward the parking lot before she remembered Caleb had driven her. Caleb. The boy who'd made her laugh and the man who made her feel beautiful inside and out. She wouldn't pull him down with her.

With a glance back at the pavilion, she reached down and freed her feet from the three-inch, blush-pink heels Odalie had thrown in with the dress. Two miles to home wasn't that far to walk.

Could she lay claim to a home, though, in a town where she wasn't wanted?

If it was just herself, she wouldn't think twice. She'd muddle through even if it took a lifetime to win back people's approval. Mattie and Ethan, though, were innocent in all of this and too young to comprehend the magnitude of how their lives had changed.

She blinked. It wasn't just Mattie and Ethan, or even her pets, she had to consider anymore. A staff of five now depended on her for a paycheck. Gritting her teeth, she'd make her way through this. As long as she could find her way home, she could make it through anything.

CHAPTER ELEVEN

"THANKS, JONATHAN." Caleb extended his
hand and Jonathan brought him in close for
a second-long hug.

"I'd say I was going to miss you, but your
parents are pulling into town tomorrow
night," Jonathan joked while slipping off the
moving gloves and placing them on the coffee table in Caleb's new cabin.

"I'm ten minutes away, not a six-hour flight
away." Caleb's droll voice sounded dry even
to his own ears late on a Sunday morning.
"The Maxwell family isn't getting rid of me
that easily."

Vanessa ran over and tugged on Caleb's
untucked flannel shirt. "Then can you come
over tomorrow morning before school and
make breakfast? Your pancakes are much better than Dad's."

Jonathan staggered backward, his hands
over his heart as though he were mortally

wounded. "Betrayed by my own daughter. Will I ever recover?"

Vanessa giggled but a few tears slid down her cheeks, her hand weaving its way into Caleb's. His heart quivered.

He had missed this type of personal interaction in Montana. Coming home to family after an overnight hike or an even longer camping trip made life that much better.

It was time to start exploring whether Lucie could one day be family. For now, though, his young cousin Vanessa needed some reassurance that he was back for good.

"You know who taught me everything I know about pancakes?"

"YouTube?" Vanessa asked.

Caleb laughed so hard tears came out. He wiped them away and found his voice. "My dad, and I'll bet he'll teach you and Izzy."

"Speaking of my other daughter…" Jonathan tapped his watch. "Vanessa and I have to go round up Izzy. Soccer practice starts in twenty minutes. Got everything, Caleb?"

"Yes, Mom." Caleb smiled but, inside, the hollowness kicked in. He'd miss this group who'd taken him in for the past couple of weeks.

Ten minutes, Caleb. Ten minutes. The same distance as it was to Lucie's home.

Caleb looked around his new cabin residence. While it lacked the photos and homey touches of Lucie's or Jonathan's, it was cozy, and the furniture delivery had made a world of difference. Todd Bryant had shaken his hand on Friday night and had everything in place yesterday morning.

He'd spend quite a few nights on the comfortable couch in front of the fireplace. Logs and tools were already waiting to warm up the room. When the fire wasn't crackling, new lamps would emit a soft glow over the wooden planks on the walls. Whatever Lucie wanted to keep, he'd leave behind when he moved out, as she was charging a pittance of what he'd have paid for a house in town.

Lucie. By the time he'd extricated himself from the Whitleys, she'd already left. When he texted to check on her, she'd said her hay fever was acting up and she couldn't stay any longer. Fortunately, Georgie and Mike had left a few minutes after her and had driven her home. While he'd have thought that was just an excuse from anyone else, her consistent honesty told him otherwise. How much impact, though, had the Whitleys had on the way she'd been feeling?

Respect for what she endured on a daily

basis flowed through him. She'd rebuilt her life after it had been ripped apart through no fault of her own. What was more, she did so oblivious to the positive impact she had on everyone around her. In the less than two weeks since his return, he'd seen people like Frederick Whitley try to take her down, but she stood tall, a true morning glory, and rose above it, promoting her business in such a way as not to lower herself.

It was no surprise, then, to realize she had also rebuilt his heart, the muscle weak after Leah's admission she'd dated him to look good for her family. Now it was beating stronger with a dose of Lucie's spirit. Lucie would never do anything that went against her personal code.

And honesty was central to that code. He had to tell her about his parents. Then he could tell her she'd claimed his heart.

Caleb set to prioritizing what he should unpack first. His back twinged, and he stretched out the impacted muscles. Today was the first March day worthy of a North Carolina spring since he'd returned to Hollydale. There was no reason he couldn't perform his therapy outside in the sunshine. Nature had always been his great motivator.

Besides, finding a woodpecker to sketch would be a welcome bonus.

Whistling, he walked out the front door. With no one around, there was no use in locking it.

"Mr. Caleb." Caleb recognized Ethan's voice, his enthusiasm like no one else's. "What'cha doing here?"

Caleb could ask the same of the little fellow. Where was Mattie? Where was Lucie?

"I moved into the cabin this morning." Before he'd finished his sentence, Mattie brought up the rear, with Ladybug waddling beside her, the leash rather slack.

Ladybug grunted, a happy sound, and trotted over at a fast clip for a bulldog. Her stub of a tail wagged with all its might. He rubbed her head and grunts of pleasure were his reward. "Hey, Mattie. How are you today?"

"My mom is washing the china she brought from our attic. She said we could walk Ladybug because she only has a ten-minute exercise span. She'll walk Pita later." Her blue eyes were miniature replicas of Lucie's morning glories, the same attention to detail lurking in them. Mattie switched the leash from one hand to the other, and Caleb didn't miss how she'd evaded his question.

"It's my turn to hold the leash." Ethan swiped at Mattie's hand.

"Wait a minute." Caleb stepped between them. How did parents do it? How could he make them both happy without looking like he was playing favorites? Lucie made parenthood seem easy. She had that special rare quality of lavishing time and affection on each living thing under her roof, people and animals alike. "How about a compromise?"

"What's that?" Ethan stilled and paid attention to Caleb—a small victory, but he'd take it.

"It's when we both get something but not everything." Mattie sniffed and held her nose higher.

Caleb blew out a deep breath and placed his hand on his back before stretching out the muscles. "How about Mattie holds the leash until you turn around and head back? Then it'll be Ethan's turn." He knelt next to Ladybug, who slurped at his hand, drawing a rare giggle from Mattie. "But remember to take your cue from Ladybug. If she's happy, let her be."

"Mr. Caleb." Ethan tapped his shoulder, although Caleb wasn't quite sure why—he already had his attention. "Can we see what you've done with the cabin? And do you have any food? I'm starving."

"We ate breakfast an hour ago. How can you already be hungry?" Mattie sighed before glaring at her brother.

Caleb whipped his cell from his back pocket. "Hold that thought." He sent a quick text to Lucie and laughed at her return text emoji with the bright red cheeks. *Three, two, one.* Sure enough, his phone rang on cue. "Hi, Lucie."

"Mattie and Ethan weren't supposed to leave the front area with Ladybug." Lucie stopped and inhaled.

He kept silent as it was obvious she had something else on her mind.

"I'm sorry about leaving the soiree suddenly."

"Is your hay fever better?" Caleb waited until Lucie replied in the affirmative. "For the record, Ethan saw me on the porch and came over to investigate. Mattie followed. I texted you to see if it's okay if they have a snack." He stopped as Ethan and Ladybug both perked up. Caleb pleaded his case. "They'll be helping me. I'm already missing Izzy and Vanessa."

"Are you sure they won't be any trouble? And aren't you supposed to be resting?"

"Actually, the physical therapist taught me some new core-stabilizing exercises. The twins might have some fun doing them with me. They'd be helping me."

And they could also help him with his new project.

Last night Owen had given him strict orders to be on the lookout for woodpecker habitats. As far as Caleb was concerned, today was the perfect time to start. When the twins' attention span started to go, that would be his sign he needed to rest.

"I would get more done..."

"I'll escort them back to you the second they're trouble." Caleb glanced at Ethan, who smiled with angelic goodness, and Mattie, who frowned with eternal perseverance. "Tonight I'll get so much rest, I'll be a dead log and the Timber River woodpecker will make a nest in me."

They arranged a time for a transfer and Caleb led the kids inside. Ethan made a beeline for a particular corner. "What's this?"

"It's a Garrett AT Pro Metal Detector."

Ladybug came over, sniffed it and sat at

Caleb's feet, trying to convince him she was much more interesting.

"Yes, Ladybug, you have definite merits, but you're fun in a different way."

"This thing is fun?" Mattie approached it but stopped short. "Can I touch it?"

"Yes, and thank you for asking first." Caleb watched as first Ethan then Mattie stroked the side like they would Ladybug. "Better yet, I'll show you how it works. Then you can decide for yourself if it's fun."

They settled Ladybug in the kitchen with a bowl of water. There wasn't anything for her to destroy or eat, so Caleb didn't worry about leaving the bulldog alone for a short time. After texting Lucie and receiving her approval to search around the low ropes course, he grabbed the metal detector and the twins followed him outside.

Caleb soaked in the gloriousness of the spring sun, the warmth and brightness the best medicine for his back. He'd been so busy this morning he hadn't noticed the creamy yellow daffodils in the garden patch or the deer tracks in the mud. All around, signs of the season bolstered him almost as much as the antics of Mattie and Ethan.

And Lucie? Where did she fit into his life?

According to her, they were friends and nothing more. There was something about Lucie, though, that he didn't feel for any other friend. The way she made him feel at ease, the way she made him feel like the only person in the room even when a crowd surrounded them, the way she brought order out of the hustle and bustle surrounding her.

"Have you ever found anything with that?" Mattie picked up a leaf and tossed it in the air.

"A few quarters, some dimes and a buffalo nickel."

Caleb demonstrated how to use the metal detector. Finding treasure wasn't why he'd picked up the hobby, although it was nice to uncover something that was hidden from everyone else, a little like when he'd uncovered Lucie's true spirit when they were teenagers. Back then, everyone had a different idea of Lucie's nature. Some assumed she was a spoiled debutante, yet they hadn't seen her work hard at her parents' wedding event business, adding special touches in the cabin for every bride on her day.

Lucie was a rare butterfly, spreading her colorful wings. One in a billion.

Ethan swung the metal detector a little too high, and Caleb took his head out of the clouds. "Whoa, a little lower. That way the detector can send an electromagnetic wave into the ground. If we get lucky, an object will answer back, and we'll dig it up."

"We should just look for more woodpeckers. We can see those." Ethan handed the detector back to Caleb and ran ahead before glancing over his shoulder. "And definitely hear them. Why are those birds important anyway?"

"Stay near me, Ethan." Caleb used his ranger voice, and Ethan headed back. "One thing at a time. Woodpeckers are nature's cleaning system and so much more. Other species use their nests, and they keep the insect population under control."

"They eat bugs? Yuck." Mattie wrinkled her nose and shuddered.

"It's the mainstay of their diet, along with acorns, pine seeds and berries. They also love suet. Tomorrow, I'm setting up some special feeders, along with installing motion-sensor cameras so we can monitor where they are." Caleb swung the detector in an arc and then turned to Mattie. "Would you like to try this?"

Mattie stepped back, her apprehension clear. Cautious but careful. No wonder he wanted Mattie on his side. "It looks really heavy, and I might break it."

"It's light, only a couple pounds, about the same as a laptop. If it were too heavy, I couldn't tote it around."

Mattie and Ethan might not know about his back. He'd keep that part to himself.

"You won't break it."

He handed it to her, and she bit her lip. He showed her how to operate the detector. The second he stepped away, strong beeps echoed.

"I broke it," Mattie wailed.

"You found something on your first try," Caleb reassured her, and her face lit up.

"Lucky." Ethan ran over and stared at the ground. "What did she find?"

"Only one way to find out." With a flick of his wrist, Caleb detached the digging trowel from the side of the detector. He knelt and the kids followed suit while he dug. A couple scoops of dirt later, the trowel clunked against something hard.

"What was that?" Mattie's blue eyes grew even wider.

"Did we find buried treasure?" Ethan fisted his hands and pulled them together for a victory pump. "Way to go, Mattie."

This was no ordinary earring or coin. With

a delicate hand, Caleb unearthed the soil and pulled out an old tin canister. He squinted and made out the words on the side: Carolina Country Coffee, Blue Seal Best.

"Woohoo! Treasure!" Ethan jumped up and danced around in circles. "The kids at school are gonna love this. Can I open it?"

"I found it. I should open it." Mattie stood next to Ethan and folded her arms together.

"I think your mother should be here when we open this." Caleb replaced the soil before patting the earth with the back of his trowel, taking care the area looked the same as before. "We'll go back to my cabin."

Ethan clicked his tongue. "That'll take forever."

No, forever was the amount of time it had taken him to realize what a treasure Lucie was. The question was, when was he going to do something about it?

He'd start by sharing this with her.

Then he'd share everything else, including his heart.

LUCIE RUSHED INTO Caleb's cabin with one sneaker on her foot and the other in her hand. Now here, she felt silly for not taking time to even put both shoes on properly. In the past couple of weeks, Caleb had demonstrated his concern for the twins. If anything was truly wrong, he'd have called or rushed to the lodge.

"Hi, I'm here." She was proud of her calm voice and the restraint she was showing. Taking a minute, she looked around and appreciated the changes. In a mere weekend, Caleb had placed his stamp here, the comfortable couch winning her seal of approval along with his other simple but stylish purchases.

She sat and appreciated the comfort of his couch before putting on her other shoe. Trust came hard for her, but Caleb's patience was winning her over.

Slowly, she was getting back in touch with parts of her former self she'd hidden for self-protection. She had missed that part of herself that knew how to twist everything into a positive. Even last night, there'd been positives. She'd respected herself enough to stand up for herself. In the two weeks since Caleb had returned, a whirlwind really, something had been different. Could *she* be different? Could she be ready for a relationship?

But what if something went wrong? Another kiss could devastate their fledging friendship.

But what if it brings out something as amazing and beautiful as the kiss itself?

Ladybug trotted over and sat in front of Lucie, her tongue dangling. The normal grunts were a sign everything was right with the world.

She knelt beside Ladybug and scratched her dog's favorite spot, receiving a moan of approval. "Should I throw caution to the wind?"

Caleb emerged from the kitchen, wiping his hands with a paper towel. "About what?" His smile, visible under his beard, which was growing in fuller and getting more attractive by the day, touched her heart. "You have something splattered on your bandanna. Painting again?"

Lucie yanked off her bright pink bandanna. Sure enough, traces of white trim paint dotted the cloth. "Is everything okay? Your text was rather vague."

"Mommy's here. Hurry up." Mattie emerged from the bathroom and held up her hands. "All clean. Mommy, do I get the treasure because I found it, or do I have to share it with Ethan?"

"I was there, too." Ethan scurried out, his

small face aghast at being left out of whatever Mattie was talking about.

"You found something?" A pinprick of curiosity tickled her spine. "In the loft?"

"Mattie found a coffee tin using my metal detector." Caleb ruffled Mattie's hair and Mattie sent a small smile of approval his way.

Her daughter had blossomed quite a bit under Caleb's attention over the past couple of weeks, but what would happen when Caleb's work kept him busy to the point where they didn't see him for days or even weeks at a time? What would happen if Caleb changed his mind about wanting a relationship and found someone who didn't have so many trust issues?

Her stomach twisted at the thought of anyone else claiming Caleb's affections, bringing out the best in him, making him laugh when he took things too seriously.

"But I was there, too, and it's not fair Mattie gets it all." Ethan brought his foot back and kicked the floor.

"I don't know what's in the tin." That note of caution in Caleb's voice gave her pause. He pointed to the fireplace mantel, where a rusted tin sat in the place of honor.

"Ethan Christopher, it's impolite to act like

that in your house, let alone someone else's. We're Caleb's guests." She searched Caleb's face for advice, and it wasn't hard to read his mind. The tin had been found in an offbeat area. For all they knew, it could contain something grisly or illegal. She sought a compromise. "How about we take Ladybug outside for a quick walk? Caleb can make sure it's suitable for little eyes."

"That's not fair." Ethan's leg went up again, but he sighed and brought it down without kicking the hardwood floor. "What if it's pirate treasure and it's worth a gazillion and one dollars?"

Lucie clasped Ladybug's leash onto her collar. "I don't think pirates made it this far inland." She met Caleb's gaze, and the depth of her trust surprised her.

He'd earned something rarer than the endangered Timber River woodpecker.

"And Caleb's one of the good guys. He'll do right by us. I'm curious myself—give us the all-clear signal once you've opened it." Lucie ushered the twins outside, but her gaze stayed on the front door.

It wasn't long until Caleb called them. "Mattie can do the honors."

Mattie rushed ahead and they gathered

around a blanket Caleb had laid on the hardwood floor. Plopping onto the floor, Mattie accepted the tin from Caleb and unscrewed the lid, reaching in for the first item.

"Aw, dump it out so we can see everything at once," said Ethan.

After she arched an eyebrow in his direction, Ethan folded his arms and clamped his mouth.

Mattie pulled out a circular golden item and handed it to Caleb. "What's this?"

"It's a pocket watch." He examined it for a minute, then pressed the small golden pull at the top. The lever mechanism worked, and the front popped open. Caleb showed Mattie and then Ethan.

Mattie handed the tin to Ethan. "Here you go. I want you to take out something next."

"Really?" Ethan's face blossomed with joy. "Thanks."

Motherly love filled Lucie's heart. Her two little nestlings were growing up. Then Ethan dumped the rest of the tin onto the blanket and Lucie sighed.

"Ethan!" Mattie wailed.

He grinned and shrugged. "Couldn't help it."

Atop the blanket, several coins, marbles and some metal toy soldiers winked at Lucie.

Ethan reached for a coin. "Huh. This isn't real money. It's fake."

That didn't surprise Lucie. So much in her life had appeared to be one thing on the surface and was something different underneath.

Through it all, Caleb had dug deeper and seen the real her, the Lucie she'd kept buried for a long time. Caleb accepted her and had kissed her anyway. A feeling close to bliss settled in her chest.

"Let me see it." Caleb reached for the coin and his eyebrows knit together. "Actually, this is real currency. Considering it's been in a coffee tin for years, it's in mint condition and might fetch a good price."

Lucie wiped her clammy hands on her overalls. "You mean these might be valuable?"

Caleb rubbed the coin in his hands and pulled out his cell phone. "If there's a coin dealer near here, you might want to consult with him. This is a 1916 buffalo nickel. Depending on this mark, its value could be between seventy dollars and..."

"Or what?" Lucie laughed. "Seven hundred dollars?"

Caleb leaned over. His beard tickled her cheek as he whispered a six-figure number in her ear.

"You're kidding."

He showed her his phone screen and her stomach sank.

"You're not kidding."

Lucie glanced at the contents of the container and closed her eyes. Who would have buried this here? This windfall might not even be hers. "We have to take this to Sheriff Harrison. Until I know whether this is legally mine, we can't keep it."

Mattie and Ethan groaned. Even Ladybug seemed to get into the act by hiding her snout behind Caleb as he shrugged. "It was found on your property. Why wouldn't it be yours?"

Lucie inhaled and exhaled. "I don't know how long it was buried there, or who buried it."

"Isn't it finders keepers?" Caleb still looked as though he wasn't connecting the dots.

"Better safe than sorry. If the coins are valuable, I have to turn them over to the authorities until they determine if they are ours or not."

Caleb's face crumpled. "You don't think—"

Oh, she hoped Justin hadn't buried them there. The odds were slim, but she wanted a second opinion anyway.

"But, Mommy, don't we even get to keep the soldiers?" Ethan pouted.

"Or the marbles?" Even her sweet Mattie's voice was tinged with slight resentment.

Lucie collected the contents and placed them back in the tin. "Until I hear otherwise, we can't keep this." Her weak smile probably wasn't much consolation. "What's important is that we found it and can return it to somebody."

She'd rather err on the side of caution than have anyone accuse her of impropriety or any crime. Not for the first time, Lucie wondered if life would have been simpler for Ethan and Mattie if she'd moved them away from Hollydale, but with the house and lodge tied up in litigation, she hadn't had anything more than the clothes on their backs to start over.

For Mattie's and Ethan's sakes, she hoped Hollydale would move on, and soon.

CALEB OPENED THE door to The Busy Bean for the three Deckers, two of whom had the longest faces he'd ever seen. Lucie was rather stoic, though, proclaiming you can't miss something you just found.

She was wrong. Tonight, when he told her the truth about his parents, she might decide he'd waited too long to confide in her and cut him out of her life completely.

His heart pinged. He wanted time with Lucie, Mattie and Ethan, not to mention every lovable animal in the Decker household.

More than that, he wanted a lifetime, and that wouldn't change even though he'd only been back in Hollydale a short while.

"Hot chocolate isn't as good as antique marbles," Mattie softly voiced, her depth quite remarkable for someone so young.

"It is if there's whipped cream." Ethan bounced into the coffeehouse and shrugged under Mattie's glare. "What? Whipped cream makes everything better."

Ah, the joys of being seven, when your stomach ruled the world. Caleb entered the coffeehouse and his eyes adjusted to the dim light. There were quite a few people inside on this Sunday afternoon. The table by the bay window was occupied by three women, one of whom bore a strong resemblance to his mother.

"Caleb! Surprise!" The woman ran over and hugged him.

Caleb hugged her back before extricating himself. "Mom. I thought you and Dad weren't arriving until tomorrow night." Caleb glanced around the coffeehouse, trying to find his father, who was nowhere in sight.

"I missed you and Jonathan. The girls are so big now. I didn't have the heart to wake up your father. He's asleep at Jonathan's. But I so wanted to see my friends again." With some reluctance, Tina released him and tilted her head. "What haven't you been telling me on the phone? It's your back, isn't it? Did something happen?"

"Are you Caleb's mommy? I'm Ethan Decker, and Caleb's the best." The little boy inserted himself between the two, something akin to hero worship in his eyes.

"Thank you. I happen to agree with you. Caleb is my favorite child. Decker?" Recognition flared in his mother's eyes as she glanced from Lucie to Mattie to Caleb then back at Lucie. "It's been a long time."

Not long enough. With his mother's early arrival, Caleb had to keep her from discussing Justin until he talked to Lucie first. With genuine regret, he might be able to convince Lucie he'd kept it from her for a good reason. But the news had to come from him, not his mother.

"Is that Diane Harrison at your table?" Caleb

rubbed his eyes. "I must be seeing things. That looks like Beverly Bennett with her."

Tina nudged his ribs and motioned for him to come close so she could whisper. "I know Beverly used to be…well, Beverly. Apparently, she wants to turn over a new leaf. One thing I've learned since my breast cancer diagnosis is life is too short to hold grudges. We're catching up on all things Hollydale."

Looked like he needed a refresher course as well, since he'd somehow missed the news about Beverly's transformation. "We'll join you after we order."

"Hold on a minute," Tina cautioned, smiling at Mattie. "I've met this fine gentleman, but who is this pretty young lady?"

"Matilda, ma'am." Mattie gave a small curtsy and hid behind Lucie.

Lucie offered a lopsided smile. "Mattie is only shy until she accepts you. Then she's a chatterbox."

Caleb wasn't quite sure whether Mattie had accepted him or not. While she talked more and more around him and didn't hold back with the questions, a level of cautious wariness still existed.

Time would be the best means to overcome that, but he was running out of hours fast.

Caleb's mom brightened instantly. "A bit like you, Lucie, if I recall."

Caleb inserted himself into the conversation before his mother could say anything else. "I promised Mattie and Ethan something to drink and a small snack. Let's go."

He ushered the three of them toward the counter, aware of his rudeness but not sorry about it.

Lucie looked over her shoulder. "I think your mother was about to say something else."

"What about me?" Ethan tugged Caleb's shirt. "Am I like Mommy and Mattie?"

Lucie hugged him. "You're all Ethan and that's what matters."

When they reached the counter, Mattie ordered apple juice. "Are you sure that's all you want?" Caleb pulled out his wallet. "My treat. I thought you were a hot cocoa girl."

Mattie shrugged. "It's not a hot cocoa kind of day. I'm sad Sheriff Mike had to keep the tin. I hope we get it back."

"Me, too," Ethan chimed in, although he had, in fact, ordered hot chocolate with extra whipped cream. Caleb was learning fast that nothing could get between Ethan and his stomach.

"I'll carry your apple juice for you so it doesn't spill." Caleb reached for the plastic cup and nodded at Deb, sticking a five in the tip jar.

Tina stood when they arrived at the table.

Caleb looked around. "Where did Diane and Beverly go?"

"They thought I might like some time with you. We tried to get here in time to attend last night's Sunset Soiree, but it didn't work out." Tina patted Caleb's shoulder before looking straight at Lucie. "And we definitely have a lot to catch up on."

Jarred, Caleb catapulted forward, forgetting he held Mattie's drink. He tripped over the chair and Mattie's apple juice landed all over his mother's blouse. Loud gasps came from everyone before Mattie burst into tears.

"Oh, Mattie. Don't cry. It's only spilled juice." Tina reached for napkins at the same time Lucie rushed to his mom with a handful. "Thanks, Lucie. It's been a long day and Drew will start to worry if I'm not home soon." She laughed. "If he's up from his nap, that is."

"I'm sorry, Mom." While he hadn't planned to spill Mattie's juice all over her, he couldn't have come up with anything better if he'd tried.

She smiled and shrugged. "This isn't the worst thing to happen to me." She reached for her purse and pulled out a couple dollars. "Here you go, Mattie. This should be enough for a new juice."

"You put your money away." The owner, Deb, came over with a full cup—this one with a lid—and a mop. "I saw what happened."

"Thank you, Deb." Lucie's sincerity rang through. "You didn't have to do this, cleaning up our mess and all."

"Sometimes helping each other makes life more manageable." Deb cleaned up as Caleb's mother tapped his elbow.

"Dinner at Jonathan's house tomorrow night. Don't be late." She glanced at her shirt, which was sticky and wet. "I'd hug you good-bye but…"

His mother left the coffeehouse, the lingering apple smell dissipating with the strong aroma of rich coffee and cinnamon. No sooner had he sat than the barista called out the rest of their order. Caleb stood, intending to retrieve the drinks, but Lucie applied the slightest amount of pressure to his biceps. "I'll be right back."

He'd been granted a reprieve, but only a short one. Tomorrow morning he'd be placing suet feeders out for the woodpeckers, and tomorrow night he'd see his parents.

It had to be tonight. He'd talk to his parents first, then go to Lucie's and tell her the whole truth about the money.

WAS CALEB PUTTING the cart before the horse? Walking up the path to Jonathan's house, he figured he'd find out in a few minutes.

Welcome back to Hollydale, Mom and Dad. By the way, I'm falling in love with Lucie, the same person whose ex-husband stole your life savings. Just thought you should know.

Not a great speech, but better to hear it from him than someone else.

He knocked on the front door and heard a muffled command to enter. Wiping his clammy hands on his jeans, he entered, and a missile almost flattened him. "Caleb! I knew you wouldn't stay away for long." Vanessa crooked her finger and he bent to her level. "Uncle Drew snores. Everyone's out back. Come on."

Vanessa dragged him toward the backyard patio.

Jonathan waved from his spot at the grill.

"Hey, Caleb. Great timing, as usual. Dinner's almost ready. You're more than welcome to stay."

Mom came over and hugged him, her new outfit free of the sticky drink of earlier. "As long as Vanessa doesn't share her juice with you." She laughed.

Dad rose from the Adirondack chair and embraced Caleb. "Good to be back in Holly-dale." His father sent a fond look at his mother, their strong bond one of the constants in Caleb's world. "Heard about the mishap today."

"It was an honest accident."

"Then you weren't accompanying that woman and her children into The Busy Bean?" An edge crept into his father's voice, and Caleb's stomach tightened. "I wish I'd been there to set Lucie straight for the pain she caused your mother."

Jonathan handed Caleb the spatula. "You take over the grill. I'll bring Izzy and Vanessa inside to get everything else ready." A current of sympathy passed between them—Jonathan must have already figured out Caleb's feelings for Lucie.

The sliding door closed behind Jonathan and his daughters.

Mom laid her hand on Dad's arm and shook her head. "Justin's in jail, and Hollydale is a small town. We'll have to see Lucie once in a while. Life's too short to hold grudges. Let's move on, for all concerned. If you'd seen her with her children…"

"I saw you having to work during your chemo treatments in order to pay our bills." Dad's lips pursed into a thin white line. "What you went through, I went through. We have no secrets from each other. And remember Caleb's senior year? Lucie was so intuitive—sometimes she knew what was going on with Caleb before we did. There's no way she didn't know about Justin. She should be in jail, too."

"She's rebuilding her life. She lost everything."

His father's jaw clenched and he shook his head. "No, she has her home, she has her kids, she has her health." Dad's voice broke, and he sat back in the chair and turned his full gaze on Tina. "And I still can't afford to take you on that trip you scrimped and saved for. One month to luxuriate in the sun. That's the least of what you deserve."

Caleb flipped the burgers, his hand gripping the spatula so hard his knuckles were white. His father wasn't going to budge from his position. Instead, he rose from his chair and excused himself.

Mom came over and covered Caleb's hand with hers. "I saw how you and Lucie looked at each other. Your father will come around."

For so long, Caleb had been sitting on the fringes of the world, looking at what others had. In high school, Lucie had dulled the pain of watching his friends celebrate their senior year. At Yellowstone, he'd watched those three boys reunite with their families, the burning ache of Leah's betrayal fresh. But here in Hollydale, Lucie had opened her home to him, and he'd been part of someone's life. He'd laughed with the Decker family. He'd felt their pain when Mattie and Ethan had to leave the coffee tin at the police station. And seeing Lucie in that pink dress? That might be his most cherished memory of all.

Lucie had showed him how to find a real home, not as a stray or an outsider, but as Caleb. She'd accepted him for who he was, not because of his job or because he'd look good around town. She'd brought him into her family fold, and he'd loved every minute of belonging.

He loved Lucie Appleby Decker, the teenager she'd been and the woman she was now.

But he also loved his mom and dad. Going against his father wasn't an option.

THE TWINS INSISTED on an extra game night to make up for their disappointment about the tin can. They'd start as soon as Lucie finished her routine Sunday cleaning of the bunny hutch. The three bunnies hopped around their gated enclosure while Lucie finished tidying the rabbits' space. Pita whined from downstairs, but the border collie always stole the bunnies' honey sticks, their weekly treat. She'd just returned the bunnies to their clean hutch when the doorbell rang. Glancing down, she quickly swatted at the bits of bedding and pine attached to her sweatpants, but soon gave up.

Lucie hurried downstairs, with the dogs barking and jumping around the entranceway. She squinted through the peephole and cracked the door a sliver.

"Caleb."

The single word reverberated in her heart. In such a short time, he'd become her best friend all over again. Maybe more because she didn't feel the same about this man as she felt about her pals Natalie and Georgie. Not at all.

"Can I come in before Ladybug and Pita escape?" Caleb brought his face to the crack.

She racked her mind for a single excuse and came up empty. If he didn't run off into the night at the sight of her with bunny bedding all over her, she'd come clean about her feelings for him. She wanted more than friendship. This was Caleb, a good guy for keeps. He was no more capable of deception than Ladybug.

"Of course."

Caleb entered and gave each dog his attention. Midnight halted at the top of the stairs before darting toward the hallway, most likely heading for Mattie's room—the cat preferred Mattie to Ethan, who'd pulled her tail when she was a kitten.

Caleb's gaze roved over Lucie's outfit. "How can I help?"

A man who offered to help on pet maintenance night was more than a keeper. She wanted more kisses in a gazebo and a genuine relationship. She wanted to reach for the stars.

"I finished with bunny cleanup and was about to get ready for a special bonus edition of family game night. It's Ethan's turn to pick the game. You're more than welcome to stay."

"For the moment, I'm all yours." He winked.

"Mr. Caleb!" Ethan ran down the stairs and stopped short, yawning. He shook his head as though fighting sleep. "Thank you for the hot chocolate." He leaned against the railing and yawned again. This time he rubbed his eyes as though that would help. "Game night will be that much better."

Caleb had worn Ethan out without even trying.

"Let me go check on Mattie." Lucie went upstairs and found Midnight weaving in front of her daughter's closed door.

After a soft knock with no answer, Lucie opened the door. Midnight darted in and jumped on the bed, curling up in a similar fashion to the ball that was Mattie asleep. Lucie edged the picture book out of her hands and turned out the light.

She found Caleb and Ethan in the living room, Ethan cuddled on the couch under a blanket, his eyes closed. Ladybug rested nearby and Pita guarded everyone from her perch on the rug.

Caleb brought his index finger to his mouth

before nodding toward the foyer. Lucie followed and they slipped outside, keeping the front door ajar in case anyone cried out.

The stars twinkled and the spring air caressed her arms. For the first time since last year, night insects chirped for mates and the promise of new beginnings filled Lucie with something she hadn't felt in forever: hope.

It was glorious to step into her old self and find her glass slippers still fit after all this time. Never before had her porch swing beckoned with such promise, such romance. Building a bridge between her past and her future started now.

"Lucie—"

"Caleb—"

Their voices intertwined and she laughed at how well they fit together. Nature, animals and shared core values brought them close. Those flutters in her stomach whenever he came near confirmed her feelings for this good man.

Finally, Lucie could trust her own judgment.

She entangled her hand in his and led him over to the swing. "It's a beautiful night."

Caleb halted and glanced at the porch steps. "The stairs are a better place to talk."

"Mattie, Ethan and the entire Decker menagerie are asleep. That doesn't happen often, so we'd better relax and enjoy the evening." She pulled on his arm and he followed, sitting next to her on the swing. "Besides, this has to be more comfortable for your back."

"If we stay here, I'm going to kiss you."

The porch light provided a soft glow that highlighted the dark brown streaks in his hair. Before he could change his mind, she leaned forward and kissed him first.

Home had never felt so right.

Lucie poured herself into the kiss, his beard tickling a little, but she soon grew used to the soft hair against her skin. His lips demanded little, but she wanted more from him. She needed more—his truth, his joy, *him*. Everything faded away until it was only the two of them on the swing. His hands caressed the back of her head and threaded through her hair.

The kiss lasted for forever, but it was still too soon when Caleb pulled back and rested his forehead against hers. "You kissed me first."

"Yes. You're a good man, Caleb Spindler."

He winced and scooted to his end of the seat, the soft metal clinking sweet music. "Don't make me into something I'm not."

"How am I doing that? You're a kind, loving person. I'd stake everything on that." She lowered her voice and steepled her fingers. "I'm staking my heart on that."

He licked his lips and glanced away from her, staring straight ahead. "I didn't come to the center the first day because of your email. I came because Justin stole a substantial amount of money my parents invested with him. Fifty thousand dollars."

Her heart thudded and crashed. She shook her head. "The authorities would have known about them. They weren't on the list of people Justin swindled. I'd have recognized your last name. Twelve families, not one of whom was named Spindler."

This wasn't happening. Drew and Tina must be the mystery couple the authorities had questioned her about at some length. Since they hadn't come forward and she hadn't been involved in the theft, her lawyer had managed to smooth her end of the matter. She wouldn't let Justin control this situation. She wouldn't let him dominate everything about her life for always.

The harsh whistle of her blood rushing into her ears drowned out everything around her. All this time, she'd believed Caleb was being honest with her, yet, for two weeks, he'd held back something important. Calming herself, she promised to listen. After all, this involved his family.

"Justin was arrested just after my parents handed over their money to him. They waited for some word from authorities, but then my father's company transferred him. My mother was embarrassed about the swindle—she's a bookkeeper and thought, who'd hire someone like that to protect their money if they couldn't protect their own? So my parents stayed quiet.

"Not long after my mom found a job, she discovered she was sick. The battle they chose to fight was cancer, not Justin. Now that Mom's in remission, they asked me to find out if it was a good idea to hire an attorney to approach the authorities to see whether there's a restitution fund or if Justin's conviction ended any chance of seeing any of their money again."

Tina and Drew were two more people she'd have a hard time looking in the eye.

No—the *old* Lucie would have had a hard time with that. Last night had taught her something. With a little respect and a lot of integrity, she could hold her head high.

Besides, this was Tina and Drew. The three of them had shared many cups of coffee in the cafeteria while waiting for nurses to finish procedures. They knew her and had to believe she wouldn't willingly put people's livelihoods at risk.

She inhaled a deep breath and fingered the metal chain links. "I'll go over to Jonathan's house tomorrow and talk to them. Clear the air. Tonight would be better, if you'll stay with Mattie and Ethan."

"No." Caleb didn't look at her, and everything caved in.

"Why didn't they go to the police?" Her legs stopped pumping and she stayed still, the rocket rhythmic beat of her heart faster than ever before.

The question hung in the air like a dark cloud above them.

Caleb rubbed his beard and then rose, pacing the length of the porch, making her more light-headed than she already was. "I told them to do just that. I'm also trying to convince them to consult an attorney and try to get their money back."

"You've known this all along." She paused for breath before she made this worse than it was. Caleb was different from Justin. She had to put everything, including her heart, on the line. "Are you hiding anything else from me?"

He wouldn't meet her gaze.

"What else aren't you telling me?"

"My father is upset."

She'd lost her parents; no matter what, she'd never tear a family apart. "I won't get between you. Family is too important. If there are any issues with the cabin, send an email and I'll resolve them as soon as I can." She rose and moved toward the house, wanting nothing more than to hold her dogs and find some comfort in their straightforward nature.

"You included me."

Her hand stilled on the door. That was the most honest thing he'd ever said to her, but it wasn't enough to turn family members against each other. She glanced over her shoulder, her sadness penetrating a deeper fissure than she'd ever thought possible. "It's a small town, so I can't promise I won't run into them, but I won't try to talk to them, either. Not until they're ready."

She hadn't done anything wrong, but she'd lost more than anyone would ever know.

Including her heart to Caleb.

CHAPTER TWELVE

LEAVES CRUNCHED UNDERFOOT despite the new growth surrounding them. Sunlight streamed through the overhead canopy of spruce-fir trees, and Caleb glanced at the Timber River at its narrowest point. The rushing water filled his ears and his soul, the clarity of it showing the rock layer below. He kept his eyes open for evidence of any wildlife in the area. Black bears in North Carolina tended to come out of hibernation this month and the beginning of next.

Gray clouds swirled overhead. Unless Caleb was mistaken, and his back told him he wasn't, Hollydale was in for rain later today, with dipping temperatures after that. Some Monday this was turning out to be.

Although the weather had teased residents with warmer temperatures over the past few weeks, Caleb believed there'd be at least one more taste of winter before spring settled in.

Owen walked alongside—he'd agreed

Caleb could accompany him. They both knew it was a test, one Caleb intended to ace. They combed the forest for evidence of the Timber River woodpecker. If Caleb jumped over a few rocks, he'd be on Lucie's property rather than on the Park Service's land. For some reason, though, the woodpeckers preferred her woods.

Caleb couldn't fault them. For over a week, he had longed to cross the distance between his cabin and the wellness facility and talk to Lucie, see if they could work through this together. He missed Mattie and Ethan, Fred and Ethel, Ladybug and Pita.

More than that, he missed Lucie. Even his return to desk duty, which he'd thought would keep him so busy he wouldn't have time to dwell on her absence from his life, didn't fill that empty void like it had in the past. The space had a distinct Lucie-sized shape.

As of yet, he had no ideas about how to bridge the gap between his father and Lucie. Until he did that, he couldn't find his way home to those he loved.

Owen stopped and staked his six-foot walking stick into the dirt of the main trail. "I've been keeping an eye out all week, but I still haven't found a single woodpecker nest in any of the decaying logs or tree hollows."

Caleb scrubbed his beard and settled his own stick into the dirt. "Me neither. At least, not on this side of the river."

"Have you seen anything more than the one nest on Lucie Decker's property?" Owen twisted his walking stick before reaching for his reusable water bottle from the mesh netting on the side of his backpack.

"She gave me permission to set up the suet feeders and motion-sensor cameras." At least she had when they'd signed the rental agreement. "I reviewed footage last night at my cabin. There were some promising leads."

Owen squinted and left the main trail. He navigated his way to the river's edge before glancing back at Caleb. "You have permission to be on her land? Is that in writing?"

"The rental agreement is in writing." Caleb joined him near the edge, the water calmer here than a couple miles down the road, where kayakers often launched their boats. "She gave me verbal permission for the feeders and cameras."

"Get that in writing. Then conduct a more thorough search for nests and map out what you find by the end of next week.

"I also want a written report of her planned uses for the facility and the impact on the land, along with photographs of the nests and any woodpeckers you come across." Owen glanced up at the sky, the clouds looking more ominous by the minute. "We better get back to base. I have a feeling this might turn to sleet by tonight."

Caleb now had an excuse to see Lucie again. He intended to make the most of it.

LUCIE BANGED HER head against the wall before she collected herself and entered the finished spa at the lodge.

"Honey, that thump can only mean one thing. Someone's having a bad Monday and is going to have a grade-A awful headache later." Mitzi bustled from one side of the room with a giant cardboard box in her arms. She lowered the box and wiped her hands. "Want to tell me all about it?"

"Not particularly. I haven't had a chance to really talk to you since the Sunset Soiree. How was your date with Caleb's boss?"

Mitzi's eyes glazed over with happiness. "Owen might look like he wouldn't know his way around a dance floor, but I'm happy to report that man can move. And I enjoyed our second date last Friday. He might not talk much, but then again, I talk enough for half of Hollydale as it is." She laughed, picked up a box cutter and slit open the top of the nearest box. "Then again, I guess everything's a matter of perspective. I have to wheedle information out of some customers and stand back while others spout like gushers. You'll have to learn to do the same, but you'll catch on when this place opens next week."

And the bookings only covered the first three weeks. That baseball friend of Caleb's was supposed to call this weekend with a decision about an endorsement. That might help. What she needed was a top-tier client who would provide a reference as well as book return visits. The Whitleys would have been perfect, but she was sure it would be a snowy July day in Hollydale before she heard from them again.

Lucie brushed her hand against the burnished dark granite countertop. Everything in the room exuded peace and elegance, right down to the fluffy white towels and gray robes. "I don't know how long we'll be in business." Defeat tasted bitter, and the thought of losing Mitzi's hard-earned money hurt almost as much as distancing herself from Caleb.

"Oh, honey." Mitzi slipped an arm around Lucie's shoulders and led her over to the soft couch. The buttery leather felt like a warm hug. "My mama told me a long time ago never to put all my eggs in one basket. Mind you, my mama never had two eggs to crack for breakfast or any other meal, and neither did your grandma on your mama's side, but we had lots of love. Same as your mama loved you. She'd be mighty proud of you rebuilding your life and making a difference for others. Everyone'll come around."

"I have more bad news." Lucie sniffled but kept the tears back. After Caleb, she wasn't sure she had any more tears anyway. "The bookkeeper I hired called this morning. She received a full-time offer closer to her home, and she quit before she even began."

"Then we'll find another one, someone who'll make your books as shiny and pretty as this room and you." Mitzi squeezed her shoulder. "Speaking of beautiful, I didn't get a chance to talk to you at the pavilion. Why didn't I run into you and that handsome fellow of yours on the dance floor?"

Lucie's throat tightened and she glanced at her watch. "Staff meeting in ten minutes."

She started to rise, but Mitzi pulled her back. "Then that's plenty enough time to tell me everything. I might not be Patsy, but she'll haunt me tonight if I don't get what's wrong out of you." Mitzi's serious expression proved she truly believed every word.

"Turns out Justin stole money from Caleb's parents. Fifty thousand dollars. I won't get between Caleb and his parents."

"Tina Spindler's a good woman, and she raised a good son. Have you talked to her?"

Mitzi made it sound so simple, as if Justin's acts could be erased with a few kind words.

"I don't want to hurt his parents any more than they've already been hurt." Lucie tapped her foot against the gorgeous cherry hardwood she'd worked for a week to restore. At least that work had paid off. "For the best part of two years, all I've faced are people who want to believe the worst in me. They won't forget."

Mitzi smiled. "Patsy was no stranger to having people think badly about her, you know."

"What do you mean?" Lucie glanced at Mitzi, whose dark eyes were alight with memories of a strong friendship. "Everyone loved my mom."

"Not everyone." Mitzi waved a hand. "Some of the older folk in town, bless their souls, thought your mother was a gold digger, someone who should have stayed on her side of town. Patsy worked hard, supporting the Appleby business and foundation. She made each bride feel like a princess. She helped behind the scenes, too. When Dwayne left me, she supported me with the money to buy into the salon."

Mitzi didn't talk of Dwayne often. Lucie stiffened her spine, sitting a little straighter. "I should have taken a page from your playbook and focused on my business instead of getting involved with Caleb."

Mitzi frowned and folded her arms against her ample chest. "That's what you're taking away from all this?"

Lucie nodded. "Dwayne burned you, and you threw yourself into your work. Nothing wrong with that."

"Honey, I'm fifty-two, but I don't have one foot in the grave yet. And Owen's a couple years younger than me…it's early yet, but there's potential. When it's right, it's right. The way Caleb looks at you is right."

"But Caleb's father doesn't approve. I won't get between him and his father." No matter how much she wanted a relationship with Caleb, she wouldn't ask him to choose her over his father.

But getting over Caleb? That wasn't like flicking a switch. Losing his friendship and missing out on love would take a lifetime to recover from.

Lucie's phone buzzed with an incoming text and she pulled it out. "Sorry, but I have to check this in case it's the kids' school." She read the text. "It's Sierra—she says the staff's assembled in the conference room."

Lucie rose but Mitzi cleared her throat. "Honey, Justin and Caleb aren't anything alike. The person who has to decide about his father is Caleb. You're running from yourself. You've surrounded yourself with so much activity these past couple years because you've been afraid to live again. Trust me, I know."

Stunned, Lucie tried to make some sense of what Mitzi was saying. Mitzi headed for the door, and Lucie said, "I'll be there in a minute."

Mitzi was right. Lucie had been on the defensive ever since Caleb came back to town. That very first night, she'd sent Caleb away rather than ask him to explain. Instead of running toward something positive, she was running away from him because she was afraid to live, afraid to feel, afraid to give her heart to someone else.

If it hadn't been for his father, she would have found another excuse to drive him off.

It was easier to reject someone than to lose everything. Love, though, wasn't about losing yourself—it was about finding something so incredibly strong and uplifting it got you through anything.

Then her phone dinged with another text from Sierra, and she hurried along.

CHAPTER THIRTEEN

AFTER A QUICK tuna sandwich for dinner, Caleb kicked off his boots and reclined in his new living room chair. Silence surrounded him—no Izzy and Vanessa quibbling over space, no Ethel jumping onto the shed couch, and no Lucie helping him balance work and life. He reached for his sketchpad and his favorite Palomino Blackwing pencil. Rather than the fawn he'd seen this morning, Lucie's face stared back from the paper. Family meant everything to her, and she wouldn't go against her principles. That was one of the qualities he loved about her.

He didn't want to live in this quiet cabin. He wanted to be part of the Decker noise. With Lucie, he'd found the best of everything. His back twinged, and he looked longingly at the fireplace. A fire might liven the space and provide some much-needed warmth. He picked out three logs from the carrier alongside the hearth and laid them in the fireplace.

A knock on his front door brought a smile to his face and a leap to his step. He'd emailed Lucie earlier today about exploring her back property for woodpecker nests. She must have decided to deliver her verdict in person.

He threw open the door and found his mother lowering her umbrella, a couple bags at her feet. "Hope you don't mind I dropped in. I cooked some soup today and ran out of space in Jonathan's freezer, so I'm bringing you chicken noodle and corn chowder to get you through this cold snap."

Mom reached for the bags, but Caleb beat her to the handles. "I've already eaten dinner tonight, but this will be great for the next few days. Thanks."

"We haven't had a good long talk since I've come home." Mom stepped inside, her brief murmur rather disconcerting. "This cabin isn't anything like I remember it."

"Lucie sold most of the contents to raise money to start her business." And too late he remembered Lucie probably wasn't someone his mother wanted to discuss. He ran his hand through his hair, the chilliness of the cabin getting to him in more ways than one. "Mom, about your money and Lucie …"

Mom patted his arm, and he halted halfway

to the kitchen. "Someday your father will forgive Lucie. I'm working on him." She rubbed her hands together and pointed at the fireplace. "Are the logs in there for decoration or were you about to start a fire? Georgia doesn't get as cold as Hollydale."

This wasn't a courtesy call to drop off soup, then. If his mother had made enough soup to fill both Jonathan's and Caleb's freezers, something was wrong. "Did you get some bad news?" His heart raced. "Is the cancer back?"

"Heavens, no." She rolled her eyes and walked toward the kitchen. "And let's clear the air right now. Whenever something's wrong with me, we're not going to jump to thinking it's cancer every single time, okay?"

Caleb piled the bags on the counter, pulling out container after container of soup, all neatly labeled with the contents and date. "You cook when you're upset."

"And you take walks. It's our way of getting the stress out." Mom folded the bag into smaller and smaller squares while he rifled through the contents of the second. "Can I have a glass of water? You'd think after all the rain this afternoon, I wouldn't want to look at the stuff."

"Glasses are in the cabinet above you." He'd

unpacked those last night when the silence had gotten to him. He pulled out one pie, then another. "Are there three pies in here?"

"Your father and I had a disagreement. I told him life was too short and Hollydale was too small to hold a grudge." She shrugged, filled her glass and pulled up a stool. "And I didn't get that job I applied for."

Jobs around Hollydale didn't grow on trees, so that must have been a double whammy for his mother, who believed a day without work was a wasted day. Like mother, like son. Hence the pies and the soup. Lousy for her but great for Jonathan and the girls and Caleb. "If I hear of anything…"

Another knock at the front door, and his mother jumped to her feet. "That's your father."

No visitors to his cabin since Mattie and Ethan, and then two in one night. At least it was breaking up the oppressive silence. Caleb hurried into the other room, his mother on his heels. "It's nice to know your father is willing to admit he was wrong."

Caleb opened the door. Instead of his father waiting there, he found Lucie shuffling her feet. "Oh, you do have company…" She pointed to his mother's frilly pink wisp of an umbrella. "I thought the car in the parking lot belonged to the furnace installer, who said he might take some measurements tonight. I'll come back later."

"Come on in out of the rain." His mother ducked around him and waved Lucie inside. "Would you like a container or two of soup to take home? Maybe a nice pie? Which do you like more—apple or blueberry?"

Lucie sent Caleb a puzzled look as his mother ushered her into the kitchen. "Since I had to head this way, I only came over to give Caleb written notarized permission to search for the woodpeckers on my land." She reached inside her raincoat and pulled out an envelope.

Caleb's mom glanced at Lucie's unsettled face and then at him. "You know what? I'll let the two of you talk without me." She went over and kissed Caleb's cheek, smooshing his beard. "If you hear of any job openings, let me know."

"Natalie mentioned her friend Shelby is getting ready to open a lunch café." Lucie snapped open her raincoat. "You could contact her."

"If she needs someone in accounts receivable, I'm her person." Tina sent a nervous smile Lucie's way and laughed. "You'd think with my bookkeeping experience, I'd have known better than to invest with your husband."

"You're a bookkeeper? I'd forgotten." Lucie rubbed her hands and appeared undecided about something. "Are you looking for something part-time or full-time?"

Another knock at the front door stopped Caleb's mother before she could answer. Instead, she looked at him and smiled. "This time it's your father. The hair on my arm is standing on end."

Caleb rolled his eyes but excused himself to answer the door. Sure enough, his father was waiting on the porch with a suitcase. "It's too noisy at Jonathan's." He frowned as his gaze settled on the umbrella. "I see your mother already arrived."

"Come in, Dad." This might be the first fight he'd ever witnessed between his parents, and it was over the woman he loved. He stiffened his shoulders. He wanted his parents to accept his decisions. After all, Caleb was the one who had to live with them. "She's in the kitchen."

Caleb bumped into his back when Dad halted without warning. "You didn't tell me you had company."

Mom jumped up and clapped her hands. "Great news, Drew. I have a job."

Lucie's chin rose and she stepped toward Caleb's father. "I know Justin hurt a lot of people, but I've spent two years apologizing. It's time for me to move on, and hiring Tina makes perfect sense. Accountability and openness will be the only way I can convince the town I'm here to stay."

His mother picked up her glass, walked up to his father and dumped the water on him.

"Tina!"

"Oops, look what I have done." Her monotone and deliberateness left no doubt of her motive. "Now we'll have to leave the two of them alone to straighten everything out." She glanced over her husband's shoulder and met Caleb's gaze. "Sorry you have to clean up my mess. Soup and pie are a fair exchange. Come on, Drew."

"But—" his father spluttered, raising his arms, water dripping everywhere.

"Our son is involved with the woman who divorced the man who stole from us. We'll figure it out as we go along." Mom grabbed Dad's arm and pulled him away. "See you tomorrow morning, Lucie."

Lucie nodded. A second later, the front

door slammed, leaving the two of them alone. Her phone pinged with a text. "The furnace installer won't be here until tomorrow, so I'll leave since you have the notarized statement. Mitzi is taking care of Ethan and Mattie at my house, and she's meeting Owen for dinner." She started for the living room.

"I've missed Ethel and Ladybug." Huskiness coated his voice and he longed to sweep her into his arms until the feeling of home engulfed him and would never let him go again.

Her gaze clouded over as she gripped the doorknob. "I won't tell Fred. He'll feel left out."

"I have enough patience for both of us to get through this."

"The documents in the envelope give you and Owen permission to scout out my property." She opened the door. "This isn't about patience anymore. If anything, my feelings for you are that much stronger. You stand by those you love. Your father is one of those people, and he should be."

With that, Lucie left. But she still had feelings for him. The talk on the porch hadn't changed that. Hope gripped him with a promise they might get through this, after all.

CHAPTER FOURTEEN

SWEAT DRIPPED OFF her forehead, despite the cooler temperatures. This challenge wall lived up to its name.

Lucie gripped the head counselor's hands while glancing over her shoulder for a signal Tina and Sierra could handle her weight. Before one came her way, Trent pulled her over the climbing wall, his muscular arms a sure sign he was strong enough for this job and well suited given his always positive attitude.

Once Lucie was over the wall, that only left Caleb's mother and Sierra on the other side. Before too long, Tina smiled at Lucie from the top of the wooden structure. "I had no idea I'd be jumping into the fray of things so quickly. This is what I needed more than anything. For coworkers not to treat me like a fragile violet but like a resilient dogwood flower." Tina laughed. "Although, next time, I do admit I'd like to test the spa rather than the outdoor ropes course."

"You're sure your doctor would approve?"

"I'm not dead, and it's been a long time since my reconstructive surgery. I'm good." The tone of Tina's voice told Lucie to move on.

Trent balanced Lucie on his shoulders while Sierra worked her way up the wall, and Lucie helped lift her over the top. Sierra landed on the ground while Lucie extricated herself from Trent, thankful for her two years of cheerleading experience.

"Good call letting Sierra come over last." Trent clapped and glanced upward, the gray sky becoming more ominous. "I recommend cutting this short. My four-wheel drive is at Max's Auto Repair, and I'm borrowing my wife Audrey's compact today. I want to get back to town while the getting's good."

"Agreed. Great work, team. We're ready for the grand opening on Monday." Lucie took a few deep breaths and then walked alongside Tina for the short trek to the center. They discussed which new computer apps and programs Tina favored for bookkeeping. Tina's chatter reminded Lucie so much of her mother's happy nature.

They reached the upstairs staff conference

room for a quick wrap-up of the morning's activities.

"Does Caleb know how lucky he is?" asked Lucie.

Tina stared at her and grasped Lucie's hands. "I think that should be my line. I know it's tough, but time will help, along with the two of us working together. Caleb's father is slowly coming to terms with everything."

Until he did, Lucie wouldn't be able to accept a role in Caleb's life. She knew what it was like to lose a family member, and she'd never get between Caleb and his parents. Family, whether family by blood, or the family you chose, was too important.

Tina squinted and shook her head. "My husband is a mite stubborn at times, but he has a good heart."

Lucie's cell phone rang and she glanced at the Caller ID. Frederick Whitley? She held up her finger. "I have to take this."

"Ms. Decker, is this a good time?" It was the man himself, not an assistant.

Lucie's pulse sped up. "It's a perfect time."

Tina waved and entered the conference room without her.

"My wife stands up for people she believes in. You made a good impression on her." Frederick's tone made it clear she still had to win over one more Whitley.

Allowing her business to speak for itself was her best option. "The Hollydale Training and Wellness Center would love to make a good impression on both of you. Anytime you'd like to tour the place, I'll escort you personally. Then I'll present an attractive proposal package that'll give you an overview of our services and pricing structure. Good group morale can always be made better. We strive to bring authenticity and cooperation to the forefront."

A pencil tapping in the background encouraged her that Frederick was considering her offer. That was a step in the right direction. "How does next Tuesday afternoon work for you?"

Lucie had to hold back a cheer. "My staff and I will be at your service."

After the call ended, Lucie entered the conference room and whooped for joy. "That was Frederick Whitley." At Sierra's blank stare, Lucie elaborated. "He runs a manufacturing plant. He's turning more toward philanthropic efforts and is building a new nature conservancy. He's a big supporter of using environmentally friendly products."

Tina cleared her throat. "That name sounds familiar for a different reason." Lucie winced. "The Whitleys invested in Justin's Ponzi scheme and lost a good deal of money."

"What made him call you and ask for a tour?" Tina opened her laptop and stared at Lucie.

"I spoke to him at the Sunset Soiree. Since I hadn't heard from them, I wasn't holding out much hope. He said his wife convinced him to give us a chance." Lucie smiled. "And if Mrs. Whitley succeeded in changing her husband's mind…"

"This gives you hope Drew will come around." Tina finished her sentence for her.

A little hope might be exactly what the doctor ordered. The business was coming together, with the baseball manager, Jared Engel, agreeing to endorse the center, more Hollydale residents were seeing the real her, and Caleb's patience was a hopeful sign, too.

Life was looking up.

CALEB STUCK HIS hickory walking stick in the ground, the log where he'd spotted the original nest in plain sight. The suet birdfeeders he'd placed in various areas showed signs of activity. He'd examine the footage on the motion-sensor cameras later for verification it was the Timber River woodpecker.

The decaying oak rested a ways off, and Caleb turned to Owen. "Are you up for examining the log, or do you need to get back to the station?"

"Let me check to see if I have any messages." Reaching into his jacket pocket, Owen pulled out his cell phone. "Amazed I still have service."

"I talked with Lucie about that before I signed the lease. She has a signal booster amplifier for her business. It must reach out this far." Caleb picked up his stick, the extra stabilizing force helping to control the twinges in his back. While the exercises and physical therapy were good, the weather aggravated his herniated disk. There was no way he would admit that to Owen, though. Better to rest tonight.

Coming home to a silent, empty cabin felt as gray as the overhead clouds. He should go to the animal shelter this weekend and check out the dogs.

Better yet, Lucie had rescued him since he'd been back. It was his time to make a stand and fight for her. Tonight, he'd take her and the kids out to dinner and plead his case.

She was worth fighting for. That thought alone lifted his spirits.

Owen planted his phone back in his pocket. "We have time to investigate. The National Weather Service issued a statement saying the front is moving slower than expected. It's stalling over Kansas. No precipitation expected until the middle of the night."

They narrowed in on the decaying tree where Ethan had first showed Caleb the nest. Without disturbing anything, Owen extricated his digital camera from his pocket and converted his walking stick to a photo mount, which he planted in the packed soil. He centered the camera and snapped pictures while Caleb checked out surrounding logs, finding evidence of two other nests.

Caleb returned as Owen was packing up his camera. "Four eggs in one a couple hundred feet away and six in the other." Caleb had checked the site for common grackles or other predators of woodpecker eggs. With the weather taking a backward dip into winter, snakes wouldn't come out of hibernation until next month. One less worry.

"This one has three." Owen reached for his walking stick, lifting it from the ground and filling in the slight hole left behind from the divot.

The hesitation in Owen's voice was clear, and Caleb didn't like it. "What aren't you telling me?"

Owen glanced at the log then at Caleb. "Once I receive your final report about the woodpecker habitats, I'll talk with Lucie about restricting activity in the area. I'll work in conjunction with the other area agencies, but we have to preserve an endangered species, especially one with such an important role in the local ecosystem."

"Lucie is trying to start her corporate training and wellness business out here." Even to his ears, his words sounded hollow. He reached for his reusable water container and swallowed a big swig. "Can I tell her first?"

"Of course. Working with her instead of around her is always the preferable approach."

Owen left no doubt. His boss would find a way to protect the woodpeckers' habitat, even if it signaled the downfall of Lucie's livelihood.

LUCIE LOCKED THE door of the lodge behind her, checking it was shut and the security system activated. The sound of a car pulling up in the parking area gave her pause. A police squad car approached the circular drop-off area, and her legs wobbled for a second. Mattie? Ethan? Had something happened to either of them? She blinked and dismissed the notion—she had just received a text from Natalie that they were okay.

Mike emerged from his squad car with the coffee tin in hand while whistling a jaunty tune.

Lucie met him halfway. "Good news, I take it?"

"I checked with District Attorney Stuart Everson at city hall. I also put out feelers to a couple other agencies. Everyone said it's yours." Mike presented the tin to Lucie, and she accepted it. "Stuart paid particular attention to the soldiers. He said they're in good condition—he looked rather distraught at having to give them up."

They laughed. "Thanks." She held up the tin, the faded blue label peeling on the sides. "Mattie and Ethan will love this."

She hesitated, but it was best to go full speed ahead so there'd be no accusations down the road. "There's no chance anything in here could be ill-gotten gains? I don't want that hanging over me."

Mike shook his head and folded his arms. "We made all the checks we could. And besides, the coins in there aren't worth much. Inside you'll find an inventory. We consulted with a coin shop in Asheville. The dealer said the coins are worth sixteen, seventeen dollars tops for the lot of them. If anything, they'll make a great display for your center."

Relief exhaled out of her. No one could accuse her of covering anything up. "Good to know."

"The weather's supposed to take a turn for the worse. Do you need me to follow you into town?"

"No, I have to send a few texts before I start driving. Then I'm heading home."

"Be sure to let Georgie and me know you got home safely."

Lucie waved goodbye and clutched the tin to her chest. Mattie and Ethan would be thrilled with this surprise. This might perk them up as they'd taken Caleb's absence harder than expected lately. Even Mattie.

Caleb deserved to be there when she announced the tin's return to the twins. She texted him, inviting him to dinner. His acceptance was immediate. This evening she didn't know what Mattie and Ethan would welcome more: the tin or Caleb. Of course, there was no contest. Ethan, Ladybug and Ethel would fawn over Caleb all night. Lucie would be lucky if she got a word in edgewise.

They weren't the only ones who'd missed him, though. Rather than delegating Caleb to the far recesses of her heart, Lucie had found the past week without Caleb excruciating.

When his father accepted her, Lucie and Caleb might stand a chance, especially after she explained the revelation Mitzi had gifted her with: Lucie had been running away from her heart, fearing commitment, fearing herself.

That was no way to live. Loving meant opening yourself to someone and sharing the good and the bad, the funny and the serious, the pigs and the dogs.

Love was all about chance. You didn't choose who you loved—you just loved them. To some, Ladybug, with her doggie overbite and constant slobber, might not be the most beautiful dog, but she was all Ladybug, loyal and sweet. And Lucie loved her.

Did Lucie love Caleb? That scared her. Although his patience with Mattie and Ethan, his commitment to nature, and how he made her feel respected and loved was proof that he was worthy of her love. More than that, they'd shared kisses—short ones, long ones, ones she felt all the way to her toes. That went beyond friendship. He'd been patient with her, and together they could show patience and mend the rift with his father.

For once, she'd fallen for someone who would believe in her, would fight for her, would cherish her. While the treasure in the coffee tin had turned out to be a shadow, more of a curiosity and a talking piece rather than a substantial find, Caleb was no shadow and neither were her feelings for him.

She loved Caleb.

Starting her car, she smiled, knowing tonight would be the night she found out whether Caleb loved her.

Tonight could be the best night of her life.

CALEB STRETCHED HIS back muscles on Lucie's front porch, clutching the planter with morning glories trailing over the sides. Red roses might be the usual expression of love, but he didn't want something here today and gone tomorrow. With a little care and diligence, this planter would cultivate vines that they could plant in her yard when spring came to stay.

For he'd arrived tonight with a mission. No more buried treasure under the surface, no more burrowing a nest into a log. Only honesty moving forward. From the beginning of their friendship, they'd laughed together and found common ground. Now, all these years later, there was something scary about leaving friendship on the porch, seeking something more with the person who, ultimately, knew him as well as he knew himself. But it was right. He loved Lucie. She made him feel so at ease, so loved.

He glanced at the glider and shivered. Too cold for an outdoor kiss tonight, but if she forgave him, there'd be another round of kisses before he left for his cabin with enough time to settle in before the storm.

With perseverance, there'd be a lifetime of kisses ahead with a blonde dynamo whose depth of caring amazed him every day.

Shoring up his resolve, he knocked, the familiar cacophony of barks livening up the evening air.

The door opened, Ethan's face popping around the side. "Mr. Caleb's here."

Mattie came running. "Mr. Caleb. I finally lost my first tooth. See? Now Ethan and I are twins again."

Caleb closed the door and knelt in front of her as she beamed a wide grin. "I see the gap." Committing to Lucie meant committing to her children, and he intended to be there for them. Always. "You never stopped being Ethan's twin."

Mattie shuffled her feet and sighed. "Some of the kids at school say we're not twins because we don't look alike."

Ladybug trotted over and must have sensed Mattie's genuine dismay, as she wagged her tail in Caleb's direction but hunkered down on Mattie's feet, giving a doggy grunt of understanding. Out of the corner of his eye, he saw Lucie in the doorway, wiping her hands on a dishtowel and heading their way. He held up a finger and she stopped.

"There's no written rule saying twins have to look alike. Fraternal twins don't. When people think about twins, they often think about identical twins." Caleb looked Mattie in the eye. "Your bond as twins is more than skin-deep. It's what's underneath that counts. Take your mother, for example—underneath it all, she's one of the strongest and most honest people I've ever met. She's as beautiful on the inside as the outside. Same with the two of you. You might not be able to tell on the outside you're twins, but you are through and through."

"Told you so." Ethan nudged Mattie and poked Caleb's shoulder. "Can you come for dinner more often? Mom made pie."

"Actually, Caleb's mother made the pie. I only warmed it up." Lucie emerged, her blue eyes shining. "The next time we see her, we'll thank her."

The doorbell rang, and Lucie furrowed her brows. "I'm not expecting anyone."

Ethan stepped toward the door, and Caleb rose and planted his hand on Ethan's shoulder. "Let your mom see who it is first."

Lucie elbowed her way up to the door and checked the peephole. "Well, we won't have long to wait to thank your parents for the pie." She opened the door and smiled. "Come on in out of the cold. I've heated up your apple pie if you'd like to share a slice. Perhaps some coffee to go with it?"

His mother and father entered the foyer as Pita came from the kitchen area, barking and joining the general melee. His mother's amusement was clear, while his father held back, his preference for long walks where he could process everything at odds with the Maxwell and Decker households. Just as

Izzy and Vanessa had already won him over, though, Dad would come around to Ethan and Mattie, and the whole menagerie of pets, as well.

"We're not staying." Tina nudged her husband while Pita sniffed the bottom of her puffy blue coat. "And we don't need any coffee at this time of the evening. While I've met Mattie and Ethan, I don't believe they've met my husband, Drew. And who's this sweet girl?"

Tina bent down and petted Ladybug while Lucie handled the introductions. She tilted her head toward the shed. "I'll save Fred and Ethel for another time when it's still light outside."

This was pure Lucie, warm and inviting.

Glancing around the room, Caleb understood why his father was protective of Tina, who brought out the best in his dad. Caleb's best was here, in the place that filled his heart, the place he longed to call home with the woman he loved. He hoped they could see that.

More than that, he had to make sure they did. Caleb stepped forward and exhaled the breath he'd been holding. "Dad, there's something you need to know." Any chance of making this a private moment between him and Lucie had disappeared a long time ago. Then again, he had nothing to hide and he wanted Lucie to understand that. He went over and twined his arm around Lucie, a vision in a pink apron with a smudge of whipped cream and a brown coffee stain dotting the front. "I love Lucie."

"I told you so." Mattie turned to Ethan, a smug smile showing off her tooth gap. "I told you he looks at her like Sheriff Mike looked at Miss Georgie at their wedding." She stuck out her tongue for good measure.

"Matilda. That's not polite." Lucie reprimanded her daughter, and Caleb's stomach sank. Of all the reactions to his declaration of love, it didn't bode well that she'd addressed Mattie first.

All his life, he'd retreated into nature, always feeling as if he'd missed out. Returning to Hollydale had been his refuge, his saving grace.

Instead, he was another stray fighting for Lucie's attention.

She reached for his hand, her warmth seeping in. He forced himself to meet her gaze.

"I want my life to be an open book for all to see, but I also want you to have my undivided attention. You deserve that." She let go, reached up and caressed his cheek, the beard bristles bending under her touch. "You deserve so much."

"For a second, I wasn't sure you felt the same way." Caleb's voice broke. "Never again."

The doorbell rang and Caleb stopped short of throwing his arms up in the air as Ladybug and Pita started another round of barks. Even Midnight showed up, weaving her way down the stairs.

Lucie rubbed her forehead. "Excuse me a minute."

This time she didn't look through the peephole before opening the door. Franklin Garrity, the town banker, stood on the doorstep, a black leather briefcase at his side. "Mrs. Decker." He stepped inside, his jaw clenched.

Pita yelped and rushed to Caleb's side. Ladybug planted herself at Mattie's and Ethan's feet.

Smart dogs.

Caleb bent and scratched Pita's ear, keeping a wary gaze on Garrity.

"This is an unusual time to pay a visit." Lucie glanced at her watch before placing protective hands on Mattie's and Ethan's shoulders. "While I want an answer about the mortgage, I'm quite busy tonight. Tell me your first available appointment time tomorrow, and I'll rearrange my schedule and meet you at the bank."

"We should talk tonight." Garrity pursed his lips into a straight line as he tightened his grip on the briefcase's handle. "That way, if you want to obtain counsel based on the findings of the underwriter and the forensic accountant, you'll have an opportunity. Tonight is a courtesy call because of your children."

"This is an inappropriate discussion to have with me in front of my children. Official business should take place at the bank or another public setting. I have nothing to hide."

Caleb's father's glare darkened with every second, almost as if he'd made up his mind as soon as Garrity mentioned an attorney, almost as if he was judging Lucie before any evidence was presented. One word alone, along with Garrity's body language, was enough to condemn Lucie.

"We should leave." Drew made a motion, but Caleb's mother laid a hand on his arm.

"Lucie hired me. I'm staying." Tina lifted her chin.

Lucie patted her children's shoulders. "I

don't want Ethan and Mattie here while Mr. Garrity and I have this conversation. Caleb, will you take them to Georgie's house for me? She and Mike will take care of them until I can get there."

Cut to the core, Caleb remained still. She didn't trust him enough to stand by her. Every fiber of him knew Lucie hadn't done anything wrong. She'd no more betray Mitzi or her aunt than she would turn away an animal in distress.

"I'll take them to my cabin, and we'll talk when you're done."

Watching over Mattie and Ethan was his way of showing her he wanted them in his life as much as her. When she picked them up, they'd get everything in the open, starting with the reason Garrity showed up tonight and ending with why Caleb loved her.

Maybe he should start with the love and work his way to Garrity.

Lucie hesitated and glanced around. Even the dogs were on their best behavior, as if sensing the tension in the foyer. "Mattie and Ethan need their coats. My car's unlocked, so you can get their booster seats. I'll text you and you can bring them back here when I'm done."

Along with his parents, he bustled Mattie and Ethan out the door, despite their protests. Lucie flicked on the porch light before she closed the door, shutting him out.

Shivering, his mother gripped Mattie's and Ethan's hands and led them to Caleb's car. "Caleb's father and I will be right behind you. We'll make an evening out of it. Popcorn, a fire, the works. Right, Drew?"

Mom glanced over her shoulder and made eye contact with Dad, who hovered behind her. "Caleb and I will get the booster seats and join you in a minute," he said.

Caleb strode to Lucie's clunker of a car, proof she wasn't living extravagantly. Opening the back door, he extricated one of the seats while his father stuck his head in on the other side. "I can't believe she turned out to be such a swindler."

A blast of cold air bit through Caleb's jacket—it numbed his insides as much as his father's words. This was exactly what Lucie had fought against over the past couple of years as she'd worked hard for her children and to restore her reputation. "Dad, she's not a fraud."

"Then why would Franklin Garrity show up at her door telling her she needs counsel?

Sounds like she's in deep trouble. Why would you want to risk everything to stand by that?"

His father's gaze challenged him. Caleb considered the facts. Garrity was here on business on a weeknight.

Garrity mentioned a forensic accountant. That alone sounded damaging and accusatory.

Had Lucie lied to Garrity? Had she been lying to the town all along? Caleb felt sick and gripped the handle of Mattie's car seat to steady himself. Leah had lied to him, using him to promote an image to her family to get her trust fund. Had Lucie used him to promote the image of her center? After all, she'd admitted she'd contacted him to gain his endorsement, and he'd gone one better, nabbing the endorsement of a star baseball player.

Had she played him like Leah?

Had he given his heart to someone phony, someone who valued image above everything else?

Everything about Lucie was real, from her devotion to animals to her love for her family, whether four-legged or two.

He believed in the woman he loved.

"I'm staying and fighting for her, Dad.

Lucie and I will meet you and Mom at the cabin."

"You're in too deep. What if this ends badly, like it did the last time for her?" Dad met his gaze, a face Caleb knew so well, a face that had been there when Caleb woke from surgery scared and unsure of whether he'd walk again or resume a normal life, a face he'd seen supporting him in every way since Caleb could remember. "You're really willing to stake everything on her?"

"Yes."

A simple word, and one he truly meant. As sure as he was about the hibernation habits of the black bear, the nesting habits of the woodpecker, and that the sun would rise in the east tomorrow, he was sure about Lucie. "She'd never do anything to hurt her family, and she includes all of Hollydale as her family." Whether everyone in Hollydale knew that—or accepted it—wasn't at issue. Lucie loved this town, and she cared what the residents thought of her. That they believed the truth about her.

"How do you know she didn't do something criminal for her children's sake?" Dad lifted Ethan's dark blue booster seat out of the back seat.

"I know it like the air I breathe. Lucie would never hurt those children, and she wouldn't do anything for them that went against her true self." Caleb would shout it from the rooftops if it would do any good.

His father reached out his free hand over the back seat of Lucie's car, and Caleb met him halfway. More than a handshake, it was his father's way of accepting Caleb's decision. "You and your mother are very convincing. All right, so what are you still doing out here? We'll take care of those kids. Lucie needs you."

Truer words had never been spoken. Since he'd been back, he'd seen Lucie blossom and fight for herself. More than anything, he wanted to be a permanent part of her life, wanted her alongside him in the good and the bad. If there was some kissing and dancing and pink dresses involved, so much the better.

The fact they were starting with the bad? That would make the good times that much sweeter.

CHAPTER FIFTEEN

LUCIE SHUDDERED AS she shut the door. Franklin Garrity wasn't her favorite person, but she had to stay calm and listen to what he had to say. *Counsel?* What on earth would she have done that would require an attorney?

And Mr. Garrity making himself comfortable in her dining room was only the beginning of her troubles. Her heart had ripped in two when she'd glanced at Drew's face. Clearly, he wasn't going to support her and Caleb's relationship—any chance of a future with Caleb was over.

When she cleared this up, she'd probably have to find a new bookkeeper, as well. Ladybug nudged one of her legs while Pita nosed the other. She bent down and petted them before she eyed the mahogany dining room table where her mother brought love and laughter to many family meals. The table served as a reminder she'd get through this.

Of course, she'd have to get through it without Caleb.

She settled in on the opposite side of the table, folding her hands in an attempt to stop quivering. When she kept shaking, she moved them from the tabletop to her lap.

"The underwriter noted irregularities in your mortgage application." Mr. Garrity withdrew papers from his briefcase and slid them her way.

Her heart thudded in her ears. *Irregularities?* Reality sank in fast. He was accusing her of fraud, a crime that could send her to jail, unable to protect Mattie and Ethan from the town's glare, unable to build her business, unable to keep any respect she'd regained.

You're strong and elegant. Words from her best friend Natalie.

One of the strongest and most honest people I've ever met. She's as beautiful on the inside as the outside. Caleb's earlier statement hit home. Others believed in her, but she had to believe in herself. She'd done nothing wrong. Her strength and self-respect would help her through this. As would the people who had become her second family, including Mitzi, Georgie and Natalie.

Then there was Caleb.

While she knew she loved him, forces conspired to keep them apart.

Ladybug trotted into the dining room, her supportive grunts endearing. Pita remained at the threshold, pacing back and forth as though standing guard. Her pets had her back.

With more confidence, Lucie picked up the top paper and checked it over. "This is the mortgage application I submitted so I could pay for a new furnace. I own the title to this house free and clear, and I've reached out several times about the status. What's the problem?"

Mr. Garrity sneezed and pulled a tissue from his suit pocket. "For one thing, your dogs. I'm allergic and they're most distracting."

Lucie bristled at his condescension. She left the dogs in the mudroom with an apology before hurrying back, more than done with whatever stunt Mr. Garrity was pulling. She wanted a simple life, and tonight might have ended any chance of sharing that life with Caleb.

She claimed her chair and passed the paper back to Garrity. "I fail to see why this application attracted any special attention." *Why stop there?* Getting everything out in the open had been her mantra over the past couple years. "And I'd appreciate it if you contact Drew and Tina Spindler tomorrow and set the matter straight."

The creak of the front door stopped her. Lucie rose, ready to fetch whatever Mattie and Ethan had forgotten. If they'd forgotten an extra hug, so much the better.

Caleb was there on the threshold—even if she hadn't seen him, she'd have known who it was from Ladybug's and Pita's welcoming barks.

But why?

Was it to get a firsthand glimpse of whatever Garrity claimed to have against her? She didn't want to look into those hazel depths for the answer, and yet honesty began with clear communication.

Slowly, surely, she lifted her gaze and the answer knocked her into next week. Belief, respect and—dare she even think it?—love radiated forth.

"You came back." The words slipped out of her mouth, her doubt betraying her sincerity. She searched for her children beyond him. "Where are Mattie and Ethan?"

"They're safe. They went with my parents to my cabin."

Caleb walked over and sat next to Lucie. She stayed alert, her muscles as tight as a jack-in-the-box coil. "What's the issue here?"

Garrity waved the paper toward Caleb. "Take note of the value Mrs. Decker assigned to this house."

"If anything, I lowballed the value at a hundred and three thousand." Lucie racked her brain for the reasons she'd chosen that number: an online estimate, last year's property taxes and recent sales in the neighborhood. All seemed like fair ways to establish her house's value.

Caleb pushed the paper toward her. "The paper says one point three million."

The world exploded around her. There was no way she'd inserted an extra zero by mistake. She'd read over her application at least five times.

There it was in black-and-white, though. She'd signed her name to a document where she had claimed the value of her house was over a million dollars.

"I have a proposal." Garrity raised a brow. "It may seem irregular, but I wouldn't present this option if I didn't know it would help so many people in town."

While she was processing the banker's

words, Caleb's nearness almost undid her. What must Caleb think of her? *A liar, a cheat, a fraud.* Same as Leah, same as Justin. Her mind reeled and she struggled to breathe.

Caleb folded his arms and closed himself off. He must believe she'd purposely tried to defraud the bank to gain money for a mortgage. Bile rose in her throat and she gripped the table, eager to find anything solid, anything dependable.

"What's your suggestion?" Caleb's wry tone didn't escape her, and her mind kept spinning.

"Simple, really. Mrs. Decker sells this house, as well as the wellness property, to the bank. The proceeds will benefit the victims of her and her ex-husband's schemes. After all, this might be the proof the district attorney needs to connect her crimes to Mr. Decker's. If she sells and the proceeds are distributed in a fair manner benefiting those who've lost so much, I'm sure the DA will look favorably on you over such an action."

Garrity's words hung over the table, and every muscle in Lucie's body melted away to nothingness. Of course, Caleb would want her to go along with this. His parents' future would be secure again.

Everything she'd worked for was gone—

her family's house, her business, her honor. Franklin Garrity was ripping it all away over an honest mistake.

But how could she convince Caleb of that? How could she convince anyone? How would she look Mitzi in the eye, or Mattie or Ethan? How would she look at herself in the mirror?

Caleb reached for his phone. Her stomach roiled as he unlocked his screen. Was he calling the district attorney, or his parents to let them know of their windfall?

She wouldn't be able to protect the woodpecker habitat, and she could no longer protect Mattie and Ethan from the cold ugly truth that people would believe the worst of them no matter what they did. Maybe it was for the best they'd have to move away from Hollydale now. At least she could take Mattie and Ethan somewhere people wouldn't know about their father.

Never before had she felt so alone.

"I find it interesting that Lucie entered your bank late in the afternoon, yet these papers are stamped with the next morning's date. When I went to your bank to apply for a mortgage, your employee stamped the documents in front of me." Caleb didn't open his phone contacts but instead scrolled through his photos.

He was fighting for her. He believed in her.

"You're mistaken about Mrs. Decker's timing. She must have submitted her application in the morning. It's bank policy to stamp it when received, and this has 'a.m.' in the corner." Garrity nodded once for emphasis.

Caleb enlarged the photo on the screen, but it was too far away for Lucie to tell the details.

"These two photos aren't mistaken." Caleb handed his phone to Garrity. "Neither is the date on my phone, which doesn't match the date stamped on the document. These are photos of the paperwork Lucie submitted. Have a close look."

Franklin Garrity held the phone almost to his nose and his face paled. "This can't be correct. This picture of the paper shows the figure Lucie quoted."

She noted she was Lucie again. She pulled out her phone—Caleb had forwarded her the pictures in question. She hadn't been mistaken, after all. Caleb believed in her when evidence appeared to the contrary and even she had lost faith in herself.

Caleb took back his phone. "What's stopping me right now from calling Sheriff Harrison about you?"

Franklin Garrity squinted his beady eyes. "What do you mean?"

"Extortion." Caleb's answer came without hesitation.

"There's been an honest mistake somewhere. I didn't stamp the papers. I was only following up on an irregularity." A bead of sweat popped out on the banker's forehead. "You have my word I'll get to the bottom of it."

"My bookkeeper, Tina, also has a scanned copy of the document I sent to her. That's more proof in my favor." Lucie searched her mind for an explanation before she connected the dots. "You might want to start by questioning your new teller. Her sister invested five thousand dollars in Justin's Ponzi scheme." Then she sighed, wanting this behind her. "If she falsified the date, I don't want any publicity. No arrests, nothing like that. Just a promise I'll be treated fairly from now on."

Lucie extended her hand toward Mr. Garrity, relief zinging through her.

"Why?" He kept his hand to himself.

Lucie inhaled and exhaled a quick breath. "I am building a business and my children's futures. I want them to be free to make their own choices with the support of the community. Hollydale is my family, and I want the residents to be their family." Her voice caught on the last part and she stopped talking.

Besides, she had nothing else to say to Franklin Garrity. Nevertheless, she kept her hand extended.

"If the teller did this, she'll be fired. The bank's integrity always comes first." Mr. Garrity pushed his glasses up to the bridge of his nose. "I don't understand why you'd let off someone who did this. That makes no sense."

Lucie kept her hand held out, hard as it was. "She made a mistake, a bad choice, but I know what it's like to have people lose faith in you. I don't want that for her."

Garrity held up his chin. He snapped his briefcase shut and walked away without shaking her hand. The front door slammed behind him.

Caleb jumped to his feet and pulled Lucie into his arms, surrounding her in a firm embrace. For now, she surrendered to the peace and calm he offered. This was pure Caleb, everything good in the midst of a maelstrom. She snuggled into his chest, allowing herself one minute of bliss. If nothing else, she was thankful for his trust in her. She drank in his acceptance. With some luck, it would sustain her through what she'd have to do next. Drawing strength in his support, enough for a lifetime, she moved away.

"You came back," she said.

As much as she wanted to move forward with him, there was no future for her in Hollydale. If Garrity refused to shake her hand even after she'd been wronged, how could she ever set things right here?

"I'm only sorry I left in the first place. You needed me." He reached for her hands.

Midnight entered the room and entwined her body around Caleb's legs.

So much of Lucie's life had become intertwined with his over the past few weeks, and it was best to rip off the bandage and move on. Pita's barks and Ladybug's grunts from the direction of the mudroom gave her the opportunity she needed to distance herself. She moved toward the kitchen, but Caleb held on to her hands.

"They can wait for a minute. And I want to talk to you before we get Mattie and Ethan."

His use of *we* caught her off guard. Her parents had found true love against the odds. Georgie and Mike had worked everything out after a bumpy beginning, scaling their own version of the high ropes climbing wall. She wanted to rely on someone, to lean on them in the hard times, to laugh in the happy ones. But she needed to go before anything bad happened to Mattie and Ethan. If she was destined to end up alone, so be it.

"What's to talk about? I'll make sure the new owner of the center honors your lease." If she'd kicked him, he'd have looked less hurt.

"What are you talking about?"

"I'm done, Caleb. For the past couple years, I've worked hard to rebuild bridges, but someone just framed me for a crime I didn't commit. Someone has to think about Mattie and Ethan, and that person is me. They're not going to grow up in a town that doesn't want them." She'd held it together when the police officer had informed her of her parents' deaths, and when the FBI agent had informed her of Justin's crimes, and she'd hold it together now.

At least until tonight. There were no guarantees once she slid under her covers for one last time before she sold her house and the center property. Then she'd repay Mitzi and her aunt. No new mortgage applications for her.

"They won't grow up alone here. They'll have Mitzi, Georgie and Mike, Jonathan and the girls, and me. And my parents."

"What do you mean, your parents?"

"They know I came back."

"Oh." An hour ago, that would have changed everything. Now, she still felt empty inside.

Caleb stepped toward her, real concern on his face. "When I came to Hollydale, I received a hero's welcome, but it was nothing compared to the welcome in this house. Everyone else patted me on the back and went on with their business. But your family became my family. I love you, Lucie."

His eyes glinted with the promise of a real home, of fidelity, of love.

Mitzi was right—Lucie *was* running. But she had to. If she stayed here, she'd lose all self-respect. No matter how much she loved Caleb, she'd never lose herself again.

"Be my family," Caleb whispered.

His earnest gaze almost ate through her resolve. It would be so easy to stay and build something more romantic than her wildest dreams, but her children and his father needed her to keep her feet planted on the ground. "You already have one."

She ran to the mudroom and released her dogs. It was time to reclaim her family and move on.

CHAPTER SIXTEEN

CONCENTRATION LINED Lucie's face, and Caleb tried to keep his gaze focused out her car windshield. Dusk gave way to evening. While the gray clouds still hovered, not yet pouring forth their bounty of sleet and ice, the temperatures were taking a turn for the worse. Lucie's car heater vented lukewarm air the best it could, its system humming and groaning along.

She pulled in behind Caleb's car in the cabin's small parking area. The minute she engaged the emergency brake, her hand was already reaching for the door handle.

"Lucie, talk to me."

He owed it to them to try one last time to get through to her. Lucie was everything he'd ever wanted, and so much more. Long ago, he'd have given anything for a day in the sun, free of the hospital bed; so much so, he swung the pendulum the other way and devoted himself to his work. Lucie brought balance into perspective for him. Work and home coexisted hand in hand, respectful of each other.

She sighed and turned to him, pain etched in her eyes. "If anything ever happened to Mattie and Ethan because I chose to keep them here…" She gulped as she composed herself and closed her eyes for a minute. "I have to protect them from the slings and arrows the town might hurl at them."

"What about you? Who looks out for you?" Caleb wanted to reach over the console and connect with her, hold her hand, let her know she wasn't in this fight by herself.

"Why does anyone else have to look out for me? Mitzi pointed out I run away to protect myself. It's easier to look out for myself than have someone disappoint me again."

Even she appeared taken aback by her honesty.

"People aren't perfect. We have to take a chance on each other. Besides, if anyone knows about running, it's me. I ran from Hollydale, seeking an escape from my past, wanting to start over where no one knew about my surgery or my scars. Just because you can't see them doesn't mean they're not there, though. We all have scars. But confronting the past, staying in one place for a future? That's everything. That's love."

The raw huskiness of his voice breathed truth into everything. Her blue eyes held the proof she was considering everything he'd laid on the line.

Then she blinked and clenched her jaw. "My scars are too deep. I won't let Mattie and Ethan stay in a town where they're not wanted."

She turned and opened the car door, the cold rushing in. Giving his heart to her hadn't made a difference. She'd rejected him anyway. Lucie hurried up the stairs to his cabin.

Watching her sprint away from him proved to him that something was missing from his life. Love.

For the first time, he'd found the love he sought, but she'd thrown it back in his face. Instead of finding his way to a home with love and acceptance, he was back to square one.

In a few minutes, everyone would file out of the cabin and, once again, he'd be alone while everyone else went and lived their lives.

Then again, home wasn't a cabin or a house or a town. Home was being with the people you loved, the people who loved you back.

Lucie had never said she didn't love him, just that she couldn't live in a town that didn't have the backs of her children.

Finding his way back home to her was what mattered, not the street address or the place. Caleb hopped out of the car, ignoring the twinge in his back, determined to tell her it didn't matter where they lived as long as they had each other.

Home was with Lucie and Mattie and Ethan. Caleb hurried into the cabin, intent on her hearing him out one more time.

CHAPTER SEVENTEEN

LUCIE STARED AT the cozy room, expecting to see Mattie and Ethan.

"The kids were tired, so we got them to lie down in Caleb's room," Tina explained. "We checked on them a couple of minutes ago. They didn't even budge from where they buried themselves under the covers. Poor dears were exhausted."

As much as she wanted nothing more than to scoop up Mattie and Ethan and take them home, the questions in Drew's eyes demanded an answer. "Mr. Spindler…"

"Drew. We don't have to stand on formalities anymore." He glanced at his clothes. "Besides, I'd like to stay dry tonight. My wife and son both vouched for you, and those kids talk about Caleb like he hung the moon. I only have one question for you, and I'll take your answer at your word."

Lucie clenched her fists at her side. "For the last time, I didn't know what Justin was doing, and Mr. Garrity was mistaken about something and he knows the truth now."

Drew shook his head. "My question is this. Do you love my son?"

His question sank into her core. When she'd emailed Caleb before he'd returned to Hollydale, everything was supposed to have been simple. For once she'd had a plan that would help her win back the respect and hearts of the citizens of Hollydale.

Then Caleb had come back and everything had gone topsy-turvy. She'd reconnected with that part of herself long gone, the side that believed in rainbows, soul mates and happily-ever-afters. Caleb had helped her see that a dilapidated log, which others would gladly pass by without looking for any value within, could be the home for a nest with a treasure of endangered bird eggs inside.

Preconceived notions were just that, and they kept people from looking within. Someone had seen a nuisance and discarded Ladybug but, over time, the scared bulldog rebuilt trust and had become a beloved family member. Someone had dropped off Fred and Ethel, and now they lived in her shed, happy with an old couch and leftovers and lots of love.

Seeing past the surface could bring so much more to life.

With Caleb and Lucie in their corner, Mattie and Ethan would grow up secure in the knowledge that the surface didn't matter as much as what was underneath—honesty and love.

"Yes, I love your son, and it's time I stop running from him."

The door opened behind Lucie. Caleb entered and only the crackle of the fire snapped the silence. "Do you mean that?"

"Absolutely. Let me get Mattie and Ethan and then I'll say it again. I'll say it every day for years to come."

Lucie went to Caleb's room, opened the door and frowned. The room shouldn't be this cold. Her gaze went to the open window, and chills rocked her body. Racing to the bed, she whipped back the covers to find stacks of pillows forming the lumps Tina must have seen earlier. Mattie and Ethan. Where were they?

A scream pierced the air and Lucie barely registered it as her own. Footsteps sounded behind her and Caleb's woodsy scent reached her as he wrapped his arms around her.

"What's wrong?" He shivered. "Why is the window open?"

"Mattie and Ethan." That was all she could get out.

Caleb snatched a paper from the pillow. "I can't read this."

She gathered herself together. Mattie and Ethan needed her to stay strong. "Let me see."

Caleb handed her the paper, and Lucie placed the puzzle pieces together.

"They went in search of treasure."

Everyone in town knew who Franklin Garrity was, even Mattie and Ethan. The twins must have thought they were helping her by going in search of a new treasure. Didn't they know they were her treasure?

Caleb touched her shoulder. "Wait here a second."

She turned as he passed his parents standing in the doorway—Tina's face ashen, Drew holding her up. Less than a minute later, Caleb returned. "My metal detector's missing." Caleb faced his parents. "Call 9-1-1 and tell them the kids are gone."

There was no use standing there anymore. "Tell the authorities I'm out looking for them. If they come back to the cabin, call me." Lucie ran to the door and Caleb reached out to hold her back. She looked up. Every minute was precious.

"We'll find them." Caleb put his arms around her. "We need a logical plan."

"My children are out there in the dark, and it's getting colder by the minute. You and Mike figure out a plan. I'm bringing them home."

"MATTIE! ETHAN!" LUCIE'S voice reverberated around the high ropes course.

"My mom's at the wellness center, searching room by room. Dad's staying at the cabin. They'll call if they find them." Caleb caught up to her and she stopped, her tear-streaked cheeks taking hold of his heart and twisting hard. "Sheriff Harrison should be here any minute, and he's put the word out for volunteers to help search."

The wind whistled around them, the tops of the pines softly swaying. Only a sliver of the new moon peeked through the forest, no glow aiding them in their search. The murmur of the rushing river, so close, lulled him into a false sense of calm. There could be no peace while Mattie and Ethan were out there somewhere, no comfort in the green mountains that had been his mainstay for the past few weeks.

No, he had that wrong—the mountains

hadn't been his mainstay. Lucie and her family had been that and now his family was suffering, the danger threatening to rip apart the best thing that had ever happened to him.

Seeing the doubt and horror in Lucie's face, he embraced her. "We'll find them. We'll bring them home and make it clear that if they ever pull this disappearing stunt again, they'll be grounded until they're eighty."

Her chuckles turned to sobs. "You can't promise me we'll find them before it's too late."

"I promise you I won't rest until we find them."

Yet he'd found no trace of them so far, no trace of the metal detector being dragged through the dirt, no sign of their footprints or other tracks that would lead to the twins.

"Ethan! Matilda!"

Voices came from behind, beams of light from LED lanterns. "Who's there?" he shouted.

"Owen Thompson!" His boss's voice rang out as the beam of light on the ground became stronger and more concentrated.

"And Mitzi!" Another voice echoed in the darkness as the two emerged out of the shadows. Mitzi wrapped Lucie in an embrace and whispered something.

"How'd you get here so fast?" Lucie shifted

her weight in an apparent effort to keep moving and, most likely, stay warm.

"The sheriff called me and, since then, Harriet, the dispatcher, has been texting and organizing." Owen held up the lantern and Caleb caught sight of Lucie's relief that more people were on the trail.

"Between the four of us, we should find them soon." The quiver in her voice hit home.

Caleb sounded so much more sure when he told her, "We'll find them."

"Darlin', don't you know?" Mitzi stepped in and grasped Lucie's hands in hers. "It's not just the four of us. Mike and Georgie are searching the center with Tina. Natalie said to tell you she'll check the shed, as well. Ashleigh has every high school student around driving up and down Hollydale, searching. Connie and Deb are bringing boxes of coffee for the volunteer station. And get this, Franklin Garrity is searching on the other side of the lodge. All of Hollydale will bring them home to you."

A sob escaped from Lucie's throat and she launched herself into Caleb's chest, her muffled tremors cutting to his core before a final shudder came along with a sniffle and she stepped back. "Hollydale cares."

It was a statement rather than a question, and Caleb wrapped her in his arms. "So do I. We're family. Always."

That was his promise to her.

Lucie met his gaze, and the beams from the lantern showed her acceptance of him. "I already searched the area where you found the coffee tin treasure with the twins. They weren't there."

Treasure. Where had he heard that before? *In the hollow over there. That's where Miss Natalie said the treasure was. Bird eggs.* Ethan's voice echoed in his mind. Caleb knew where Mattie and Ethan were headed. His gaze met Lucie's and the same idea must have clicked in her mind.

"The woodpecker nest." Her voice blended with his in the chilly March air.

Caleb turned to Owen and filled him in on where they were heading. He and Lucie started off at a fast clip. He only hoped he was right.

LUCIE RAISED HER flashlight and there on the ground were two lumps huddled together. "Mattie! Ethan!"

They were safe! Later on, she'd tell them how they'd scared her out of her mind and shaved five years off her lifespan. The first pellets of sleet hit her face as she broke into a full sprint, their shivering bodies her only priority.

"Mom. Mr. Caleb." Tears streaked down Mattie's face. "Ethan's not moving. I'm so scared. I want to go home."

Caleb was at their side in a second, removing two small rectangular packages from a pocket of his coat. "These are emergency blankets." He handed one to Lucie while breaking open the other. "Wrap it around Mattie. Can you carry her?"

"Of course. I can't carry both of them, though." The days of lifting both at the same time had ended when they were less than six months old.

"I've got Ethan." Caleb spread the silvery Mylar thermal blanket around Ethan, no response coming from her son.

Lucie stopped the moan before it escaped. Fear already ringed Mattie's eyes, and Lucie wouldn't escalate that fear. As much as she wanted to carry Ethan to safety and make sure he'd be okay, Caleb could carry him that much faster and surer. "I'll call Mike and carry Mattie to the center." She couldn't help it as tears edged her eyes. "Thank you."

"Always."

Caleb scooped up Ethan while Lucie reached into her coat and pulled out her cell phone. Removing her right glove, she swiped the screen and delivered the news to Mike. Lucie swaddled the blanket around her daughter before cradling her close and setting off for the center.

A CHEER ERUPTED as Lucie straggled into the center. Mike and an EMT rushed to her side, taking Mattie for observation. Hollydale residents embraced each other, giving Caleb a moment of respite before he turned his attention to Ethan, who was being monitored by another EMT. As much as he wanted to be a part of the celebration, he couldn't, the pain from his herniated disc overbearing. He'd be heading to the emergency room next.

The EMTs went over and spoke with Lucie. She nodded, then joined Caleb and laid her hand on his arm. "They want to take Ethan and Mattie to the hospital for further checking, but they're both going to be okay." Hesitation lurked in her eyes before she raised her chin and inhaled. "I don't know whether to ground them or hug them."

Before he could answer, Connie made her

way over. "Hug them. Like I said, you make your mama proud. If you need anything, day or night, you call me." She extended her hand. "Agreed?"

Lucie shook Connie's hand. "Got it. Thank you—we'll talk later."

Connie nodded and walked away.

"I wish they'd let me be with the kids, but the EMT told me to wait here."

"Part of me is over there, too." He met her gaze, which was full of love and worry.

"My running ends now. The scars of the past can only fade if I let them."

"How do I know you won't run the next time something bad happens?" The pain in his back magnified and he clenched his hands.

She offered a slow smile. "I'll work on it day by day. When we celebrate our fiftieth anniversary together, you can tell me if I've gotten any better."

"Fifty years, huh? That's a long time." Caleb unclenched his fists and massaged his lower back. "I haven't even filled out my change of address form yet."

"Good. If you play your cards right, you might get to move again. Ethel and Ladybug will fight me for you, too." Her sense of humor was back.

"Shouldn't we go out on a second date first?"

"When was our first date?" Lucie wrinkled her brow and playfully shrugged.

"The memory of you in that pink dress will help me through many a hard time in my life." He had to share what was going on with his back, in case she didn't want to commit to seeing him through more surgeries. "Speaking of hard times…"

"I'll be there in the hard times and the good. Come with me to the hospital and help me take them home." She met his gaze, her blue eyes burning bright and beautiful.

He longed to reach for her and embrace her, but the pain was crippling. "I'm going to the hospital with you, but I'll be heading straight to the ER tonight. I might be facing surgery."

Alarm spread across her face. "Your back? You sacrificed your back for Ethan?"

"It wasn't a sacrifice."

Her lips silenced him as she kissed him with the intensity of a thousand Coleman lanterns lighting their way. The pain didn't entirely disappear, although it did fade for a millisecond.

She pulled back and stared into his eyes.

"Whatever you go through, we'll go through together. If you have surgery, I want to be the first face you see, not the third. If you have to find another job, you have one here if you want it. I love you."

An EMT walked over to tell Lucie they were ready for her to join them.

"I have to go," she told Caleb, her gaze hopeful.

"I'll meet you there."

She nodded and squeezed his hand.

With Lucie at his side, he could endure this surgery. He'd done it once before, and he could do it again.

Lucie was his home, and there was no other place he'd rather be.

EPILOGUE

IN A FEW HOURS, the ballroom would bustle with people waiting for Lucie to walk down the aisle. It was only fitting that her wedding would take place here at the events center, the site where her parents had presided over so many happy occasions. Even the drenching rains of the past week couldn't stop the festivities, although she and Caleb were now set to marry inside rather than outside.

Lucie ran her hand over the woodwork she'd labored over only a few months earlier. She glanced at the windowsills and breathed a sigh of relief that no surprise bats lay in the nooks and crannies. Instead, pink roses and white ribbons decorated the space.

The soft swish of the taffeta that lined her champagne-colored, floor-length wedding dress rustled, and she soaked up the scene, one of the few times silence had presided over the area in the past three months. Since the night of the kids' impromptu treasure hunt, the center's calendar had been full. Surveys invariably revealed the spa was everyone's favorite amenity, followed by the yoga and the nature walks.

"There's the bride." Mitzi's buoyant voice came from behind, and Lucie turned, her full skirt sweeping the ground. "Your mother would have loved seeing you so happy."

Happy at last. This marriage felt different, lighter, right. A commotion came from the foyer and she glanced at Mitzi before hurrying toward the noise.

Tina's voice issued from the reception area, and Lucie spotted her future mother-in-law and father-in-law all dressed up for the main event. When Tina met Lucie's gaze, she waved a paper in front of her face. "What's the meaning of this?"

"Exactly what it says. That each family involved in the Ponzi scheme can go to my attorney, who will reimburse you half of what you lost." Lucie was glad Mattie and Ethan wouldn't hear any of this. They were in the basement playing a board game with Mike, Georgie and Rachel, along with Aunt Rosemary, who'd flown in from California. Lucie treasured the long talk they'd had last night.

Tina's face blanched. "You didn't sell the corporate center to the Whitleys, did you?"

"Hear me out…"

Frederick Whitley had made a generous offer to purchase her business and incorporate it into the nature conservancy. He wanted to make the center the cornerstone of a new environmental preserve that would monitor the woodpecker population along with other protected species in conjunction with the Park Service. But she'd only accepted part of his deal because she wanted to keep the events center intact.

"Remember how we talked about our new nature trail and our plans for keeping the back acres off-limits? I sold them that land, not the lodge. They won't build on it, and the Park Service checked to make sure the woodpeckers and other animals who make their homes there are protected."

And the money from the sale of the land went toward repaying some of the wrongs from the past. She and Caleb had talked about that, and so much more, as he'd recovered from his most recent back surgery.

Drew placed his arm around his wife's shoulders. "We talked about it. We've come a long way in the past few years. Except for airline tickets and a deluxe suite for a long vacation, most of our share of the settlement should go toward our grandchildren's futures."

"I'm getting my month in the sun and grandchildren in one swoop." Tina's excitement touched Lucie. "If my boss will let me have the time off, that is."

One of the best parts about accepting Caleb's proposal was Mattie and Ethan's gaining a set of grandparents, although Mitzi insisted she'd known them first and had claimed the honorary title, which Lucie had only been too happy to bestow.

"I think we can arrange a leave of absence. And about Mattie and Ethan, thank you, but Caleb and I had a long talk…"

Before she could say anything else, muffled barks came from the entrance and Pita and Ladybug emerged. Pita bounded forward and shook the rain off her long coat while Ladybug trotted in. Drew and Mitzi made a human wall before either dog could get too close to her wedding dress.

"Caleb Andrew, what are you doing? You can't see the bride before the wedding, and you can't bring dogs in here," his mother exclaimed.

Caleb stopped at the doorway, his jaw slack

when his gaze drank in the sight of Lucie. Then his eyes brightened, and the widest smile graced his face. "Today is the best day of my life, seen or unseen." He whistled and the dogs came to sit at his feet. "I'll compromise and wait until Lucie leaves to bring in Fred and Ethel."

"Caleb Andrew Spindler, you can't bring all these animals to a wedding." Tina huffed.

The basement door flew open and Mattie and Ethan rushed to her, the commotion undoubtedly too much for them to resist. For a few seconds, at least, they appeared to be proper angels, with Mattie resplendent in her pink dress and Ethan handsome in his miniature tuxedo. They looked at Caleb. "Mom said yes? Hooray!"

All eyes went to Lucie, who shrugged. "Okay. Fred and Ethel and Ladybug and Pita are family, after all. Weddings are about family." And rainbows and promises and slow kisses. All things she'd believed happened to other people, not her.

She'd been wrong to lose sight of herself.

With Caleb as her partner, she wouldn't be sidetracked like that again.

Caleb hugged his parents and pointed to the piece of paper Tina still held in her hand. "I see you received the notice about Lucie's decision." He moved to Lucie's side and bent his head, his lips brushing hers with the promise of more to come. "This is the best time, then, to also tell you guys that Lucie supports my decision to leave the Park Service."

She leaned into him as he wound his arm around her waist. The news shouldn't come as a shock to anyone, his recent back surgery and subsequent physical therapy bringing about a change in his classification.

Drew stepped forward, the concern in his eyes real. "If you need a loan…"

Caleb shook his head. "We're fine, Dad. I already have a new job. You're looking at the new director of the nature conservancy. I'll be busy, especially with overseeing the mapping and tracking of several species in this area and working *with* Owen instead of for him."

Lucie's heart filled with joy. This was the future meant for Caleb—the best of nature with the promise of home waiting for him every night. Sharing it with him was all the sweeter.

Caleb turned toward her and grasped her hands. "No matter how much is going on around us, I will always find my way home to you, Lucie."

The minister popped his head in. "Excuse me. Did I see a pair of miniature pigs in the car?"

Everyone laughed as Lucie hitched up her dress, her pink heels a perfect complement for the creamy satin. "That's my cue to go upstairs with Mattie and Ethan until I become Lucie Spindler."

"Before you do, one more kiss?"

"Always."

Caleb's lips met hers and the sweetness in that kiss brought promises of love and a treasure beyond compare.

* * * * *

If you missed Mike and Georgie's sweet romance in The Sheriff's Second Chance, *or for more enchanting stories from Harlequin Heartwarming, visit www.Harlequin.com today!*

Get 4 FREE REWARDS!

We'll send you 2 FREE Books plus 2 FREE Mystery Gifts.

Love Inspired books feature uplifting stories where faith helps guide you through life's challenges and discover the promise of a new beginning.

FREE Value Over $20

YES! Please send me 2 FREE Love Inspired Romance novels and my 2 FREE mystery gifts (gifts are worth about $10 retail). After receiving them, if I don't wish to receive any more books, I can return the shipping statement marked "cancel." If I don't cancel, I will receive 6 brand-new novels every month and be billed just $5.24 each for the regular-print edition or $5.99 each for the larger-print edition in the U.S., or $5.74 each for the regular-print edition or $6.24 each for the larger-print edition in Canada. That's a savings of at least 13% off the cover price. It's quite a bargain! Shipping and handling is just 50¢ per book in the U.S. and $1.25 per book in Canada.* I understand that accepting the 2 free books and gifts places me under no obligation to buy anything. I can always return a shipment and cancel at any time. The free books and gifts are mine to keep no matter what I decide.

Choose one: ☐ **Love Inspired Romance Regular-Print** (105/305 IDN GNWC)   ☐ **Love Inspired Romance Larger-Print** (122/322 IDN GNWC)

Name (please print)

Address   Apt. #

City   State/Province   Zip/Postal Code

Email: Please check this box ☐ if you would like to receive newsletters and promotional emails from Harlequin Enterprises ULC and its affiliates. You can unsubscribe anytime.

Mail to the **Reader Service:**
IN U.S.A.: P.O. Box 1341, Buffalo, NY 14240-8531
IN CANADA: P.O. Box 603, Fort Erie, Ontario L2A 5X3

Want to try 2 free books from another series? Call 1-800-873-8635 or visit www.ReaderService.com.

*Terms and prices subject to change without notice. Prices do not include sales taxes, which will be charged (if applicable) based on your state or country of residence. Canadian residents will be charged applicable taxes. Offer not valid in Quebec. This offer is limited to one order per household. Books received may not be as shown. Not valid for current subscribers to Love Inspired Romance books. All orders subject to approval. Credit or debit balances in a customer's account(s) may be offset by any other outstanding balance owed by or to the customer. Please allow 4 to 6 weeks for delivery. Offer available while quantities last.

Your Privacy—Your information is being collected by Harlequin Enterprises ULC, operating as Reader Service. For a complete summary of the information we collect, how we use this information and to whom it is disclosed, please visit our privacy notice located at corporate.harlequin.com/privacy-notice. From time to time we may also exchange your personal information with reputable third parties. If you wish to opt out of this sharing of your personal information, please visit readerservice.com/consumerschoice or call 1-800-873-8635. **Notice to California Residents**—Under California law, you have specific rights to control and access your data. For more information on these rights and how to exercise them, visit corporate.harlequin.com/california-privacy.

LI20R2

Get 4 FREE REWARDS!

We'll send you 2 FREE Books plus **2 FREE Mystery Gifts.**

Love Inspired Suspense books showcase how courage and optimism unite in stories of faith and love in the face of danger.

FREE Value Over **$20**

YES! Please send me 2 FREE Love Inspired Suspense novels and my 2 FREE mystery gifts (gifts are worth about $10 retail). After receiving them, if I don't wish to receive any more books, I can return the shipping statement marked "cancel." If I don't cancel, I will receive 6 brand-new novels every month and be billed just $5.24 each for the regular-print edition or $5.99 each for the larger-print edition in the U.S., or $5.74 each for the regular-print edition or $6.24 each for the larger-print edition in Canada. That's a savings of at least 13% off the cover price. It's quite a bargain! Shipping and handling is just 50¢ per book in the U.S. and $1.25 per book in Canada.* I understand that accepting the 2 free books and gifts places me under no obligation to buy anything. I can always return a shipment and cancel at any time. The free books and gifts are mine to keep no matter what I decide.

Choose one: ☐ **Love Inspired Suspense Regular-Print** (153/353 IDN GNWN) ☐ **Love Inspired Suspense Larger-Print** (107/307 IDN GNWN)

Name (please print)

Address   Apt. #

City   State/Province   Zip/Postal Code

Email: Please check this box ☐ if you would like to receive newsletters and promotional emails from Harlequin Enterprises ULC and its affiliates. You can unsubscribe anytime.

Mail to the **Reader Service:**
IN U.S.A.: P.O. Box 1341, Buffalo, NY 14240-8531
IN CANADA: P.O. Box 603, Fort Erie, Ontario L2A 5X3

Want to try 2 free books from another series! Call 1-800-873-8635 or visit www.ReaderService.com.

*Terms and prices subject to change without notice. Prices do not include sales taxes, which will be charged (if applicable) based on your state or country of residence. Canadian residents will be charged applicable taxes. Offer not valid in Quebec. This offer is limited to one order per household. Books received may not be as shown. Not valid for current subscribers to Love Inspired Suspense books. All orders subject to approval. Credit or debit balances in a customer's account(s) may be offset by any other outstanding balance owed by or to the customer. Please allow 4 to 6 weeks for delivery. Offer available while quantities last.

Your Privacy—Your information is being collected by Harlequin Enterprises ULC, operating as Reader Service. For a complete summary of the information we collect, how we use this information and to whom it is disclosed, please visit our privacy notice located at corporate.harlequin.com/privacy-notice. From time to time we may also exchange your personal information with reputable third parties. If you wish to opt out of this sharing of your personal information, please visit readerservice.com/consumerschoice or call 1-800-873-8635. **Notice to California Residents**—Under California law, you have specific rights to control and access your data. For more information on these rights and how to exercise them, visit corporate.harlequin.com/california-privacy.

LIS20R2

THE WESTERN HEARTS COLLECTION!

19 FREE BOOKS in all!

COWBOYS. RANCHERS. RODEO REBELS.
Here are their charming love stories in one prized Collection:
51 emotional and heart-filled romances that capture the majesty and rugged beauty of the American West!

YES! Please send me **The Western Hearts Collection** in Larger Print. This collection begins with 3 FREE books and 2 FREE gifts in the first shipment. Along with my 3 free books, I'll also get the next 4 books from The Western Hearts Collection, in LARGER PRINT, which I may either return and owe nothing, or keep for the low price of $5.45 U.S./$6.23 CDN each plus $2.99 U.S./$7.49 CDN for shipping and handling per shipment*. If I decide to continue, about once a month for 8 months I will get 6 or 7 more books but will only need to pay for 4. That means 2 or 3 books in every shipment will be FREE! If I decide to keep the entire collection, I'll have paid for only 32 books because 19 books are FREE! I understand that accepting the 3 free books and gifts places me under no obligation to buy anything. I can always return a shipment and cancel at any time. My free books and gifts are mine to keep no matter what I decide.

☐ 270 HCN 5354   ☐ 470 HCN 5354

Name (please print)

Address   Apt. #

City   State/Province   Zip/Postal Code

Mail to the **Reader Service:**
IN U.S.A.: P.O. Box 1341, Buffalo, N.Y. 14240-8531
IN CANADA: P.O. Box 603, Fort Erie, Ontario L2A 5X3

Get 4 FREE REWARDS!

We'll send you 2 FREE Books <u>plus</u> 2 FREE Mystery Gifts.

FREE
Value Over
$20

Both the **Romance** and **Suspense** collections feature compelling novels written by many of today's bestselling authors.

YES! Please send me 2 FREE novels from the Essential Romance or Essential Suspense Collection and my 2 FREE gifts (gifts are worth about $10 retail). After receiving them, if I don't wish to receive any more books, I can return the shipping statement marked "cancel." If I don't cancel, I will receive 4 brand-new novels every month and be billed just $7.24 each in the U.S. or $7.49 each in Canada. That's a savings of up to 28% off the cover price. It's quite a bargain! Shipping and handling is just 50¢ per book in the U.S. and $1.25 per book in Canada.* I understand that accepting the 2 free books and gifts places me under no obligation to buy anything. I can always return a shipment and cancel at any time. The free books and gifts are mine to keep no matter what I decide.

Choose one: ☐ **Essential Romance** ☐ **Essential Suspense**
(194/394 MDN GQ6M)   (191/391 MDN GQ6M)

Name (please print)

Address   Apt. #

City   State/Province   Zip/Postal Code

Email: Please check this box ☐ if you would like to receive newsletters and promotional emails from Harlequin Enterprises ULC and its affiliates. You can unsubscribe anytime.

Mail to the **Reader Service:**
IN U.S.A.: P.O. Box 1341, Buffalo, NY 14240-8531
IN CANADA: P.O. Box 603, Fort Erie, Ontario L2A 5X3

Want to try 2 free books from another series! Call **1-800-873-8635** or visit www.ReaderService.com.

---

*Terms and prices subject to change without notice. Prices do not include sales taxes, which will be charged (if applicable) based on your state or country of residence. Canadian residents will be charged applicable taxes. Offer not valid in Quebec. This offer is limited to one order per household. Books received may not be as shown. Not valid for current subscribers to the Essential Romance or Essential Suspense Collection. All orders subject to approval. Credit or debit balances in a customer's account(s) may be offset by any other outstanding balance owed by or to the customer. Please allow 4 to 6 weeks for delivery. Offer available while quantities last.

Your Privacy—Your information is being collected by Harlequin Enterprises ULC, operating as Reader Service. For a complete summary of the information we collect, how we use this information and to whom it is disclosed, please visit our privacy notice located at corporate.harlequin.com/privacy-notice. From time to time we may also exchange your personal information with reputable third parties. If you wish to opt out of this sharing of your personal information, please visit readerservice.com/consumerschoice or call 1-800-873-8635. **Notice to California Residents**—Under California law, you have specific rights to control and access your data. For more information on these rights and how to exercise them, visit corporate.harlequin.com/california-privacy.

STRS20R2

COMING NEXT MONTH FROM

♦HARLEQUIN
HEARTWARMING

Available November 10, 2020

#351 MONTANA MATCH
The Blackwell Sisters • by Carol Ross

Fiona Harrison's dating app attempts haven't gone according to plan. What better way to make things worse than allowing Simon Clarke to play matchmaker? She's falling for the handsome bartender, but he doesn't see marriage in his own future.

#352 THE COWBOY'S HOLIDAY BRIDE
Wishing Well Springs • by Cathy McDavid

Cash Montgomery is stuck covering his sister's absence from their wedding barn business with event coordinator Phoebe Kellerman. Then come his three former fiancées, all to be wed and each ready to impart their advice about the bride who's right under his nose.

#353 AN ALASKAN FAMILY CHRISTMAS
A Northern Lights Novel • by Beth Carpenter

Confirmed skeptic Natalie Weiss is in Alaska to help a friend, not spend the holidays with a stranger's family in their rustic cabin. Tanner Rockford finds himself drawn to the cynical professor, knowing full well her career will take her away.

#354 MISTLETOE COWBOY
Kansas Cowboys • by Leigh Riker

Ex-con Cody Jones discovers that the love of his life is engaged to someone else. Is there any way the cowboy can turn his life around and convince Willow Bodine to choose him over her successful lawyer fiancé?

**YOU CAN FIND MORE INFORMATION ON UPCOMING HARLEQUIN TITLES,
FREE EXCERPTS AND MORE AT HARLEQUIN.COM.**

HWCNM1020